THE
Devil's
KETTLE

J.J. OLLMAN

outskirts press

The Devil's Kettle is a forked waterfall located on the North Shore of Minnesota. One fork drops thirty feet and flows into Lake Superior. The other fork drops twenty feet and empties into a hole in the rock. No one knows where it ends up. Scientists have lowered cameras, dropped tennis balls and dye into the water, and they have never discovered where the items reappeared. It is a waterfall to nowhere.

CHAPTER 1

S eth Tryton stood at the top of Palisade Head, staring at white-caps that splashed across Lake Superior. The wind whistled. The day was full of gray clouds that hinted of rain. He walked to the three-foot tall rock wall lining the edge of the cliff and looked down to the rocks and water a hundred-seventy feet below. He shivered. His fedora blew off and rolled across the rock and grass before it stopped at the feet of a man sharing the view.

"Gotchya," said the stranger. He plucked the hat from the ground and stepped toward Tryton, holding the hat in an out-stretched hand.

"Thought sure I lost it for good," Tryton said, planting the hat firmly back on his head. "Thanks."

They shook hands. The stranger was a little younger than Tryton, probably fifty something, and short: no taller than five-foot seven, a round face with dark, brown hair of medium length, a friendly smile, and a hell of a strong grip.

They sat and visited on two boulders set back from the wall. Seth shared that he was traveling alone with no spouse, children or grandchildren accompanying him. He was there for a holiday, he said, just to relax and enjoy the North Shore of Minnesota.

"I actually live near here," said Peter Karonen. "Up near Finland."

Tryton cocked his head a little.

Karonen acknowledged the questioning look and said, "It's a little town inland, not far from Silver Bay. I come up here often—just to look out across the lake. It always makes me feel alive when I sit with the breeze in my face, a memory in my heart... and drink in that." He nodded toward the inland sea. "Sometimes the lake's rough like today, and other times it's as smooth as old whiskey. The North Shore is like no other place in Minnesota."

Tryton's interest peaked at the mention of whiskey. In fact, he salivated a little.

They talked on for a while, getting acquainted, enjoying each other's company. Karonen stood, signaling an end to the conversation and began the short walk to his truck. Tryton followed and opened his car door.

Karonen turned suddenly toward Tryton and said, "Hey, if you want to follow me to my place I'll give you a beer... whiskey... or whatever, and I can tell you about some great out of the way places to visit around here."

Tryton only hesitated a moment before accepting the offer. He followed Karonen's truck to Finland. Twenty minutes after they left Palisade Head, Tryton pulled up beside an isolated two-story house at the base of a four hundred foot hill covered with dying paper birch and quaking aspen.

Stepping slowly from his vehicle, Tryton stood and looked at the hills. "Looks like a lot of the North Shore here. Lots of dying trees."

Karonen, who had emerged from his F-150 a few moments earlier said, "Climate change. Since the 1890's, the average temperature has risen two degrees up here. That's not the only reason they're dying, of course, but the scientists say that seems to be the major one. Several years ago we also had an infestation of armyworms. They destroyed a hell of a lot. The birch and aspen are being replaced by scrub brush like alder, hazel, and common tansy. It's sad. The north woods has changed from red pine and white cedar, most of which were logged to near extinction, to paper birch and quaking aspen, to what you see now. It's a long story if you want to hear it."

Tryton scrunched his lips together and muttered, "Some other time. How about that whiskey you mentioned?"

"Come on in." Karonen motioned Tryton to follow him into the living room.

The house had an airless, dank smell that hit Tryton's nose as soon as he entered. The smell made his eyes water and blink.

Karonen didn't notice. He moved quickly to the liquor set out on a countertop in the nearby kitchen. "Pick a chair and sit down. I'll be right back with a tall one. Jameson whiskey okay with you?"

Tryton rubbed his nose trying to eject the stench of the house, and answered, "That'll be more than fine." He selected a newer looking, straight back chair and plopped down.

A minute later, Karonen appeared with two glasses. "Hope you don't mind, I mixed 'em with sour."

Tryton accepted the glass. "Sounds great to me!"

They conversed about the history of the North Shore until Karonen finally got around to mentioning areas Tryton could visit: the Tofte dump, great for bear watching; Carlton Peak; Hog Creek; and the Superior Hiking Trail.

Tryton felt tired and mentioned that he should be getting back to his motel before he got too bad to drive.

Rising to his feet, Karonen said, "You want to see one last thing before you go?"

Tryton shook his head slowly as he stood, "Oh no, I've got to go straight to the motel. I'm not feeling really great."

"It'll just take a minute. And it's right here in the house."

Tryton began to protest, but Karonen waved him off with a follow me gesture.

He led him to the back of the house to a monstrous looking bookcase bloated with books.

Karonen beamed as he directed Tryton's gaze to it.

Tryton pursed his lips, squinted, and then said, "That's very nice."

"You're going to be more impressed when I show you what's behind it." Before Tryton could respond, Karonen latched onto a book and partially pulled it to the front.

Tryton covered his ears as he heard a sound like fingernails screeching on a chalkboard as the bookcase moved forward. "What the hell?" Tryton looked stupefied.

When it was completely opened, Karonen stepped inside the darkened area and flipped a switch. Rock and red clay walls, supported by stout timbers, were exposed.

"I found this by accident," Karonen began. "I have no idea who built it, but as you can see from the look of the timbers, it's been here for a while."

"Is it safe?"

"I've been in here lots. Come on in." Karonen beckoned him with his hand and then walked deeper into the opening.

Tryton hunched over and walked in. Fifty feet into the tunnel it widened and became a chamber. "I'm a little dizzy, Peter, I... I... need to sit down."

Karonen watched Tryton stumble, but not lose his footing. He approached and took Tryton by the elbow to support him.

"Here, sit down here." Karonen guided him to what looked like a stool carved out of the rock wall.

Tryton dropped to the rock chair and held his head.

"Something's not feeling right. Maybe I can't hold my liquor anymore." Tryton took several deep breaths, moaned, and held his head in his hands. His vision was getting fuzzy and the room was spinning.

Karonen supported him as he collapsed onto the dirt and gravel floor. He checked Tryton's pulse. It was strong, but slow. Satisfied that Tryton was merely feeling the effects of the drug he had slipped in his drink, and not suffering from a heart attack or stroke, Karonen let him lie on the floor while he prepared the next chamber for Tryton's stay.

CHAPTER 2

G erald Hodges was arranging the dishes in his special way; each had to be in its proper place. The telephone rang. He picked up on the third ring.

"Gerry?" the voice asked. Hodges recognized Earl Mancoat's voice.

"I'm sorry," he lied. "There is no Gerry here. You have the wrong number."

"No, Gerry, don't hang up. It's Earl. Earl Mancoat. We gotta talk. Seth Tryton's missing. Maybe killed or murdered."

Seth, missing. Killed? Murdered? He brought the phone nearer his better ear. "I'm listening."

Mancoat started up again, "I'm here in Tasmania. I came to find you and get your help." A long pause.

"I'm sorry, I can't help you." Hodges began to hang up again.

"Lucille told me to call you. She gave me your number."

Hodges lifted the phone to his ear again. "Lucille? She told you I was here and gave you my number?"

"I always thought she helped you get away, Gerry. I was sure of it, but I never told the police anything. I swear it, never said a word. When this thing happened with Seth, I thought we'd better get ahold of you. You'd be able to figure it out."

Mancoat was breathing hard, and then he blurted, "We need you! Lucille said she'd give you the money to slip back into the country and figure it out for us." He paused and waited for Hodges to respond.

Hodges twirled the handset between his fingers like a baton before saying, "You're telling me the truth?"

"Yes, yes!"

He decided to trust his old friend. "I'm assuming you know where I live," Hodges said.

"I got your address written down right here, uh, Tasmania—"

"I'm in Devonport. The state is Tasmania."

"I was gettin' to that. You're on Cricket North West, uh, 7311, right?"

"Correct. How soon can you be here?"

"I can be there in, I don't know, an hour."

"That won't do. Where are you?"

"I'm in Burnie."

"Why did you go to Burnie? You had to have flown to Devonport first from the mainland, and then driven to Burnie from here. If you knew I was here, why did you go to Burnie?"

"That's a story for the road!"

Hodges shook his head and sighed. "You're only thirty-five minutes away. I'll pack and be ready by the time you get here."

"Hey, I've gotta..."

Hodges hung up.

"Get my stuff together. It'll take... Son of a bitch!" Mancoat slammed the receiver down and rushed to pack his belongings.

It took him a little while to find Hodge's place, but he arrived forty-five minutes later.

"You're late," Hodges snapped as he threw his gear into the trunk.

"If you hadn't hung up the damn phone, you'd have heard that I had to pack shit, too! I got here as fast as I could!"

A focused Hodges said, "No matter, we'll catch a flight to Melbourne."

They drove to the airport and talked during the fifteen minutes it took them to get there.

Showing off his newly learned knowledge of Australia, Mancoat said, "Melbourne's in Oceania. I flew there from the states." He then added, "Takes an hour to get there from Tasmania."

Hodges was preoccupied. "Tell me more about Lucille. Did she contact you first?"

"No, other way around. I needed to get ahold of you, Gerry. We tried looking for Seth, but it's like he vanished. His car was left in Duluth, but there's no sign of him. Nobody, nothin'. The people we talked to never saw him. Police know nothing. It's crazy! He told us he was going up for a holiday. Only you talk like that, so we thought maybe that was code for meeting you, but we found out different."

Hodges interrupted. "Right now, I want to know about Lucille."

"Well, I knew she was in Melbourne. I got that much from her butler in Massachusetts. You'd be proud of me. Tracked her down like a regular PI." His wrinkled face cracked a smile, but lost it quickly. "But I was surprised to find out you two weren't livin' together anymore. What happened?"

Hodges said, "What always happens to us. We found out... again... that we can't live together. It was best, given our situation, and my, uh, problems in the United States, that I move. Tasmania seemed the perfect place for me. Isolated and far from the madding crowd."

"Have anything to do with you, Lucille, and *somebody* else in the picture?" Mancoat turned away in embarrassment when Hodges, his face like a mask, stared at him. "Uh, no, guess not."

After dropping the car at the rental office, they entered the airport, rolling their bags behind them. They bought tickets to Melbourne, using the credit card Lucille had given Mancoat. She had also arranged to get a new passport for Hodges, under a different name.

The flight was full so they spoke in hushed voices, not wanting anyone to overhear them.

Hodges busily rearranged the flight magazines in the seat pocket in front of him. When he was finally satisfied, he asked, "How is Lucille?"

Mancoat paused before responding. "She seemed sad. She talked about what you did in Minnesota."

Hodge's chin dropped and he took a deep breath.

"She loves you, Gerry. That's clear, but I can't figure out why." There was another pause before Mancoat got mad. "Hell, I can't figure out why you killed those people, Gerry. None of us can. Seth, Boston... none of us!" Mancoat slammed his fist into the back of the seat in front of him.

The man in front erupted, "Hey, what's up, mate?"

"Uh, sorry!"

Resuming his hushed voice, Mancoat said, "It's like we never really knew you, Gerry. But, but... we know you're not all bad. We had some damn good times at the Muni!" His voice rose until Hodges put a gentle hand on his arm.

"I'm different now." He looked straight at Mancoat who was staring back at him. "I realized, after I shot that woman deputy, and I almost killed myself... that I had a purpose in life. Something better, something far more important than being wrapped up in the internal workings of my own mind. Lucille knew it when she rescued me and brought me to Australia." He detached his hand from Earl's forearm and placed it in his lap, all the while looking directly into Mancoat's eyes. "I do good things now. I help out at the hospital, the library, I read to children in school. Earl, if I do enough good, maybe I can make up for a few of the bad things I've done."

A long pause before Mancoat said, "You're a murderer, Gerry. We can't forget what you did to those people and we'll never understand you, but..." He threw up his hands and looked away. "But you're the best hope we got to find Seth, dead or alive. Hopefully, the old guy's alive. You'll help find Seth?"

"I'll do my best. If I find him that will be one more mark on the good side of my ledger." Hodges turned, closed his eyes, shook his head, and then said, "My life has been one monumental, internal struggle. The differences between me and normal people are extreme, and I have only recently touched the surface of who and what I really am. I'll make no bones about it, Earl. I was sick. I was a monster, and I can't excuse the things I did in Rose Creek. The beginning of my self-realization took form as I kneeled in the snow, away from the cabin, pressed a gun to my temple and squeezed the trigger half way."

A flat expression covered his face as his eyes opened. He looked at Mancoat again. "I'll never kill again, Earl. I can't. And if I'm caught while we're back in Minnesota, so be it. I'll spend whatever time I have left helping others."

Touched by Hodge's confession, Mancoat reached over and patted Hodges on the arm. "Well, lucky for you, Minnesota doesn't have the death penalty—just life imprisonment." His face turned to the window and he watched the land disappear, replaced by ocean.

An hour later, they touched down in Melbourne, disembarked and picked up tickets for the states. Twenty hours later, they arrived in Minneapolis, paid Mancoat's park and fly charges, and were on their way to Duluth. Two and a half hours after pulling out of Minneapolis, they entered the outskirts of Duluth.

They drove down the long, winding curve of Thompson Hill and felt the temperature change immediately. Lake Superior acted like a gigantic cooler for at least a mile inland. It wasn't uncommon for there to be a ten-degree drop in temperature from the top of the hill to the bottom.

"It hasn't changed much since I was last here thirty years ago," Hodges said.

"Wait till we get down farther. There's tunnels, a new highway, and the Canal Park area is all built up. In fact, that's where we're staying. A place called The Suites, right by the old lift bridge."

Hodges watched the scenery without commenting as they drove through the former industrial area that was now home to restaurants, hotels, and a convention center.

They parked in the lot and registered under Mancoat's name for a two-bedroom suite with two bathrooms and a Jacuzzi.

Hodges finally registered approval when they looked the room over.

"I'll have to get used to calling you Jasper out in public," Mancoat said.

"Call me Jasper all the time. It'll be easier. We don't want any slip ups since we may be dealing with the police."

"Jasper Green. I'd better keep repeating that to myself so I don't screw up." Mancoat threw his bag in the first bedroom.

Hodges disappeared into the other bedroom, inspecting for dust before placing his bag on a dresser near the flat screen TV. He sighed and shook his head as he gazed around the room. He noticed the drapes were wrinkled, and the remote control for the TV was not centered on the nightstand, so he changed that immediately. The drapes? He would have to live with them, as difficult as that would be. Moving to the bathroom, everything seemed in good order, except the soap was on the left side. He preferred it on his right, so he moved that, taking care to position it just so. Obsessive Compulsive Disorder mixed with some characteristics of Asperger's Syndrome had been a part of him all his life. Things were not going to change now.

A minute later, he was satisfied with the bathroom decor and returned to the common living area where Mancoat had plopped himself comfortably into a recliner.

"We gotta talk about a plan of action, Gerald—I mean Jasper."

Hodges sat across from Mancoat and loosened his buttoned up shirt collar and stretched. "I'm very tired right now. I'd rather wait for the morning."

"Well, I'd rather do it now," Mancoat said.

Hodges, not in the mood for arguing, emitted a long sigh. "All right give me a minute." He rose, crossed to the mini kitchen, grabbed a bottled water, and returned to the chair. "Tell me everything you know."

Mancoat said, "I pretty much already did, Ger... Jasper."

Hodges said, "Pretty much doesn't cut it, Earl. I need to know every detail, every bit of knowledge you have."

"Ah, I see where you're going with this. You're the detail man, always were." Mancoat chuckled.

Hodge's eyebrows arched.

"Yeah, well, start from when Seth left Rose Creek?" Mancoat asked.

"That'd be appropriate, but first, did he say he was meeting anyone, or does he have relatives in this part of the state?"

"No, not at all, no relatives around here. They're all down in Illinois. He never said he was meeting anyone, lady friend or other. Come to think of it, I've never known Seth to have any lady friends at all. Us old dogs is all he's got, as far as I know, Jasper. By the way, see how good I'm getting at this name stuff, Ger... damn it!"

"You mentioned you thought he was meeting me up here."

"Well, yeah, because he used that word holiday instead of vacation, just like you do with your fake English way of talking and all."

Hodges looked at Mancoat. "It's not fake, at least not anymore. This is the way I talk now."

"Whatever, Jasper, I'm just tellin' you we know it's fake and that you're not really English."

"I lived in England for many years and their manner of speech became ingrained in me. It's perfectly natural to assume the manner of speech where you live, especially when you enjoy talking like that, and really especially when you've acted in the British theater, as I did for several years. Now can we please get on with this?" The irritation was evident in his voice.

Mancoat harrumphed, but continued. "Okay, Seth told us at our last meeting that he was leaving on a holiday, like I said. Said he needed to see the North Shore before he died. Pretty melodramatic, but Seth could get that way sometimes."

"Go on," Hodges encouraged, sounding like a dime store psychotherapist.

"Said he'd be gone for a week then be back. A week went by and we didn't think too much about it for the first couple days, and then we had some newswoman down here asking us questions about Seth and telling us the police found his car in Duluth. That's when me and Boston got concerned, thinking, what the hell is goin' on here?"

"That's when you and Boston came up here and investigated?"

"You got that right, Jasper." Mancoat smiled, pleased that he used the cover name properly.

"Continue," Hodges ordered.

"We drove up here in my old Buick. I didn't know if it would make it, but it—"

"I don't need to know that, Earl."

"Yeah, yeah, yeah. Anyway, we got up here, stopped down here at Canal Park first and called that newswoman. Got her card right here." He dug it out of his wallet and handed the card toward Hodges. "Sheila, Sheila..."

Hodges projected a perplexed look and interjected. "Her first and last names are Sheila?"

"No, no! It's Cadotte, Sheila Cadotte."

"Interesting name, French?"

"Kind of. I guess she's actually Ojibwa. She told me the whole story when I met her. About a quarter of the Indians living in Minnesota and Wisconsin, have French names." Mancoat withdrew his handkerchief from his back pocket and blew his nose. It sounded like several high-pitched snorts from a horn.

Hodges waited.

"Anyway, she said she'd meet us for a drink at Carmody's. So one o'clock rolls around, Boston and me are downing a couple fingers of brandy, and Cadotte walks in, spots us and rushes over. Says she doesn't have much time, and then asks us more questions about family, friends, what Seth does, if he's into drinking a lot, that sorta thing. Boston looks at her and says, 'We told you about the family in Illinois and we're the only friends he's got. As far as the drinking, hell yeah, he does that. Look at us!' She doesn't look impressed, and in fact, gets a little testy with Boston."

Hodges interrupted. "Did she give you any new information?"

"I'm gettin' to that!" Mancoat turned his head like he was trying to relieve a stiff neck. "Okay, I'll cut to the chase. I asked her that very same question. He paid eighty-nine bucks a night for three nights at the North Star Motel."

"Where's that?"

"It's up by Tofte. We drove up there that afternoon. It's not that far away, little more than an hour. The woman that runs the place remembered Seth. Liked him, I think, because he paid her cash. Curious thing though, he didn't stay the third night. She never saw his car after the second day. And, she said he didn't return the key. The other thing we got from Cadotte, and this was earlier when she came down to Rose Creek, was that Seth stayed in Duluth for four nights, right here at The Suites."

"That's interesting. I'm assuming he stayed here before he was at the North Star," Hodges said.

Mancoat's eyes widened a little. "Well, yes, and no. He stayed at the Suites on June eighteenth through the twentieth, then had the room at Tofte for the twenty-first through the twenty-third, but didn't stay there on the twenty-third. He stayed back here at The Suites, in the same room for the twenty-fourth."

Hodges broke in. "Not the twenty-third?"

"Nope."

"So, we had better speak to The Suites people, and..."

Mancoat interrupted, "We did. The front desk people who checked him in were two different clerks so they really couldn't vouch it was the same person checking in each time; another curious thing. He paid in cash for the twenty-fourth."

"That is interesting. No security camera tape to verify it was Seth both times?"

"Police went over that and couldn't see a difference. Tape was kind of bad, and you only got a look at him on the twenty-fourth from the back. We were asked to look at it. It looked like the fedora he always wore, so we assumed it was him. Looked like his coat, too. For sure it was Seth on the earlier days he was here. There was a real, nice front video of him as he turned and walked out of the lobby."

Hodges condensed the timeline, "So, we have a mystery as to why he didn't stay in Tofte for the twenty-third, or where he stayed at all for the twenty-third, because he didn't check back in here till the twenty-fourth. If indeed, that was Seth who checked back here on the twenty-fourth. What about his vehicle?"

"Parked up by the lift-bridge in the public parking area. They towed it on the twenty-fifth. Expired parking," Mancoat said.

"But if he stayed here on the twenty-fourth, why wouldn't it be parked in The Suites parking lot like our auto?" Hodges asked.

"Damn right!" Earl blurted. "Seth could have walked to that area easily from here. He wasn't in bad shape."

"I think we first have to establish if that was really Seth on the hotel video tape," Hodges postulated.

Mancoat seemed to agree, but also seemed confused. "You know, it sure looked like him from the back, but I don't know... we'd have to be able to look at that tape again. The police have it now, and I'm not sure that's such a good idea for you to be talking to the police, Gerry."

"Jasper."

Mancoat shook his head, "Yeah, Jasper... Sorry, but are you sure you should do that?"

Hodges projected confidence when he said, "It won't be a problem, Earl. Does Cadotte have a copy of the video taken at The Suites?"

Mancoat rubbed the stubble on his chin. "I could call her and check."

"Good, you do that while I shower. If she has the tape, tell her you have a friend visiting from Australia, a good friend that knows Seth better than anyone... a friend that is sure to recognize if that is Seth in the second check-in video. She'll be anxious for a break in the story and not want to pass up the opportunity."

"Do you think you can recognize Seth for sure, Jasper?"

Hodges smiled. "I'll know." He retreated to his bathroom along with a change of clothes. Thirty minutes later, he emerged.

"She's coming to our suite tomorrow morning at eight, with a player and the tape. She seemed awfully excited."

"Indeed, very predictable." Hodges sneered.

CHAPTER 3

I t was 8:05 a.m. when Sheila Cadotte knocked on Suite 316 and Earl Mancoat greeted her. She walked into the room with a bag slung over her shoulder, sporting a wide smile.

"You must be Jasper Green," she put down her bag, and pushed a hand toward Hodges.

"I am the one and only. You must be Sheila Cadotte," Hodges said as he shook her hand.

"The one and only," she said brightly.

They spoke for several minutes. Cadotte learned where Hodges had lived, and how long he had stayed there. It was all standard newspaperman talk. Hodges accepted all of her questions with patience.

After ten minutes, Hodges finally said, "I suppose we should look at the footage of our friend."

Evidently not quite ready to move on from the interesting topics presented by a visitor from Tasmania, Cadotte paused before answering, "Yes, well, we should. You're right! We should!" She reached over to open the bag holding her equipment, but Mancoat beat her to it and lifted it to the table.

Her look communicated, *don't touch my stuff again*, and then she opened the bag containing her laptop.

"I thought it was on a video tape!" Mancoat said.

"It was easier to transfer the tape to my laptop. Don't worry, it has excellent clarity, about as good as it could get." She turned the machine on, waited for it to load the operating system and quickly found the file.

"Now, watch closely," she said.

Mancoat and Hodges crowded around the laptop. They both put their reading glasses on and focused on the images. Almost immediately, Seth Tryton appeared on the video, facing the camera.

"That's him for sure," Mancoat said as he pointed at the image. Tryton walked in front of the desk, conversed with the clerk and appeared to pay for his room. He then picked up his bag and disappeared from view.

"All right, next one." Cadotte tapped the keys and brought up the next video. Tryton came into view, but this time, from the rear.

Again, Mancoat was the first to say something. "That's his fedora. I'd know it anywhere."

The figure on the screen walked to the desk, set a bag on the floor and engaged the clerk. The build seemed to be the same as Tryton's, but it was difficult to tell definitely because of the coat he was wearing.

"Can you freeze the video, please?" Hodges asked.

Cadotte froze the image.

Hodges put his face closer to the screen.

Cadotte glanced at Hodges. "Do you see something?"

Hodges looked at her. "Can you put the two images together on the screen? The first one we saw and this one."

"I can put them on a split screen," Cadotte said. She opened up the first video and it began to play.

"Get it to the point where Seth turns his back to the camera and is right in front of the desk," Hodges commanded.

Cadotte did it.

"Now, bring the other video in and find the spot where the two are in the same relative positions."

She did it.

"There, do you see?" Hodges asked.

Mancoat stared at the still videos. "I'll be damned. The second Seth is shorter than the first. It's not Seth. He's wearing his hat and it looks like his coat, but it's not Seth."

Cadotte squinted and leaned in closer to the screen. "Are you sure?"

"Use the painting behind the desk as a guide and look where the fedora lines up in relation to the stallion's head," Hodges said.

Cadotte looked again. "You're right, the first Mr. Tryton is half-way up the head and the second is at the bottom. You have a sharp eye, Mr. Green."

"Call me, Jasper, please."

"Okay... Jasper."

Hodges nodded his head in appreciation before he said, "I think it would be prudent to visit the North Star Motel and interview the individuals who work there."

"Agreed! I'll get my camera and go with you," said Cadotte.

Mancoat frowned. "I think he meant me and him," he said.

Cadotte stopped. She started to speak, but Hodges beat her to it.

"I, uh, think Ms. Cadotte should accompany us, Earl. She might come in handy."

Cadotte smiled. "It'll only take me five minutes to get my note-book and camera from my car. Meet you downstairs in five?"

Hodges smiled and said, "That would be splendid!"

After she left and closed the door, Mancoat lit into Hodges. "Whaddya mean, lettin' her go with us? She's just gonna get in the way, and maybe even discover who you really are! She is a news-woman, after all."

"She may be of use to us, Earl. She has resources and skills we don't."

"Resources, skills? Like what?"

"Her technological know-how is impressive, and she has some inroads with the police department up here. She can be our go between when we need more information from them," Hodges answered.

Mancoat rubbed his chin thoughtfully before he grunted his approval. "Just so long as she doesn't take my place as second in command," he said.

"I wasn't aware there was a second in command," Hodges said.

Hodges and Mancoat plucked their coats from the closet. Mancoat had stuffed a notebook in his coat pocket along with a pen he had swiped from his insurance agent.

Sheila Cadotte was entering the lobby of The Suites as they stepped from the elevator. She insisted that all of them ride in her Lexus. Mancoat raised his eyebrows and nudged Hodges as he gazed at the expensive vehicle.

He spoke in a low voice, "Pretty expensive car for a news lady, wouldn't you say, Jasper?"

Being only ten feet in front of them, and blessed with the typically superhuman hearing acuity of women, Cadotte overheard the question and turned toward them. "I've been very frugal and saved my money so that I afford what I wanted. Do you have a problem with that, Mr. Mancoat?"

Mancoat blinked and stood up straighter. "No," he said. "No, not at all."

Cadotte enjoyed the shocked look on his face. She led them across the street to the parking lot as the men vied to see who would sit in the front seat.

Hodges won out. Mancoat sat in silence, enjoying the view of the lake and the hills as Cadotte drove north on Highway 61. A couple of lake freighters were visible on the horizon of Superior.

"It's a beautiful lake," Hodges said flatly as he looked toward the freighters.

"The North Shore is a wonderful place to live," Cadotte began. "I went to college in Duluth and stayed here after graduation because I loved it so much. The winters can be a little rough, but I'm more than willing to put up with that."

"Where are you originally from?" Hodges asked.

"Chippewa Falls, Wisconsin."

"Must be a beer drinker, huh?" Mancoat interjected.

"Only Leiny's," Cadotte responded. She laughed and then said, "It's only the best beer ever!"

"I'm more partial to Guinness Stout," Mancoat said.

"That's good. How about you, Mr. Green?" Cadotte asked.

"I'm not really a beer connoisseur. Most of the time I like a full-bodied cabernet," Hodges said.

Cadotte and Mancoat restrained their comments. Hodges didn't notice as he studied the entrance of the Silver Creek Tunnel they were approaching. Ten-seconds later they entered the lighted tunnel that had been blasted through some of the oldest granite in North America. They passed through and seconds later emerged on the other end. Spectacular views of the lake appeared now and then as Highway 61 curved around the shoreline. They passed the Cut Face and Knife Rivers as they continued north. Beaver Bay and then Silver Bay were left behind as they approached Palisade Head, a prominent outcropping of rock standing a hundred seventy feet above the lake.

"The North Star Motel is five miles up the road," Cadotte said, and then added, "It's set back from the lake about a mile."

Hodges nodded, but Mancoat filled the silence with his observations of the clerk he and Boston Whitley had interviewed two months earlier. "She's a looker who's been up here only about a year. Comes from New Mexico, I think she said."

"Interesting that's what you focused on Mr. Mancoat," Cadotte said. "Here your friend's missing, and you talk about the good looking motel clerk."

Mancoat shrugged and mumbled something about a man just being a man, and let the matter drop.

Ten minutes later, they turned off Highway 61 and drove nearly a mile inland.

Cadotte's Lexus rumbled over a bridge in need of repair. Mancoat held his breath, and then let it out as they crossed to the other side.

"Sorry, I forgot to tell you about the crumbly bridge," he said sincerely.

"Ya think?" Cadotte blurted.

The North Star Motel was tucked snuggly between a narrow waterfall and a gorgeous stand of old growth red pines on the right. The entrance was a paved, circular drive lined with stout, cedar logs that had been cut at precise angles revealing no seams.

Hodges didn't say a word as he exited the auto and walked briskly through the motel's front doors. He scarcely noticed the animated bickering between his two car mates who lagged behind. An attractive woman, in her late forties, greeted him warmly.

Nyla Borchard had several streaks of gray in her dark shoulder length auburn hair. She looked bright and cheery, and wore a smile that never seemed to stop.

Hodges was always interested in an attractive woman, and he smiled as she greeted him. He introduced himself as Jasper Green, told her the purpose of their visit, and asked if she would mind answering some questions about their missing friend, Seth Tryton.

Nyla hesitated for a moment. "I've already spoken to the police and your friend there, behind you."

"Hmm, surprised you recognized me," Mancoat said, obviously delighted that she remembered him.

Stepping forward and getting in front of Hodges, Cadotte extended her hand and introduced herself.

Nyla said, "I know you. I've seen you on the news. In fact, you reported on the disappearance of that Tryton guy a couple of months ago. I remember!"

Nyla Borchard stepped around from behind the counter and motioned all of them to a round table situated in a small nook where the motel served a deluxe continental breakfast with waffles and cheese omelets. They all sat comfortably. Her shapely figure, set off by her tight jeans and sweater did not escape Mancoat's and Hodge's attention.

Hodges looked around. "I must say, the inside of this motel appears to be much more than just the small-time operation I expected when we drove across that bridge and into your driveway."

"Ah yes, it's a nice little spot. Here... let's have some coffee. It's on the house." " She stood and snapped up four cups from the serving counter and poured coffee for everyone.

"You mentioned the bridge. We've been after the county to fix it for the past five years now. I hope you make it back across without it crashing into the river!"

They all gave her horrified looks. "Just funnin' ya. It'll be fine...I'm sure." The horrified looks didn't vanish. "For real, folks, it'll be fine. Last year they did do some reinforcement work on the foundation. All that's left is cosmetic. I promise." She heard a collective sigh of relief.

Hodges got back to business. "We realize you've spoken to the police and my friend, Mr. Mancoat, before, but we hope you don't mind detailing everything you can remember about our friend one more time," Hodges said.

Borchard smiled.

"Call me Nyla, please. And I don't mind at all. Business has been kind of slow, and to tell you the truth, I enjoy the company once in a while." She brought the coffee cup to her lips, took a sip, and waited for a response.

"Well, Nyla, please tell us what you know...," Cadotte said.

Nyla rose from her chair, "Let me get my book first." She moved behind the counter and retrieved her reservation notebook. She sat down and flipped through the pages until she reached June 21, 2014. "Here it is, Mr. Tryton checked in at one o'clock in the afternoon. Paid in advance for three days at eighty-nine dollars per night... including tax. Eighty-nine bucks a night, total, is a good deal up here during the prime season," she added a little defensively.

"We don't doubt you on that point," Hodges said with a smile.

Nyla lost the defensiveness and continued on. "I liked him. He seemed like a nice, old guy who was curious about the area. I gave him a few brochures and a little advice about where to eat. He said he'd been up here before and liked to hike trails along the rivers. He seemed especially interested in going to Tettegouche State Park, Split Rock Lighthouse, and Palisade Head, so I gave him all the information I could, naturally telling him he was in the center of it all right here." She paused and smiled. "He reminded me a little of my uncle back in New Mexico."

"Did you notice anything unusual about the time he was here, other than not showing up for his last night?" Hodges asked.

Nyla sighed and sat back in her chair. "Not really. He came and went like everyone else. I didn't keep tabs on him."

"Did he mention anyone else that he'd met up here?" Cadotte asked.

Nyla turned her gaze to Cadotte. "Not that I can remember, no. He kibitzed a little with me during breakfast and then headed out to sightsee."

"Did he kibitz with any of the other guests, or go sightseeing with them?" Hodges asked.

"The others pretty much kept to themselves, not that there were all that many of them, but I suppose..." she looked at her notebook. "Looks like we had about a dozen other guests then, and like I said, I don't keep track of everyone."

"Since he seemed like a stand-up fellow, I imagine you were surprised when he didn't return on the twenty-third," Hodges said.

"Exactly. He didn't strike me as the type to do that sort of thing, although I was grateful that he had paid in advance." She looked a little guilty after she said it, realizing that she suddenly appeared to be too concerned with money when a human being's life was in question.

Recognizing her discomfort, and trying to reassure her that he didn't think less of her, Hodges said, "That's all right, Ms. Borch... uh, Nyla."

She gave him a relieved look.

"Did he give any indication where he was going the last day you saw him?" Hodges asked.

"He said he was going to climb Palisade Head, and then he laughed."

"He laughed," Hodges said.

Nyla chuckled, and then said, "Well, you don't climb Palisade Head; you drive to the top on this windy, narrow road... unless... he meant he was going to rock climb. It's a popular place for rock climbing. But no, that couldn't be true. He was too old for that, and pardon me for saying so, but he wasn't in any kind of physical shape to do that, regardless of his age."

"You're right," Mancoat said. "There's no way he'd try that."

"I think we can safely rule that scenario out then," Cadotte said.

A young couple entered the motel. Nyla excused herself and rose to greet them. As she checked them in, Cadotte, Hodges, and Mancoat compared impressions, and came to the same conclusion; they would visit Palisade Head first.

They waited until Nyla was free, thanked her for all her help and left for Palisade Head. It was a ten-minute drive to the turn-off for the well-known landmark.

Cadotte maneuvered the Lexus up the narrow asphalt roadway. She only had to stop once and pull over to allow another vehicle descending the road to pass. As the road curved its way upward, the only view was sky and treetops.

Three minutes later, they arrived at the circular drive that led to a parking area. Two other cars filled the tiny lot. Cadotte slid the Lexus into the only spot available, and all three of them got out of the car.

"Right here at the edge of the cliff it's about 200 feet down to the water. If you walk to the top of the bluff it's about 300 feet higher than the lake," Cadotte said. Showing off her knowledge, she continued, "It's formed from a rhyolitic flow which was extruded some 1.1 billion years ago. During the Mesoproterozoic era of the Precambrian eon, the continent spread apart on the Midcontinent Rift extending from what is now eastern Lake Superior through Duluth to Kansas."

"You sound like an encyclopedia," Hodges said, and then added, "You know your facts."

"I looked it up on my phone while Nyla was talking about it. Plus, I'm interested in rock climbing. In fact, I've descended and ascended this cliff, and the one at Shovel Point." She pointed north where a massive flow of the same type of rock extended toward the lake.

"I think I'll take a walk to the top. Care to join me?" Hodges asked.

"Lead the way," Cadotte said and then motioned him upward and away from the edge of the cliff. Mancoat trailed behind both of them, taking his time, stopping periodically to stare at Cadotte's shapely derriere.

A trail guided them through rock, brush and trees to the summit of the bluff where they stood and looked out over the lake and the remnants of the ancient Sawtooth Mountains. The range was given the name because from various points along the lake, the peaks resembled the teeth of a saw jutting up from the land.

"Breathtaking," Hodges said as he slowly turned his head, taking in the beauty of the landscape.

"And this is why I stayed in this area of the country," Cadotte said. She shook her head with sadness. "I don't stay for the duties of the job... especially when it comes down to missing, or murdered, persons. I should tell you... this isn't the first unexplained disappearance on the North Shore in the past two years. There are two others; a twenty-two year old woman, and a forty-three year old man."

Hodges turned to face her and stared for a moment before he said, "Similar circumstances?"

"They're complete mysteries, just like Mr. Tryton's disappearance," she said.

"What do you know about them?" Hodges asked.

"There's actually very little information to go on, just like this case. Cassie Bandleson came up here to backpack, left her car at the Superior Hiking Trailhead parking lot and was never seen again. The forty-three year old male was fishing in one of the lakes in Tettegouche State Park and was never seen again. They found his boat near the waterfall, but no sign of him. They expected to find him in the lake. They dragged it over and over again, but never found a body. The DNR and sheriff theorized the body drifted out of the lake, down the waterfall, over several more waterfalls along the way before finding its way into Lake Superior...where bodies are generally never recovered."

"Tettegouche, that's not far from here," Mancoat said.

Cadotte said, "Remember, just a few miles north where I pointed out Shovel Point? That's part of Tettegouche State Park. It contains a few lakes, a campground, a visitor center, and plenty of shoreline."

"What about the girl, did she disappear in this area?" Hodges asked.

"A little farther away... I think her car was found at the parking area just north of the Tofte area," Cadotte said. "It's about ten miles from here."

"Evidently, they were both alone, otherwise there would be at least some knowledge of precisely where they had been, were going, etc.," Hodges said.

"Yes, as far as we know, they were alone. The girl was an experienced hiker who did at least a couple solo hikes a year, and the man was from Virginia, Minnesota, up here for a weekend of fishing. From what the police reported, he was a guy who lived alone and loved the outdoors. According to his neighbors, he did a lot of recreating in northeastern Minnesota."

CHAPTER 4

The North Shore, Sixteen months earlier

Her ankle burned. It still bore the marks of leg irons. Instinctively, she rubbed it with both hands. The night was black, interrupted only by a sliver of light from the moon. Sitting on a rock, surrounded by trees, Cassie Bandleson wondered where the hell she was. The opening in the hill that she had crawled from was several hundred yards away. Which direction? She didn't know.

Perspiration dripped from her face to the sleeve of her flannel shirt. She strained to see anything that would help her decide which direction to run, because run she must.

Sooner or later he would return and discover she was gone. She needed to put distance between herself and her prison. There had been no way of telling day from night, only her sleeping patterns helped her estimate the time. Her best guess was that she had been a prisoner of the man for four days.

Cassie stood. Trying to ignore the pain, she stumbled through the dark, brush tearing at her clothes, rocks smashing into her knees, and tree branches swatting her head. *My God, I've got to make it out of here! Run!*

Her legs pumped as her steeled heart ordered her body to move. She extended her arms and hands in front to protect her face from obstacles, seen and unseen. Cassie did not wonder how her body could take this punishment. When you're running for your life, you don't care. You just move.

She pushed forward. The forest seemed to rise up against her, tearing, clutching and ripping at her clothes. And then she tumbled, slamming into trees and boulders before coming to rest at the bottom of a ravine. Breathing heavily, she slowly tried to move her limbs, first her arms, then her legs. She laughed. *Nothing broken!*

Hearing the rumble of some sort of vehicle in the distance, her hopes rose. *That way.* She pointed with her left hand and limped toward the sound, but more carefully now. *Take it slow.*

Following the ravine, which seemed more like a cut in the hillside, she knew she was descending; her momentum was always downhill, even if she couldn't see well, she could feel it. The shallow walls of the ravine gave her a sense of being protected. She even started to believe it.

Voices! She heard voices. She was sure of it. Picking her way toward the sound, she could tell it was from a radio talk show, playing much too loudly. Maybe it was a couple of kids parked, making out, whatever. They were going to be surprised by a beaten up, struggling hiker. She smiled as she worked her way closer.

She stood in the shadows, looking for signs of life from the pickup. It was getting late. The radio talk turned to jazz. *No kids would be listening to jazz.* She turned and melted further into the forest, sneaking a worried look back at the truck. The dome light was on. Someone had opened the door. She started moving away faster and breathing harder. *It was him!* Soon she was flailing at branches and running, her heart pounding so hard she thought it would burst from her chest.

A tree branch caught her in the eye, causing an involuntary, mini scream to erupt from her. Tears came quickly. Hysteria was near as she realized he might have heard the cry. Now, nearly blind in one eye, lost in the night, body aching, she calmed herself as best she could and limped away... until... a flashlight beam illuminated her. Hysteria took over, and she turned the other way, screaming, crashing through the brush and trees with the beam of light partially showing her the way until she emerged on a gravel road.

Thunderous footsteps were close behind. She screamed as loud as she could and turned to face him. She flailed her arms and struck out forcefully. The light enveloped her, and pain wracked her head as she went down, crying... and then there was darkness.

Karonen dragged Cassie toward his truck.

I shouldn't have hit her so hard! Dead or relaxed weight was heavy. He knew that from experience. Lucky for him, she had made it to the road. Carefully letting Cassie down after dragging her for twenty yards, he jogged back to the truck and drove it to her. With difficulty, he partially hoisted her onto the truck bed, and holding her upper body in place, he hefted the rest of her in. After shutting the lift gate, he closed the tonneau cover, quickly returned to the driver's seat and drove back to his home.

Once she was safely in her quarters, he waited for her to wake. An hour and a half later, she still had not awakened.

He tried shaking her, yelling her name; nothing worked. Karonen paced inside her cell. This would not do. It had been stupid of him to let her escape in the first place. *Now, what do I have to work with?*

It was an experiment gone bad. He had only wanted to study her reactions, her emotions, and then glean information from her after recapture.

Cassie stirred, then moaned.

Karonen's hopes jumped. *She's going to make it!* A smile appeared on his desperate looking face. He went to her, feverishly arranging her on the bed as she continued to moan. *She'll be okay. She'll be okay.* He didn't need another companion gone bad.

Six months prior to chancing upon Miss Bandleson on the Superior Hiking Trail, he had made the mistake of taking Tom Hecimovich, a younger man than he, who was strong and determined. Eventually, Mr. Hecimovich needed to be dealt with in a most severe manner. His body would never be found. Karonen was sure of that. The fisherman had been an error. He faulted his judgment for taking him in the first place.

The palpable relief he now felt released all emotion from him. He sat on the folding chair he kept in Bandleson's room, and breathed deeply, burying his face in his hands. Five minutes later, he walked over to Bandleson.

She opened her eyes and stared at him.

"Welcome back, Cassie," he said warmly.

She closed her eyes again and turned her face away. He patted her arm and left.

Pausing at the opening of her chamber, he glanced back, as if he wasn't quite sure she was all right. Karonen was satisfied when he observed her move to her side. He latched the gate and locked it. "Good night, Cassie," he said.

Ten hours later, Cassie opened her eyes again. She moved from her side to her back. The bed she lay in was comfortable, to the point of annoyance. She didn't want to be comfortable in her prison. Anger and despair filled her head as she ruminated about her lost opportunity for escape.

Thinking of escape again, she took stock of her functioning body parts; she moved her arms, legs, fingers, and toes. Everything worked, although her ankle and head still hurt. Cassie also noted she was not chained in any way. She was surprised, but happy for that circumstance.

Her room was a rock and timber chamber with a bed, a small bookcase filled with classic literature, a round wooden table, a mirror, a thick area rug covering half the floor, a chandelier hanging from a massive timber in the center, a portable toilet, and a wash basin. A bucket of fresh water was always provided. At least it always seemed fresh. If she thought of the room as a bedroom, it was much larger than anything she had ever possessed. It was probably thirty feet by fifteen with a ceiling height of ten. She could put a children's basketball court in here, or a wine rack.

She was disgusted with herself. *Don't start thinking of this place as a home. It's a prison!*

While staring at the walls, Cassie stood, walked to the nearest one, and ran a hand along it until she had circled the room. *Why isn't it damp? It should be at least a little wet.* She pondered the question, but didn't resolve it. *It doesn't matter. What difference would it make?*

She sat on the bed and sighed deeply, holding her face in her hands.

I can't believe I ran right into him! Idiot. Next time, I won't make the same mistake.

She heard the familiar sound of footsteps and readied herself for the appearance of Mr. Karonen.

"Good, you're awake. You had a rough night so I brought you croissants, cheese, and meats. The cheese is a nice Blue Castello. It has a soft, buttery, tangy taste. I'm sure you'll love it," Karonen said. "And the meats are fresh from the tourist trap down the highway. The water is from my tap. It's good Lake Superior water." He smiled, and placed the tray he had meticulously arranged on the table near her bed.

The tourist trap down the road? She filed another note in her head. Cassie said nothing, but stared at Karonen, who looked like a jovial grandfather. *What was wrong with this man?*

Karonen seemed to wait for her to speak, so finally, she said it without emotion. "What is wrong with you? Why are you doing this to me?"

He flinched a little before he said, "The croissant is warm and you will want to spread the cheese on it before it gets cold. Please enjoy your meal, and we'll talk later."

"Mr. Karonen, we need to talk now." Again, she said it evenly, which seemed to take him off guard.

He stared at her.

She stared back... waiting for him to speak.

"I collected you."

"You collected me."

He looked away, as if he was searching for something on the wall to her left. She turned to where he gazed. On the wall was the photo she had noticed before, but never given much thought. It was a young woman, not pretty, but pleasant looking.

He continued to stare at the photo as if he were immersing

himself in every fine detail and extracting every scintilla of emotion he could from it.

"Who is she?" She finally asked.

"Methodist is her name," he said.

"Do I remind you of her?" She asked.

He smiled wryly. "No," he shook his head. The action seemed to relieve him of his absorption with the photo. "No, you're nothing like Methodist." He paused before he backed from the cell and latched the gate. "I'll come back for your plate later."

Cassie looked down. She suddenly realized how famished she was, and plucked a croissant from the tray. She spread a thick mass of the Blue Castello cheese on it, and then took a large bite of heaven.

CHAPTER 5

Cadotte repositioned the scarf around her neck. "It's getting windy."

Mancoat lumbered up the Palisade Head trail to where they stood.

"I'd like to visit the trailhead where the young lady's car was parked," Hodges said. No one expressed an objection.

The trio walked the trail down to their parking lot, loaded into the Lexus and made their way down the winding road without incident. They headed north on Highway 61 and arrived at the trailhead near Tofte thirty minutes later.

Three empty cars were parked in the lot, suggesting hikers were on the trail somewhere north of them.

"Just what do you hope to accomplish by visiting the parking area where the missing woman's car was found? That was a long time ago," Mancoat asked.

"Not much, just satisfying my curiosity more than anything," Hodges completed a 360-degree view of the area. He then approached the trailhead and began hiking.

Cadotte and Mancoat followed. Mancoat liked his view from the rear. They walked the first mile slowly, stopping at different points to observe stunning vistas of valleys, lakes, and rivers along the way.

"I can see why people do this," Hodges said. "I wish I were younger and could go further," he said before sitting on a rock outcropping and viewing the valley below, painted in oranges, yellows, reds, and greens.

"I sure hope you're getting something out of this," Mancoat

said. "Because I'm not seeing the point to this right now. We should be out talking to people and getting clues to where Seth is... or was."

"Perhaps the key to finding Seth is linked to the other disappearances."

"We don't know that," Cadotte said.

"No, we don't, but they may all be linked somehow," Hodges said.

A visibly frustrated Mancoat drifted to the edge of the bluff, picked up a rock and tossed it over the edge, inadvertently scaring a turkey vulture that had been perched forty feet below. Surprised by the large bird taking flight, Mancoat jumped back.

"A hiker could easily access this trail at several points." Hodges had resumed walking as he made the statement. "Do you know how far the next access point is?"

Cadotte rubbed at her pockets and then shrugged her shoulders. "No map on me, so nope, I don't," she said.

They kept walking, but at a slower pace.

"Are we just enjoying a hike, or is there another purpose to this, Mr. Green?"

"I don't know about you, but I am enjoying it immensely. But, to your larger question, I am curious as to how far it is between access points," Hodges answered.

"Well, I hate to spoil your *immense* enjoyment, but I'm getting bushed, and I think I'm gonna head back right now," said Mancoat. "Could you give me the keys, Sheila, so I can have a comfortable place to sit, while you two do your hiking thing?"

Cadotte was tempted to join him, but changed her mind. She dug in her purse and tossed him the keys.

"Earl, you have your cell phone on you, right?" Hodges asked.

"Yeah, got it right here in my pocket, Jasper." He patted the bulge in his jacket.

"I think we'll hike to the next access point and have you pick us up there," Hodges said.

"I'm not really dressed for this, and that could be miles!" Cadotte said with irritation in her voice.

Hodges turned and continued to hike the trail. "Yes, it could be, but I think we're both in good enough shape to do it."

Cadotte adjusted her light-weight jacket around her waist and followed. "You be careful with my car!" she yelled back to Mancoat, who waved and told her not to worry.

Ahead of them, the trail descended steeply; sharp rocks, embedded in the red clay soil jutted toward the sky.

Cadotte assumed the lead, partly out of concern for Hodges, who was considerably older than she was. She figured that if he stumbled, she would be in position to catch him, or at least get in the way of a nasty fall.

She wasn't concerned she could be hurt in the process. Her muscle mass was densely packed on a one hundred thirty-two pound, five-foot-five frame. It was due to an active lifestyle that included hiking, kayaking, weightlifting, and Kalairppayattu, a martial art with origins in India.

Behind her, Cadotte heard the sound of a shoe catching on a rock, accompanied by an alarmed call from Hodges. She turned in time to brace herself and catch him as he fell into her. The hat Hodges had bought at the Duluth Trading Company slid halfway off his head and settled against Cadotte's shoulder.

Embarrassed, Hodges sputtered, "I'm so sorry, Miss Cadotte. Apparently I wasn't paying enough attention to the trail and caught one of the rocks. I'm surprised I didn't take you to the ground as well."

Cadotte held onto him as he regained his balance. "All in a day's work, Mr. Green. You just found out that I come in handy for more than my technological skills or contacts with the police and sheriff departments in the area." She winked. "And please, call me Sheila."

Hodges paused and then said with a bow, "And you can call me Jasper."

She smiled. "All right, Jasper, let's keep moving." They resumed their hike, eventually reaching the bottom of the trail as it inched its way next to a river. A wooden footbridge had been constructed over the river giving them an excellent view of a small chute of white water as they passed over it. Two miles and a blister on Hodges' foot later, a solitary hiker with a daypack hanging on his back came their way. He waved as he neared, and then stopped to talk. "How far you going?" he asked.

"To the next trailhead and parking area," Cadotte said as Hodges settled onto a log and took off his shoe to examine his blister.

"Well, you're pretty close. It's probably less than a mile from here," he looked over at Hodges. "Looks like you've got a problem."

"I guess I bit off a bit more than I could chew today," Hodges said.

"Lucky you don't have very far to go. It's no fun hiking with any kind of injury. Good luck to you." The hiker began walking away.

Hodges spoke up. "Say, before you go, would you mind telling us a little about this section of the trail?" The hiker came back.

"Sure, I've got plenty of time to get to the next trailhead. What would you like to know?"

"Do you know how many trailheads there are within the next fifteen miles or so?"

"They're about every four to five miles. When they made the trail, they tried to keep it fairly easy for day hikers like me, although, just over a year ago, I did a hundred mile section, including this part."

"You went alone?" Cadotte asked.

"No, I'm not the type to do that. I went with a couple friends."

Hodges jumped back into the conversation. "Did you meet anyone else on the trail?"

"Oh yeah, lots of people hike this section. It's one of the most popular. I mean I don't want to give you the impression it's Hennepin Avenue busy, or anything like that, but every few miles you meet people, kind of like the BWCA where you tend to meet a lot of people on the portages. Also, one of the best parts of hiking long stretches is that you can hike off the trail to state park campgrounds or pick designated spots right on the trail. It's very cool."

Cadotte took a stab in the dark. "You don't happen to remember meeting a young woman hiking alone? It would have been over a year ago."

The hiker laughed. "Well, that narrows it down. Remember that woman who went missing hiking this trail alone? My friends and I talked about that after it happened, and we did meet a woman who matched the description, but... who knows, could have been her, but probably not."

"Where was she, and what direction was she going?" Hodges asked.

"Funny you should ask. It wasn't far from here, in fact, it was just after the next trailhead, and she was going the way you're heading now."

"Did you ever tell the sheriff about it?" Cadotte asked.

"Yeah, we did, but we just didn't have much information beyond what I told you, so I don't think it helped them at all. They showed us pictures of her, but none of us could be sure it was the same woman, so it probably wasn't."

After a little more inconsequential talk about the encounter, Cadotte and Hodges thanked the young man and resumed their hike with a little more spring in their steps.

A visibly excited Hodges took the lead and gestured with his arms as he spoke. "This could be important. If this was the woman who disappeared, then we have a timeline and a location where she might have gone missing."

"Listen, Jasper, the sheriff and the police combed this entire area looking for her and found absolutely nothing. Dozens of volunteers walked the trail, off the trail, some searching for miles beyond where she was thought to have gone missing. There were no signs of her anywhere."

"Just like my friend, Mr. Tryton," Hodges said.

They stopped, and Hodges leaned on a tree trunk while Cadotte stood a few feet away. He slowly pulled the hat from his head and mashed it into a ball. He loved that he could do that and the hat would resume its natural form when he opened it up again.

"These people and my friend, Seth, didn't just disappear," Hodges said as he mashed and then reformed the hat. "To simply vanish does not make sense to me."

"It does if they all ended up in Lake Superior. Because of the coldness and the bacteria in the lake, bodies that go into the lake never see the surface again. Lots of people have never been recovered," Cadotte said.

"Oh please... the theory of the man falling into the smaller lake, drifting out of that lake to the river, down various waterfalls, and eventually settling into Lake Superior is absurd; that man was snatched by someone! And Seth, we have direct evidence that another man pretended to be him and then probably moved his car to the parking area near the lake to give the impression that Seth was drinking and drowned when he fell over a chest high barrier into the channel where the ore boats enter and exit the harbor. Ridiculous! They dragged the harbor and channel and found nothing. And the woman, did she also fall in the water and end up in the lake? Does that make sense?" His eyes were hot and determined as he looked at her.

She said nothing for several seconds, wavering in her own convictions until she spoke, "No, no; it doesn't." She stood still for a moment longer and then quietly said, "They could all be alive."

Hodges cooled down and nodded. "That is what I'm hoping."

He plopped the hat back on his head and they resumed walking the trail. A mile later, Hodges called Mancoat and told him which trailhead they were at and that he should come and pick them up.

When Mancoat pulled into the trailhead parking lot, Cadotte waved and made a show of inspecting the auto for any dings in the paint. After conferring, the three of them decided Hodges and Mancoat would return the next morning, and walk at least the beginning of the second trail to look for anything that would help them. Cadotte had to work the next day, but she promised that she would do some more digging on the other disappearances in the newspaper's archives, and if she had time, would review the police records of all three disappearances.

That evening, after saying goodnight to Cadotte, they returned to The Suites, and Hodges soaked in the Jacuzzi while Mancoat went downstairs to the bar and downed four Guinness Stouts. Hodges finished his soak, dressed, and took the elevator down a flight to the Timber Lodge Restaurant. Not showing any hint of inebriation, Mancoat raised an arm and waved until Hodges saw him.

Taking the stool next to Mancoat's at the bar, Hodges ordered a glass of Penfolds Grange Shiraz. The bar tender looked at him blankly before responding. "I'm pretty sure we don't have that, sir."

Bemused, Hodges then said, "All right then, I'll have a glass of D'Arenberg d'Arry's original Shiraz-Grenache."

"Sir, I'm not really familiar with that wine either," the bartender said.

Unwilling to ask for another by name, Hodges asked, "What's your best Cabernet?"

"That would be from Ravenswood in Sonoma—"

Hodges said, "I'll have a glass of that."

CHAPTER 6

S eth Tryton woke slowly. Heavy eyelids peeled halfway open and focused on walls made of rock and timber. He lay on a comfortable queen-sized bed with a comforter pulled over his chin. Moaning, he rolled his right leg over his left and pulled the comforter off his body. When he moved both feet to the floor and stood, he felt the shackle on his left ankle. The chain attached to it lay across the floor of the room and was anchored into a wall timber.

His head was pounding. He looked toward what appeared to be a gate, and above it, a video camera mounted in one corner of the ceiling seemed to track every movement he made. His mind returned to his ankle, where the shackle caused a burning ache. It was tight and bit into his skin.

"Stay on the bed, Seth." A voice he recognized floated through the air. Peter Karonen soon appeared at the barred door. Tryton recognized the click of an opened padlock, and then the door opened with very little accompanying noise, and Karonen stepped into the chamber.

Tryton squinted. "Peter, what the hell is going on?" He tugged at the shackle on his leg.

"I'm sorry, but the clamp is a necessary precaution. I can't trust you... yet."

"I don't understand. I figure you drugged me, and then chained me to this wall inside your homemade dungeon." His hands shook as the anger inside boiled over. He yanked on the chain and yelled, "Tell me what I missed, Peter! Why the hell did you do this to me? And you'd better be specific, because I am pissed beyond belief." He stood and panted. His angry soliloquy had nearly winded him.

"I need a companion," Karonen said sadly, apologetically.

Tryton didn't say anything for several moments, and then he shouted, "You need a fucking companion? That's it? Hell, I liked you. I thought you were a good guy. Intelligent, fun, you like to drink. I'd of stuck around for a while just because I liked you. You didn't need to shanghai me and then chain me to a wall in a dungeon. I would have been your friend!"

"The companion is not for me."

Tryton gave Karonen a slant-eyed look and was momentarily speechless. Disregarding his predicament for a moment, Tryton said, "A companion, not for you... but for someone else. Who?"

"When you've calmed down and are able to listen, I'll explain, and you'll meet her."

"Holy balls! You just don't do this to people and expect them to calm down and listen, at least not me!"

"Seth, if you help her, I'll be good to you, and you'll eventually get out of here. I promise. But if you don't help, I don't know if I can ever let you go."

Tryton made a rush for Karonen and let loose a bellow.

Karonen didn't move.

Seven feet short of Karonen, Tryton was jerked back by the chain. Stinging pain shot through his ankle as the shackle bit into the skin.

"Seth, you need to think about it. I'll return in an hour. Truly, think about it!" Karonen pivoted and walked away from the cell. He replaced the padlock and snapped it in place. He flipped one last look through the barred door at Seth and then left without another word.

Tryton, wracked in pain, shaking and angry, yelled, "You son-of-a-bitch! I'll get out of here and beat the living shit out of you. That's what you'll truly see!" He turned and shuffled back to the bed where he sat down and began prying at the shackle with his fingers.

An hour later, Karonen returned and Tryton yelled and screamed, "You bastard! You come in here and get close to me and I'll tear your arms off! Come on in, you son-of-a-bitch!" Tryton stood in a fighting stance with his fists beckoning Karonen.

Karonen undid the padlock and entered the cell. "Very well," he said, and approached Seth. He showed no fear as he went straight to Tryton, who struck out with a roundhouse aimed at Karonen's head. He evaded the blow and grabbed Tryton's arm. Karonen yanked downward and pulled Tryton to the floor—face down. Karonen knelt on Tryton's back, placing his knee in the middle. When Tryton attempted to get up, Karonen increased the pressure, causing Tryton to cry out.

Tryton tried to turn on his side, to no avail.

"I can do this all day, Seth," Karonen said.

"I can do this all fucking day, too," Tryton yelled.

Karonen elicited another scream of pain from Tryton by twisting his arm up and back.

"Wait, wait, stop," Tryton yelled, giving up.

Karonen stopped. "I'm going to let you go, and then I'll pull a chair up next to the bed. Will you talk then?"

In pain, a defeated Tryton replied, "Yeah, yeah, I'll talk. I'm too old for this shit."

Karonen pulled his knee from Tryton's back, let go of his arm, and slowly moved away.

Tryton rolled over onto his side, and then onto his knees. With difficulty, he crawled to the bed and waited.

Karonen placed the chair ten feet away from the bed and sat. He was still guarded against the possibility of an attack from Tryton.

"You wanted to talk. Talk! Who's the companion?" Tryton demanded.

"Her name is Methodist, and she needs someone, maybe you, who can get through to her."

"What do you mean someone who can get through to her?"

Karonen's gaze shifted to the floor and he clasped his hands in front of him. "She's in a catatonic state, has been for three years now. She can't... won't... talk to me."

Tryton shook his head imperceptibly. He was weary and his

attitude had softened. There was a long pause. "She needs a hospital, Peter, with trained staff. What do you expect an old man to accomplish that professionals can't?"

Karonen shivered and said, "No hospitals, no nurses, doctors, psychiatrists, or therapists. She wouldn't want that. I know she wouldn't. I only need the right person; someone who can bring her back to me."

Tryton, growing more curious, asked, "Have you ever tried it? A hospital, I mean."

"At first, but it didn't work, so I brought her home, set up a room with the right equipment to keep her alive while I tried to get through to her." Becoming excited and talking faster, Karonen said, "When I met you, I thought immediately that you could be the one. You're easy to talk to. You're kind, and you're a good man." His body shook when he said, "I think it could be you who makes the difference. You could bring her back!"

Tryton sat silent for several moments before asking, "Who is she? Your wife?"

Karonen looked at him hopefully. "She's my daughter."

"Peter, I've got a lot of questions about this, and I don't know where to begin."

"Just ask anything. I'll answer everything. I just need you to try to get through to her."

"What happened to her?"

"Drugs. She took too many. I'm sure it was an accident and she didn't mean to try and kill herself. They were prescription medications, and she got confused and just took too many. She'd never try to kill herself," he repeated. "She called me, and I found her in her apartment. I called the hospital and they took her by ambulance, got her stomach pumped out, but she just wouldn't wake up. Eventually, they said she was brain dead, but I knew she wasn't. I know she isn't! She just needs the right person to get through to her! It could be you, Seth."

"Where is she?"

Karonen became more excited. "You'll do it?"

Trying to buy time and looking for any opportunity to escape, Tryton said, "I have to see her first. Let me see her."

Karonen jumped up from his chair. "She's in the house. In her bedroom!"

"Take me there."

"Of course, of course, let me get one thing, though." Karonen left the cell. He returned a few minutes later holding a collar in front of him.

"What's that?"

"I'm going to have to take the leg iron off, but I'm sorry, I can't take the chance of you trying to trick me, so I have to put this around your neck. It's a shock collar... to control you. I'm sorry, but I can't trust you yet."

Tryton, who had changed his tactics to gain his freedom, looked wryly at the collar and said, "I understand."

"Please, place your hands in front of you." Tryton did as Karonen requested. He felt the clamp of handcuffs around his wrists and took a deep breath. Karonen placed the shock collar around his neck and activated it. Next, he removed the ankle clamp. Tryton's ankle felt better instantly.

"All right. We're ready to see Methodist." He made Tryton walk in front of him as they worked their way out of the cell and through the winding tunnels, passing two other locked and darkened cells. They emerged from the shaft at the point Tryton remembered entering, and walked to Methodist's bedroom. He remembered the revolting odor in the house. It was musty, but something else, something that reminded him of a sewer, or road kill.

The door was closed. Karonen moved in front of Seth and unlocked the door. When he opened it, the odor was overwhelming. Tryton winced. Karonen flicked the light switch on, and Seth's eyes needed a moment to adjust to the brightness. He stepped through the doorway, and at first glance, saw no one.

"She's in bed, Seth." Karonen pushed him into the room by the small of his back, nudging him forward.

Tryton walked to the bed and noticed a small bulge under the covers, about the length of a young adult. He blinked. The stench was overpowering. He stared at the face jutting out from the covers. It was leathery and taut. Her eyes were wide and unblinking. An IV tube dripped fluid into her emaciated left arm. On closer examination, much of the liquid appeared to just dribble out of her arm and onto the covers. She didn't move.

"Methodist," Karonen said quietly. "You have a friend who's come to talk to you." The figure beneath the covers did not move. "Talk to her Seth, talk to her."

Tryton walked nearer to the bed and leaned over, a couple of feet away from Methodist's face. "Hello, Methodist. I'm Seth." There was no movement or sound from her.

"I think she likes you," Karonen said. "Sit on the bed beside her."

Reluctantly, Tryton managed to sit on the edge of the bed next to her, the handcuffs digging into his wrists. He repeated, "Hello, Methodist, I'm Seth." There was no movement, and no answer.

Tryton turned toward Karonen, "Peter, I—"

"Just talk, Seth, she's listening." Karonen nodded his head and motioned for Seth to look at Methodist.

Tryton played along. He turned, and for the first time, noticed the bed was saturated with fluid. The section of the bed where he sat was damp; and still, there was no movement from Methodist.

"Methodist, I'm here to keep you company for a while," Seth began. "Maybe you have a favorite book I could read to you."

"Excellent idea, Seth! I'll be back in a moment." Karonen shuffled from the room.

Tryton heard the lock turn.

Foreboding consumed him, but he lifted the covers from Methodist. Immediately the odor washed over him. The sheets were covered in a mixture of green, yellow and orange colored stains. Drawing back her flannel nightgown, he gagged when he saw that it covered nothing more than bones and taute yellow skin. His head snapped back. He tried to hold his breath and not inhale any more of the decomposed corpse's odor.

He heard the lock turn and hurriedly pulled the covers back over the rotting cadaver.

Karonen entered the room holding a hardcover copy of *Pride and Prejudice*.

"She adores this book. Here." He handed the copy to Tryton, who reached out his cuffed hands to accept it. He stared at the book without seeing.

"Read, Seth, read! I know she is super excited about this. The sound of another voice will rejuvenate her; and you have an excellent voice for reading. She'll love it. Read!"

Tryton opened the book and began to read.

"It is universally acknowledged, that a single man in possession of a good fortune must be in want of a wife." He read until Karonen stopped him, getting through the first three chapters.

"I think that's enough for today. I see she is tiring a little, and may need a change in her feeding tube." Karonen directed Tryton to place the book on the nightstand next to the bed and turn off the lamp. He did as he was told, and stood when Karonen motioned to leave the room. Karonen followed, shut off the light and locked the door behind him.

They walked back to Tryton's chamber where Karonen chained his leg, undid the cuffs, and removed the collar from his neck. After Karonen left, Tryton sat on his bed. He felt mentally exhausted and nauseated. The odor of the rotting corpse mixed with the IV liquids that had soaked the bed stuck like glue in his nasal passages.

He lay on the bed and contemplated his predicament. Either Karonen was insane and Tryton was unsure of how to deal with that fact, or Karonen was merely using him in some sick mind game. Maybe Karonen was experimenting with how long his subject would put up with a fatuous situation before he chanced calling him out on the insane nature of the affair. His head pounded.

The combination of the stench of rotten human flesh, and the probability of insanity threatened to propel him into a downward spiral of despair.

CHAPTER 7

The previous evening in the Timber Lodge bar had felt like old times for Hodges. He knew he had drunk too much and listened to too many of the same tepid stories from Mancoat. But the familiarity of it all had made him realize how much he missed his old friends and previous life in the quiet, little town of Rose Creek. He stopped shaving and just stared at himself in the mirror. *I am different now, but the same.*

He put the razor on the edge of the sink and leaned on the counter. His head drooped and he closed his eyes. The sickening thud of a nightstick smashing into Laura Walter's head once, twice, three, four times reverberated in his ears until his eyes sprang open. He splashed water on his face and tried to wash the memory away. *I am different now!* Hodges picked up the razor and finished shaving.

Thirty minutes later, Hodges and Mancoat drove up the shore and returned to the trailhead they had left the previous day. The hiking boots they had purchased that morning felt vastly superior to the dress shoes they had worn eighteen hours before. Hodges had also covered his blister with moleskin and felt confident he was well prepared for today's hike.

They began on the section of the trail where they believed the Bandleson woman was last seen. Hodges felt a growing faith in his belief that the three cases of missing persons were all related, and that the young hiker they met yesterday had seen Bandleson.

"Why are you so positive the woman seen by that guy yesterday was Bandleson?" Mancoat asked.

"It's a gut feeling, Earl. I have nothing else to base it on."

"And if it was her, why do you think we're going to learn anything more by hiking this trail?"

Hodges stared at the forest ahead of them, and then answered as he walked, "I don't know where else to go right now. I keep thinking that something is going to come to me or something so obvious is going to present itself and give us another clue as to what happened to her... and lead us to Seth."

Mancoat puffed while he walked the steeply inclined rock and clay trail, but he was still able to say, "I sure hope so, Jasper, because I don't think this old, out of shape body can take much of this kind of walking."

Cadotte walked upstairs, threw her jacket onto the coat hanger next to her cubicle, and plopped down into her roller chair. The computer terminal was lit up—waiting for her to get started on a myriad of possible stories. Get started was a misnomer; she had already begun three stories that would probably be buried somewhere in the middle of the paper. Two, would be in the human interest section and the other, she hoped, would make the front page; it would zero in on the three disappearances within the past twenty-three months.

"Hey, Sheila, did you make any headway this weekend with the two old coots?" asked Sam Moller, the managing editor.

Agitated, Cadotte turned around and narrowed her eyes at him. "Don't scare me like that, Sam. I'm jumpy enough anyway just thinking about the disappearances, and then you do that!"

He gave her a halfway apologetic look before saying, "Didn't mean to surprise you, Sheila, it's just that I'm curious and..." he trailed off and shrugged his shoulders. She stared at him for another moment. He leaned on the roller chair nearby, obviously not moving until he heard something from her.

She matched his silence and stare for a few moments, and then spoke. "Actually, I think this may result in some movement on these cases. Mancoat's Tasmanian friend impresses me. He seems to have a way about him that just gives you the idea that he knows things, and if he doesn't know things, you definitely feel like he's going to figure them out. Mancoat is basically a dufus who's only there for a little comic relief."

Moller tilted his head to the other side and stepped back from the chair he had been leaning on. "Well, that's encouraging. By the way, I thought Mancoat, the dufus, had said his friend was from Australia." And then, seeming to lose interest in Mancoat, he added in a dispassionate tone, "Have you checked in with the police yet and told 'em about these two beginning their own little investigation?"

Cadotte pursed her lips like she was about to put lipstick on, and then said, "Ah... no, but I plan to... soon. By the way, Tasmania is part of Australia."

Moller walked away. "Just keep me informed," he called back to her. "We may get lucky on this thing, and if we do, we'll sell a bunch of papers."

Cadotte sat motionless for two-seconds, and then turned to her computer. Her fingers flew as she punched the keyboard and searched the newspaper archives for the past three years. She began with the unexplained disappearances of Tom Hecimovich, Cassie Bandleson, and Seth Tryton.

Hecimovich had been single, an outdoor enthusiast, and a popular science teacher at the Virginia public high school. She breezed through the information, most of which she had written after his disappearance two years ago. Cadotte then moved on to Cassie Bandleson, a young waitress from Silver Bay, who loved to hike the trails in northern Minnesota and Wisconsin; a real outdoors woman. Seth Tryton was last on her list. The article she had written about his disappearance was shorter on personal information than the other two, but made up for it in the added mysteriousness.

Her fingers withdrew from the keyboard and she sat back and relaxed. She also now possessed information which she knew she had to share with the police about the videotape of the man impersonating Tryton.

Cadotte speed dialed the local police department.

_____

Lucas Johnson, a Duluth police lieutenant, answered. "Hey Cadotte, what can I do for you today, coffee, lunch, me?"

"Ha, ha, whatever you want, Johnson."

"Man, you made my day, it's me then!"

"Yeah, you could say that. I've got some new information for you. You know that videotape of the guy who disappeared a couple months ago, Tryton? Well, turns out, I've got a guy who could ID him and guess what?" She explained who Jasper Green was and what he had noticed.

"That's very interesting! I wanna talk to this guy. You got a phone number?" His hands rummaged through his desk drawers for a pen and notepaper. He found both and wrote Green's name and number down. "I'm on this. This is the first break we've gotten on any of these disappearances."

"I don't think you could get a hold of him right now," Cadotte cautioned. "He and his buddy, Earl Mancoat, are hiking the Superior Hiking Trail where we ran into the guy who may have seen Cassie Bandleson just before she went missing. You remember him, right?"

"Yeah, not much, but it turned out it probably wasn't her. They couldn't ID her from the pictures we had."

"Just so you know... Mancoat and Green are probably in an area where they can't get reception."

Johnson sank back in his chair. He had been adrenalized by the new information and wanted to get on it right away. "Crap! I'll try anyway." He dialed the number she had given him. It immediately went to voicemail where he left a short message. He hung up the phone and rapped his knuckles on the desk.

Cadotte returned to her research, trying to discover any connection between the three missing individuals.

"Rest," yelled Mancoat. They had hiked for over an hour on a dirt and rock surface. They had ascended peaks and descended into forest-covered valleys. Both were sweating like high school boys in a grudge wrestling match. Hodges sat on a nearby rock made to order for his posterior. Mancoat found a downed tree that had been freshly cut by a volunteer trail maintenance crew and pulled off the trail.

Before long, one of Mancoat's boots was off and he was rubbing his toes. "I think I bought 'em just a smidgen too small," he muttered.

Hodges pulled a bottle of water from the daypack he was carrying and took a long swig. He doused a handkerchief he pulled from his back pocket with some water and delicately wiped his forehead and face. He looked at Mancoat.

"So... what do you think?" Hodges asked.

Still looking at and rubbing his toes, Mancoat said, "You're asking me? You're the guy with the gut feeling." Mancoat then shook his head. "I don't know, Jasper." Mancoat's gaze shifted to Hodges. "I'm thinking we could be wasting our time just hiking through these hills. I don't know what we're supposed to find: a sign from God, a torn piece of a blouse, bread crumbs that are gonna lead us to the girl?" He stopped rubbing his toes and looked around. "I'm thinking we've gotta go talk to people; maybe go back to Duluth and just canvas the hell out of the Canal Park area. Go back and look for Seth."

Hodges slapped his knees and rose to his feet. "I think you're correct, Earl. This is leading us nowhere. I thought after we talked to the hiker yesterday that we were onto something, but we're not going to find it here."

Hodges put his pack on and started back the way they had come. After putting his boots on, Mancoat slung his pack over his shoulders and joined Hodges. They had walked a mile when Hodges noticed another, narrower trail descending the hill. "I didn't notice this when we came by earlier."

"It's just a spur," Mancoat said.

"It looks like it should connect to a road below." Peering through the trees, he could see an opening far below and a yellow surface. "Let's take this and see what's below," Hodges said.

Mancoat frowned, but followed without a word.

Hodges picked his way down the narrow path, holding back branches that might have lashed back into Mancoat's face as he went. The walking was easy, even for two out of shape older men. It wasn't long before they could see the bottom, which turned out to be a gravel road that snaked between the Sawtooth Mountains and Highway 61.

They stepped onto the gravel and looked in both directions. "Are you thinking what I'm thinking?" Hodges asked.

"Maybe, I'm thinking this might be a quicker way back to our car."

Hodges sighed. "I'm thinking that this would be a perfect area to park your car, walk up this short trail, snatch some young woman hiker, and make a quick getaway."

"That assumes you knew that young woman hiker was going to cross this trail at a certain time," Mancoat said.

"If he had noticed her earlier... If he had made a point of watching for specific hikers, he could have noticed her at the last trailhead, leap-frogged her with his car, and waited for her at the intersection of the trails."

"Could have," Mancoat said. "But that's an awful lot of conjecture, don't ya think?"

"Of course, but we've got to look at all the possibilities; and it's a very real one. Let's follow the road back this way and see where it leads."

"I don't mean to be contrary or skeptical, Jasper, but this could take us way out of our way and make a long hike much longer."

"So true, but it's a beautiful day, and do you really want to hike back up that hill?"

Mancoat's face flattened as he considered hiking upward. "No... let's go."

The gravel road curved around the hill, revealing occasional vistas of Lake Superior. Blue skies domed their world and the crisp air invigorated them. A bounce in their steps returned as the walking got easier.

"Do you ever miss meeting the old group at the municipal and cracking back a few beers and whiskies... and wines?" Mancoat asked Hodges.

"Every day," Hodges said.

"Yeah, I do too. Those were good times, Jasper. I wish... I wish... we could have 'em back."

Hodges stopped walking and turned to face Mancoat. "Looks like I screwed that up forever." He paused and then added. "I think we'd better do what we came to do, and enjoy each other's company as much as we can, while we can." He waited for Mancoat to say something.

Instead, Mancoat walked past him and took the lead. But he patted Hodge's shoulder as he went by.

The gravel road turned out to be a shorter route than the mountain trail, and led to an intersection near the trailhead where they had parked the car.

"Ya know, I think there might be a little merit to your previous conjecture, Jasper."

Hodges acknowledged the affirmation and strode to the trailhead. Both of them were excited as they laid their packs in the trunk, then sat in the front seats and snacked on trail mix.

Mancoat started the engine and drove them back to Highway 61. As soon as they hit the highway, Hodges noticed the voice mail blinking on his phone. He listened to the message from Lucas Johnson.

"Was it Cadotte?"

Concerned, Hodges answered, "It was Lucas Johnson with the Duluth police."

Mancoat squirmed in his seat. "Damn! So much for our go between, Cadotte, taking care of all the contacts with the police for us."

"I'll have to call him back. He sounded very interested in our discovery about the videotape and feels like we can give him more help on the case... cases." Hodges hit the call back button and was soon conversing with Johnson. He agreed to go down to the station and meet Johnson to view the hotel videotape at three.

After getting back to The Suites, Mancoat and Hodges, showered, and had a bite to eat before the meeting.

Later, they walked through the lobby of the hotel, on their way to meet Johnson. Mancoat once again pressed Hodges. "Are you sure this is a good idea? What if this guy, or one of the others, recognizes you from the book club murder cases in Rose Creek?"

"I'm not sure at all, but I don't think we have a choice right now. This Johnson fellow seems wrapped up in this case and wants to solve it. I don't think he's going to go off track and start an entirely new investigation into something else. If we keep a low profile, and don't do anything stupid, he'll stay on point and ignore us... me."

"I hope you're right, Jasper. I hear what you're saying, but it's taking a chance."

Hodges briskly walked to their vehicle in the parking lot. Mancoat walked beside him, not expecting an answer to his observation, but hoping for some sort of acknowledgement of what he had just said.

Hodges didn't say another word.

At the police station, they spoke to the sergeant at the front desk who directed them to Lieutenant Lucas Johnson's office in the far corner of the building. After exchanging greetings, they settled into uncomfortable metal chairs opposite Johnson's seventeen-inch Dell computer screen.

He loaded the hotel video, and Hodges pointed out the difference in height.

"I can see what you're saying, Mr. Green. That was a good catch on your part," Johnson said.

Hodges gave a respectful nod.

"So," Johnson asked, "Did you discover anything on the trail you walked yesterday and today?" He raised his eyebrows a little.

Mancoat answered. "Not much, but we did find a spur to the main trail that leads to a gravel road, that leads back to the trailhead. To us, it looked like a good spot for someone to intercept the lady hiker, grab her, and get her to a vehicle down below quickly."

Johnson relaxed in his comfortable roller chair and pondered the thought. He took his time responding, as he twiddled a pencil between his fingers like a baton twirler and looked out the window.

Hodges and Mancoat waited in silence for a minute before Johnson spoke again.

"You guys should be detectives." He rolled his chair across the small room and dug in a cabinet. He grunted when he found what he was looking for and brought it back to his desk. Johnson cleared the desk and spread out a detailed topographical map of the area Mancoat and Hodges had walked. "Here's the trailhead you were at." He pointed at the spot where they had parked. "Right?"

Hodges edged closer to the desk and peered through his reading glasses. After orienting himself to the location on the map, he affirmed what Johnson had said.

"I see the gravel road you found, but the map doesn't show any spur leading from it to the hiking trail. Will you show me the spur if I take you back up there?"

Mancoat frowned, but Hodges instantly said, "Sure."

"Great, I'd like to go up there now. You guys busy for the next few hours?" He asked the question with the clear expectation that they shouldn't say no.

"It's a splendid idea, Lieutenant Johnson," Hodges said.

Mancoat nodded; though it was clear he didn't want to go and thought it was a waste of time.

They piled into Johnson's police vehicle and drove to the trailhead.

"I think we'd better walk from here, Lieutenant. The spur is difficult to see when you're driving, and we might miss it," Hodges suggested.

Johnson assented and then parked at the trailhead. It was just as easy walking the winding gravel road north as it was when they walked south.

After they had hiked about a mile and a half, Hodges and Mancoat started looking for signs of the spur. When they didn't find it, they walked farther, all the while searching for the opening to the little used trail.

In the lead, Mancoat was the first to notice it. "It's here, got it right here!" He pointed to an area where, unless a hiker was very familiar with it, most people would pass by and think it nothing but a deer path.

Johnson quickened his pace as he came to the opening, and then began following the trail. Hodges and Mancoat followed him. Ten minutes later, they were standing at the intersection of the main trail.

"I can't believe any of the searchers didn't notice this." Reconsidering his statement immediately, Johnson added, "They must have, and at least checked it out." He wiped his brow with the back of his wrist. "If I were a person bent on snatching someone, this would be a good place to do it. I'll grant you that. I'm gonna have to look back at our search records and see if this spur was ever mentioned." He turned to Mancoat and Hodges. "You two have given us some helpful information. If you don't mind, I wouldn't care if you kept on plugging away. I'm not making excuses or anything, but we've got our hands full with all of these disappearances, plus the regular crap going on, budget cuts, politics, you know." He gave them a hopeful look.

"We would be delighted to continue, Lieutenant Johnson," Hodges said.

Johnson allowed them a brief smile and a thank-you nod before the three of them hiked back down the spur and to the road.

Johnson glanced at Hodges riding in the front passenger seat. "By the way, were you ever in law enforcement, Mr. Green? You look so damn familiar to me. Maybe we met at a convention somewhere."

Hodges said, "You flatter me. No, I've never been involved in your profession. In fact, I've been in academics my entire career."

"Teacher?" Johnson asked.

Hodges knew he had messed up. Making something up on the fly could come back and haunt him and he wanted to put this conversation to bed as soon as possible. "Yes, just a high school teacher, that's all, nothing spectacular."

Mancoat, getting nervous about where the conversation was going, suddenly jumped in, "Hey, did you see that? I thought I just saw a wolf next to the highway." He turned around and kept yapping. "Yeah, I'm sure it was a wolf, for sure a wolf! Maybe we could turn around and take a look, Lieutenant."

Sufficiently distracted, Johnson said, "If it was a wolf, and I'm not saying it was or wasn't, he'd be long gone by now."

"Oh, so no point going back? Well... something to tell my grandchildren, I suppose," Mancoat said. He then kept up a running commentary on his thirteen grandchildren for the remainder of the drive back to Duluth.

Early that evening at The Suites, Hodges and Mancoat were surprised by a knock at their door. Sheila Cadotte stood at the doorway holding a bottle of red wine and a six-pack of Leinenkugel's Creamy Dark.

Mancoat's grin wouldn't quit as he opened his arms wide and bowed as he showed her in.

"Ms. Cadotte, to what do we owe the pleasure of your company... and the liquid sustenance?" Hodges asked.

Cadotte giggled as she popped the cork on the bottle of cabernet she had brought for Hodges and twisted off the caps of two beers for her and Mancoat.

Hodges went to the cupboard, found a cheap wine glass and held it out for Cadotte to pour. She did it with a smile and then showed him the label.

"Ah, Balnaves Cabernet Sauvignon. A civilized choice," Hodges said

"Better be, I paid thirty-nine bucks for this stuff, Jasper... before tax."

Hodges nodded in appreciation. "Well, thank you very much. Shall we sit at the table and discuss the reason for our apparent celebration?" He winked and edged himself into a chair.

Mancoat and Cadotte tipped their beers back, drank, and joined him.

"This is wonderful, Sheila. Creamy Dark is one of my favorites," Mancoat said.

"Be truthful, Earl, they're all your favorites," Hodges quipped.

Cadotte placed her beer on the table, and walked over to her bag. She dug out several copies of news articles and a topographical map and spread them evenly on the table. "Read through these. Wait a second. That would take too long, I'll summarize for you. The long and the short of it, God, I love that expression, don't you?"

Neither Hodges nor Mancoat responded, but only stared at her.

"Well, I guess the feeling is not mutual on the expression," she said.

Hodges sighed and tapped his fingers on the table.

She took note and continued. "I started looking into past articles about the disappearances of all three of the victims, some of which I had written, and looked at possible links between the three."

Mancoat was getting excited, "And you found some! What are they?"

The smile disappeared from Cadotte's face and her expression changed to a cringe. "Well, not exactly links between the victims— where they knew each other."

"I'm confused." Hodges stopped tapping, placed his chin in his hand, and rested his elbow on the table. "Was it another person they had in common, that they all knew?"

Cadotte's smile returned. "Possibly," she said in a teasing voice.

"Somebody we ran into as we've talked to people?" Mancoat asked.

Cadotte extended her hands and did a wavering motion, palm up, palm down while tilting her head from side to side.

"Someone we should interview that we haven't thought of yet?" Hodges guessed, irritated that he had been sucked into a game of twenty questions.

Cadotte hesitated.

A frustrated Mancoat blurted, "Come on, tell us what you got, Sheila. Seth's out there, maybe still alive."

Sheila sat down. "Okay, okay." She shook her head. "I couldn't resist having a little fun. This is what I've got." She plucked three articles from the pile and laid them out on top of the others. "Each of these articles is about one of the victims. So, there's one about Seth, the most recent; one about Cassie Bandleson, the second person to disappear; and the first one to go missing, Tom Hecimovich." She looked at Mancoat and Hodges.

They both looked back with expressions that said, *get on with it.*

"Well, it turns out that all three victims, uh, missing persons, might have stayed at the North Star Motel." She winked and smiled.

Mancoat's mouth opened and stayed open for several moments. "That's it, that's the link? *Might* have stayed at the North Star Motel? And why do you say might have stayed at the North Star Motel? I don't understand how you get a might out of your articles, and how a might, helps us!"

Hodges, ignoring Mancoat, leaned back and appeared to contemplate what Cadotte had said. "Explain further, Ms. Cadotte... please."

Cadotte pulled up the topographical map. She pointed. "Here's the lake in Tettegouche where Hecimovich supposedly fell out of the boat and was swept down to Lake Superior." Her finger traced a pathway two miles away where Hodges and Mancoat had postulated that Bandleson could have been abducted, but then her finger traced the thirty miles back to Palisade Head where they thought Seth Tryton had been last known to have visited. "And then, look at the location of the North Star Motel. It's pretty much in the middle of the three disappearances."

Mancoat heaved a sigh, shook his head, muttered something unintelligible and sat back like he was exhausted.

Hodges continued his thoughtful posture for a minute.

Cadotte remained silent.

Hodges got up and walked across the room to a window and stared out, then turned around and strode back to the table and looked at the topographical map. He traced his finger to each of the spots Cadotte had marked to signify the last known locations of the victims and the location of the North Star Motel.

"You may have something," Hodges said. "Right here," he pointed to an area where he thought the spur was, "is where Bandleson might have been abducted, not that far from the North Star, and isn't there a little town inland near there?"

"Yes," Cadotte said. "It's Finland."

"We know Seth stayed at the North Star, but we don't know about the other two. Wouldn't the police have checked on whether the other two stayed there?" Mancoat said, more like an accusation than a question.

"They did," Cadotte said. "But their names weren't in the books for those time periods."

Mancoat shrugged. "So now I'm even more confused. First they might have stayed there, and then they didn't. Which is it?"

"Because maybe they stayed under different names," Hodges said.

"Yes, yes! That's what I thought!" said Cadotte.

Mancoat shrugged again. "Why in the hell would they do that?"

"We can only speculate, but it would be worth it to go back to Ms. Borchard and ask if she would check her records and determine if there was anyone matching the description of the two who disappeared in the two year period before Seth went missing."

Mancoat rubbed the back of his head. "I'll do whatever. We don't have a whole lot to go on, but as long as it's a possibility, we should try it."

"We can go in the morning, then?" Cadotte asked and started gathering up the articles.

"Yes, would you please leave the articles, though, Ms. Cadotte?" Hodges asked.

Cadotte laid the articles back on the table and said, "Absolutely. Knock yourself out. There's some good stuff there." She gathered her coat.

"Uh, Sheila," Mancoat said. "Could you leave the beer?"

Cadotte's brow furrowed. She grabbed two of the bottles and left.

CHAPTER 8

EIGHTEEN MONTHS EARLIER

Peter Karonen slowly rowed the twelve-foot long duck boat on Nipisiquit Lake, deep within Tettegouche State Park. As often happened on the North Shore, the day was overcast and a coolness gripped the air. Karonen was comfortable in his Guide Gear pants and green flannel shirt. He wore a tan, wide brimmed hat and Sorel hiking boots.

His plan was simple, approach the young fisherman, give him the sob story about his truck being stuck, and ask for help. When the man was sucked in, Karonen would subdue and transport him back to his house.

Karonen had tracked the young fisherman since first seeing him near the North Star Motel. He had observed his kindness with others and a quiet, unassuming personality. He thought he might be just the one to keep Methodist company, and hopefully, liberate her from her unconscious state. *Was he the right type to bring Methodist back?* He would soon discover the answer.

His original plan was to wait for the young man to return to shore, but the guy appeared to be in no hurry and might stay until nightfall. He decided to act now.

The man appeared totally entranced in fish catching mode and did not seem to notice Karonen approaching. Karonen thought it would be a good, confidence building gesture to hail the young man with a shout, rather than inadvertently sneaking up and startling him.

"Ahoy there," he shouted when he was about a hundred feet away.

The young man turned and waved, thinking he was just being greeted, and then returned to retrieving his just thrown lure.

"Excuse me, sir, but I need some help, I've—"

"What's that?" The young man yelled back. He stopped reeling his line and waited for Karonen to repeat his words.

"I said I need some help, my vehicle is stuck and I think with just a little push I can get her out. Can you help me?"

Tom Hecimovich, a science teacher from Virginia, MN, and a part-time fishing enthusiast, reeled in and yelled back, "Sure thing, turn around, and I'll follow you back to shore."

Karonen shouted his thanks and prepared himself.

Hecimovich secured his rod and bait, broke out his Kevlar paddle and turned his canoe. He quickly caught up to Karonen and the two men made small talk as they travelled toward shore.

"It doesn't look too bad," Hecimovich said as he surveyed the truck. "I see you have the F-150. Do you like the size and power?"

Karonen equivocated, "For the most part I do. It's a little underpowered when I haul firewood up the hill, but it gets the job done. I like the mileage I get versus the bigger models."

"Yeah, I know what you mean. It's always a trade-off, mileage/power, power/mileage. I kind of did the same thing with my Rav4. It pulls my small trailer, so that's all I need... for now. Get in, and I think with a little rocking and me pushing, we'll get it out."

Karonen smiled and stepped into the driver's seat.

"Ready?" He shouted.

Hecimovich yelled back that he was, so Karonen began rocking the vehicle back and forth in the mud hole he had purposely parked in, and then after a couple minutes, he kept it in forward gear and drove clear of the muddy spot he had not really been stuck in. He drove several feet onto the dry roadway, walked to the back of the truck and opened the tail gate, taking care to keep make sure no one else was in view. He rolled back the tonneau cover, revealing a fishing tackle box and assorted fishing paraphernalia.

Hecimovich approached.

"As a reward for your help, I'd like to give you one of my favorite lures." He opened the box and stood aside for Hecimovich to peruse the lures.

"Oh, no, no, that's not why I did it. You needed some help so I gave it to you. I don't need anything, but thanks for the thought."

"Nonsense. I insist. I want you to have something. I interrupted your day and you came all the way back to the landing, so please, humor an old man and take something." Karonen waited until Hecimovich finally assented and leaned onto the bed of the truck to look at what Karonen had offered.

Karonen slipped the chloroform soaked rag out of his lined pants pocket, maneuvered behind Hecimovich, and held the rag against his nose and mouth. Hecimovich only struggled for a few moments, then he lost consciousness and collapsed. With difficulty, Karonen lifted the hundred-eighty pound Hecimovich, and pushed him onto the truck bed. He quickly closed the tailgate and pulled the cover over Hecimovich. Next, Karonen hurried to the landing and walked Hecimovich's canoe knee deep into the water and pushed it out as hard as he could. He watched it glide quickly through the mellow water toward the larger opening of the lake.

Satisfied that the canoe would continue toward the deeper water, Karonen backed his truck easily through the mud and into the shallower water, maneuvered his duck-boat onto the trailer and secured it. He returned to check on Hecimovich, who appeared to be solidly out, but Karonen made sure he would stay unconscious until they reached his home by reapplying the chloroform.

Karonen worried that the fisherman would wake up during the trip home. *I should have tied and gagged him.* He had never done anything like this before and was having second thoughts. *Turn around and take him back. You can stay with him until he wakes up and tell him he just passed out. You can still drop this whole thing. Find another way to get Methodist back.*

But, then again, he couldn't think of another way. This was the *only* way. He didn't want to do it, but he had to. Karonen wiped away vestiges of any thoughts of giving up on the plan. He would follow through, no matter what. God knew he didn't want to do this, but... God would understand. What man could stand by and watch his daughter just lay there, stuck between worlds, between life and death? He was fighting for his daughter's life and if this man could save her, then God would forgive him. Convinced of his rationalization, Karonen felt better now. He knew he was doing the right thing.

Half an hour later, he drove into his driveway and backed the truck into his unattached garage. He closed the garage door, left through the side door, and then crossed the short space to the front door of the house. He trekked to a closet and plucked a blanket from the shelf. He carried it to the truck, unfolded the blanket and laid it on the garage floor at the back of the truck, eased the fisherman's body onto the blanket, and partially wrapped him in it like a cocoon. Karonen opened the surround door and dragged the body to the chamber he had prepared for his helper: Methodist's potential savior.

Karonen had worked hard to make the area comfortable, and even a little homey, with pictures of the North Shore hanging on the walls, and several photos of Methodist as she grew into the beautiful young woman that he knew her to be. He made sure to provide a comfortable queen-sized bed, portable sink with a mirror, and a chemical toilet. He even considered extending his cable to the area to provide some entertainment for his guest, but settled on a TV with DVR and copies of old movies and older TV shows he had enjoyed over the years. He had copies of *Bonanza, Hogan's Heroes,* and some newer ones of *Friends*. He was quite pleased with himself for providing what he thought would be a stimulating and interesting environment for the stranger who would guide his daughter back to the conscious, beautiful being she had been.

The fisherman stirred as Karonen hefted him onto the bed. *I'll have to hurry*, he told himself. The chain and clamps, necessary to retain his guest in a controllable state until he could convince him of taking on the task willingly, were in a heap, ten feet away. He retrieved the end with the clamp and deftly placed it around the man's ankle and clamped it shut. The key dangled from a ring on the wall outside the chamber. The man moved a little more.

Karonen left and returned a minute later with a pitcher of water and a glass, which he placed on the table next to the bed. *He'll be waking up soon.* He backed away from the bed. He had positioned a comfortable recliner near the door of the chamber. He sat with his hands folded in his lap; waiting for Hecimovich to wake.

Hecimovich finally awoke and slid both of his legs off the edge of the bed, letting his muddy tennis shoes dangle over the side. His hands gripped the bed. He looked around and spotted Karonen sitting in a chair by the open doorway. "What happened to me?"

Karonen acted as if he didn't know what to say, but finally spoke. "You're a guest in my home. Everything will be all right."

Hecimovich shuddered and then said, "This doesn't look like a home, but I'm not sure if I'm seeing things right. It looks like a cave." He rubbed his now closed eyes with the palms of his hands. "I feel like I'm dreaming." Hecimovich pulled his hands away from his face and looked Karonen in the eye. "Am I?"

Karonen stared back and answered quietly. "No sir... You're not dreaming."

Hecimovich seemed to notice the clamp around his left leg for the first time, and jerked it upward.

The abruptness of the motion, and the clang of the chains, startled Karonen. He jumped to his feet. "Please, if you relax, it will be better."

Hecimovich's eyes had changed from unfocused and drowsy to wild and desperate. "You, you did this to me. I helped you, and you did this. Why are you doing this? What do you want?"

Hecimovich rushed to where Karonen stood, but his leg was jerked back by the short chain and he fell forward, just a few feet away from Karonen.

Karonen pleaded, "Please, I'll explain everything, but I need you to calm down, and listen. Please, I need your help!"

Hecimovich, who lay face down on the floor with his arms outstretched in front of him, clawed furiously at the earth, trying to get to Karonen, who didn't move a centimeter. Hecimovich clawed and yelled until Karonen made the mistake of squatting and found himself too close to the fisherman's grasp. Hecimovich's hand shot out and clamped onto Karonen's ankle with the force of a giant eel. Yelling and thrashing, Hecimovich pulled Karonen closer.

Karonen yelled, "No, wait, wait. I need your help. I'm not going to hurt you!"

"I know you won't, you bastard," Hecimovich yelled. He almost had Karonen's wrist in his other hand.

Suddenly, Karonen changed tactics and launched himself forward, smashing his body into Hecimovich's. Karonen ended on top and pummeled Hecimovich's face with his free hand.

The fisherman released his grip on Karonen's wrist and tried to protect his face, but Karonen had entered fight or flight mode, and delivered blow after blow to Hecimovich's face.

In a last desperate move, Hecimovich tried to kick the chain attached to his leg over Karonen and tangle him in it.

Karonen pulled Hecimovich's hair, lifting his head off the rock floor, and then smashed his head back down to the rock floor several more times. He released the younger man's head, and powered his fists again and again into Hecimovich's face.

Finally... he stopped.

Hecimovich didn't move.

Breathing heavily, Karonen stumbled as he got off Hecimovich's chest, fell down and then got up and staggered a few feet away. He took several deep breaths and then moved to the recliner. His head pounded; a wave of nausea swept over him, and his eyes felt as if hundred pound weights were pulling them shut. Despite the force of adrenalin sweeping through his body earlier, his energy was now escaping him. A minute later, exhausted, Karonen fell asleep.

He woke with a start. His head was clear and the nauseous feelings had vanished. He looked toward Hecimovich, who still lay where he had left him on the floor. Hecimovich hadn't moved—not an inch.

Karonen left the cell and returned a minute later with an axe handle. He held it out in front of him as he approached Hecimovich. He reached out and nudged Hecimovich's foot with the handle. No reaction. He crept closer and moved toward the fisherman's head. His eyes were open, appearing to stare at the ceiling. *A trick, he's trying to look dead to get me closer.*

Karonen cried; not a gush of tears, just a few confused tears. *He's dead. No, he's got to be alive.*

His senses heightened, he swore he heard the tick of the second hand as it ticked off the moments on his watch. Slowly, realization of the man's death embraced him. And then the tears gushed with the hiccupped crying, the self-recriminations, and the guilt. He dropped to his knees and prayed for forgiveness. *Oh my heavenly father, what have I done? What have I done?*

He sat on the floor next to the man he had killed and cried some more.

One day later, dark clouds drifted lazily across a quarter moon. It was two a.m.

Karonen transported the body to just south of the Canadian border. He sat in the truck for a long time, making sure no one else was present. Finally, he emerged and pulled the body, wrapped and tied securely in a blanket, out of the bed of the truck.

Though the evening was cool, he noticed himself drenched in sweat only a quarter mile into his trek. He was strong for his age, and graced with higher than normal endurance, but still found himself stopping and resting every hundred yards or so down the trail.

After a mile of dragging Hecimovich's body over a rough trail, he arrived at the spot where he knew he could safely dispose of the body. He found two large rocks that he tied a rope to, and then wrapped it, and the rocks, around the blanket covering the corpse. He eased the body to the edge of the Devil's Kettle. His legs nearly buckled as he worked not to slip. Dragging the body had sapped most of his strength.

Finally, he shoved the corpse over the precipice and watched it drop into the swirling, watery abyss below. One fork of the Devil's Kettle falls flowed outward toward Lake Superior. The fork that he had dropped the body emptied into what seemed to be a bottomless, churning pothole in rhyolite rock. No scientist had ever been able to trace where the water went, and even though dyes, logs, and Ping-Pong balls had been thrown into it, none had ever been found elsewhere. The consensus of the researchers was that the exit point was somewhere beneath Lake Superior.

After watching the body swirl for a couple minutes, and then disappear into the bottomless hole, Karonen shook. He said a prayer, crossed himself, hiked back to his truck, and then drove home.

He didn't sleep well for the next three days.

CHAPTER 9

2003

Karonen sat in his soft, over-sized armchair. Intermittent tears leaked down the side of his face. His wife of twenty years lay in a grave ten minutes away... cancer. The end had come swiftly for Janet—too fast for him to comprehend, and certainly too fast for his twelve-year-old daughter.

He gripped and re-gripped the ends of the armchair like he was exercising gnarled fingers, teeming with arthritis. The unconscious act continued, as did the slow drizzle of tears.

"Daddy?" The voice was quiet and shaky.

Karonen didn't move. The sound of the voice was perceived, but not understood.

"Daddy?"

He released his right hand from the chair and wiped his eyes before he turned to respond to her. "Yes, Methodist." The words were slow, soft, and kind. He cleared his throat.

She stood just to the side and behind him, looking tentative and concerned. "Are you sad about Mommy?"

He nearly lost it right there. *Of course*, he wanted to say, but that would have been uncalled for... rude, mean. This was his daughter, the only other person left in his little family; his sweet, innocent child, whom he treasured with all his heart.

So he turned, and said, "Yes dear, I am."

Methodist moved closer, opened her arms, and hugged him with all the strength she could muster.

His pulled her tight. A tear trailed down his face and caressed her cheek. They embraced for a minute, maybe more.

When they released each other, Methodist's eyes held no trace of a tear. "Should I fix something to eat?"

He cocked his head. He worried about his little girl. She should be crying and telling him how much she missed her mommy. Instead, *Should I fix something to eat?* He didn't respond, just looked at her.

The silence was too long for her, "Do you want some soup?"

He smiled a little and then said, "I'd like that."

Methodist smiled back. "Okay."

She ran to the kitchen and opened a can of Campbell's Chicken Noodle Soup, eager to do something for her Daddy.

Karonen watched her run away and thought, *How lucky I am to still have Methodist. She'll be my savior in this.*

They ate.

"Was it good, Daddy?"

"The best I ever had."

She laughed and scooped another spoonful of soup, soon cleaning out the rest of her cup.

"Not as good as Mommy's, I bet."

"Even better." He said it with conviction, looking her straight in the eye.

She smiled again.

"I'll try to be as good as Mommy, I promise."

He nearly lost it again, but recovered.

"You don't have to try. You are who you are, the best little girl I could ever have." And then he said, "I love you, Methodist, and will always protect you."

"I love you too, Daddy, and I won't ever leave you."

2010

Karonen answered the phone. Caller ID had showed him it was Methodist. She had her own place now, but only trouble and heartache had been the result. He had thought it would be better when she was on her own. He had been wrong.

Uneasiness filled him as he picked up the phone.

The slurred words hit him hard. "Dathhyyy."

His heart sank. He couldn't understand a word she said. Every syllable was unintelligible.

"I'll be there in ten minutes."

He moved as fast as he could, grabbed his coat and ran out the door. He had moved to Duluth to be near her. The fears he had when she was younger, when she didn't seem to be affected by her mother's death, when she didn't give herself a chance to grieve, were well founded.

At the time of her mother's death, Methodist must have felt the need to be strong to protect and help her father, but years later, the grief and depression surfaced, enslaving her in a never-ending cycle of alcohol and drug abuse. He tried everything he could: counseling, rehabilitation, a psychiatrist... love.

Nothing worked. And he couldn't bear it. He was watching a train wreck in process, and there was nothing he could do, just like he hadn't been able do anything about his wife's battle with cancer.

He ran into Methodist's building and bounded up the steps to her second floor apartment. Fumbling for the key in his pocket, he pulled it out, dropped it, and fumbled for it again. His hands shook as he thrust the key into the lock and burst into the living area.

She lay on the couch.

He raced to her side.

Her chest rose and fell in tentative spurts. He grabbed her shoulders and shook her, careful not to send her head and neck in opposite directions. She mumbled a few syllables he couldn't understand. Grabbing his phone, he dialed 911 and pleaded for help.

The ambulance arrived within eight minutes.

Persistent...Vegetative... State.

He cried, cried more, and when he thought there were no more tears, more came... until finally nothing was left.

After two years in the hospital, he took her home to Finland--to the house she grew up in. The doctors told him there was no hope, to just make her comfortable...

He purchased a ventilator and hooked it up with the help of technicians. The nurses showed him how to deliver IV fluids.

He kept her room just the way it was when she was a child. Everything was the same. He kept thinking it would help her when she woke.

He had never accepted the diagnosis.

Persistent...Vegetative... State.

"I know you miss your mother," he began. "But you never told me you did. You never cried. You kept it all in... I know you thought you should be strong for me. But honey, you should have cried. You should have let it out, not for me, but for you." He cried.

After several minutes sitting hunched over by her bedside, elbows on his knees, Karonen sat up straight and let out a long breath.

He talked to her for hours every day. He read her favorite books, reminisced about the times they had spent together, always hoping that something he read or said would bring her back. He rarely went out of the house except when he needed groceries. Friends stopped coming over when he became non-communicative. They ceased to exist in his mind.

Over the next year, he descended into his own personal hell. His mind deteriorated, and his thoughts became irrational. He began to think he was not the one she needed. He kept her alive in the barest definition of the word. He needed her to come back to him. He needed to explain to her, tell her how much he loved her, tell her the story of how she got her name.

He laughed through his tears as he recalled the day Janice and he discussed what they should name their baby daughter. Dozens of names had been thrown about. None of them had been acceptable to either of them. Janice, in exasperation, finally blurted, "Okay, we're Methodists, so how about we name her Methodist?"

At first, he laughed and told her no.

A minute later, his wife had asked, "Do you have a better name?"

He looked at her and admitted, "No, no I don't. We'll name her Methodist."

2013

"Wake up, please, Methodist, wake up." Karonen shouted and pushed hard on the bed, bouncing her in the air, nearly detaching the feeding and breathing tubes.

Karonen seethed with anger and frustration. *Why won't you wake up? What am I doing wrong? Please, Methodist, please come back.*

But she didn't wake up. She lay motionless except for the rise and fall of her chest forced up and down, up and down, by the ventilator.

He cried. His mind was empty, hopeless. His life had consisted of only Methodist for the past three years, and before that, before the overdose, he watched her plummet into hell, powerless to help, powerless to save her. *Why did she deserve this? If I had loved her more, this wouldn't have happened.*

He rose from the side of her bed, his body shaking, and his mind in a swirl. He cursed himself. Cursed God.

Leaving her bedroom, he walked in a haze to the living room, absent-mindedly pulled a book from the shelf, and felt the bookcase release from the wall. At first what he saw didn't register. In disbelief, he stared at the space between the wall and the bookcase. Hesitantly, he grabbed hold of the edge, and pulled. His hands shook uncontrollably.

His breath was heavy and his brain quivered with uneasiness, but he opened the structure and peered inside. *Dark. It's too dark to see. What the hell is this?* Confusion.

He raced to the kitchen and found a flashlight in a drawer. He returned and when he stepped inside, he stared at gray, dusty rock walls supported by primitive timbers. His first thought was that this was an abandoned mine. The North Shore and north central Minnesota experienced a mini gold rush from 1865-66, but hardly any gold was found.

Why was this covered up, and the opening elaborately covered by a bookcase?

He hesitated. Fear gripped him, but his curiosity won out.

Another thought occurred to him as he stepped inside.

Is it safe?

He felt his way along, carefully, slowly, shining his light ahead as he did. It was damp and warm. Beads of sweat popped up along his forehead. He wiped them away with his forearm.

He explored tunnels and chambers all afternoon, until Methodist snapped back into his consciousness. He felt guilty. He hadn't thought of her in hours. He ran back through the winding tunnels to the house and Methodist's room, where the sound of the ventilator and the drip, drip, drip of the IV fluid greeted him. He rushed to the bedside and held her hand. Tears flowed from his eyes.

"I'm sorry, dear, I... I left you for too long. But I'm back now, and you're safe."

He cradled his head next to hers. *My God, I love you!*

His accidental discovery of the system connected to his house must have been a sign. *I can use this. Yes, I can use this.* The reason someone carved tunnels and chambers out of the hill, mined it, and then later made it part of this house eluded him, but at that moment, he didn't care. His tortured mind formed a plan.

He worked in two-hour shifts for the next three months, shoring up timbers, preparing chambers, and running electrical lines. As his mind descended past delusional into nearly full blown insanity, he knew this was his opportunity; the time to find another who could do what he could not do alone, someone who would could awaken Methodist.

CHAPTER 10

2016

Cadotte arrived at 8:30 a.m. Hodges, who was the first one up and ready, opened the door and let her in. Mancoat rushed out of his room a few moments later and they drove up the shore to the North Star Motel.

They passed over the same cosmetically challenged bridge they had driven over before, but paid it no mind this time.

Nyla Borchard was sitting in the breakfast area. Three cups of coffee and glazed doughnuts sat on the small table near her. She winked and greeted the three and then took a small sip of her coffee. "I have my books for the time frame you asked about, Sheila, and if the missing folks had stayed here then, they registered under different names. And, I'm afraid my memory of their faces wouldn't, and didn't, do me any good when the police asked about them originally... although, I was only looking for their names back then, not their faces."

"I brought good quality photos of Cassie Bandleson and Tom Hecimovich along, just in case you can make an association between the registered names and faces," Cadotte said.

Hodges and Mancoat realized there was nothing for them to do, so they drank their coffee and ate their doughnuts as the other two got down to business.

Cadotte spread the five by seven photos on the table. Borchard reviewed her registration books and wracked her memory trying to match names with the two faces. She shook her head as she looked at one signature after another, really hoping for something to trigger a match, but then something occurred to her. "There's gotta be a record of what types of vehicles they both drove, right?" Borchard asked.

Cadotte's face brightened, and she flipped through the police and sheriff's reports and finally found what she was looking for. "Here, Cassie Bandleson drove a Chevy Cruze, dark blue. The plate number is LZK 409." She reached for the other report. "And Tom Hecimovich drove a yellow Rav4. The plate number is TCH 119."

Borchard pored over the books again. "Here's one. A blue Chevy Cruze, license plate number LZK 409."

Hodges leaned forward, smiled, and triumphantly rapped his knuckles on the table.

Ten minutes later Borchard said, "Okay, okay, I've got the other one, yellow Rav4, license plate number TCH119. We've got it. Both of them were here! I guess the police or sheriff just looked for names, not vehicle types or license plate numbers when they came here."

"But why'd they register under different names?" Mancoat asked.

"There might be another connection between the two we're not seeing," Hodges said.

"They came here two months apart, I just have no idea how there could be a connection between the two of them," Borchard said, and tossed the registration book on the table.

"What were the names they registered under?" Cadotte asked

Nyla picked up the book again and found the entries. "Linda Johnson, and, let me see, Richard Gabrielson."

"The disappearances happened about two months apart, correct?" Hodges asked Cadotte.

Cadotte nodded.

"Wait, this sounds a little crazy," Borchard said. "But what if Hecimovich came up here, just not wanting to be disturbed, and Cassie Bandleson came up here, not wanting anyone to know who she really was, to try to find him?"

"Yeah, crazy is what I'd say," Mancoat agreed.

"Well, maybe not," Cadotte said, conspiratorial thoughts grew from her newspaper background. "Maybe she was related to this Hecimovich guy in some way, some way that wasn't clear when we all looked at their names and where they were from."

"Yeah," Mancoat said sarcastically. "Maybe he was her long lost father from when he'd been a sperm donor and she was the long lost child looking for him." The others seemed stunned and remained silent. "You're kidding... I'm kidding! I'm not serious about that, that couldn't be..."

Hodges spoke, "It's worth a look. Sheila, could you use your connections to check into Bandleson and Hecimovich's pasts?"

Cadotte answered quickly. "You betcha. Nyla, could I connect to your Wi-Fi here and get going right now?"

"Sure, the password is North Star Motel, that's it."

Cadotte opened her laptop. Her fingers were a blur as she pounded the keys and looked for all relevant information on Cassie Bandleson and Tom Hecimovich.

"I think Earl and I should drive to Virginia and interview friends, relatives, co-workers, anyone that might help us learn why he would come here and register under a different name. Also, we could check out Earl's idea."

Mancoat rolled his eyes. "I made a sarcastic statement; it was just a joke. I meant it as a joke."

"It made sense, though, Mr. Mancoat," said Nyla.

The three of them left. Mancoat and Hodges took Highway 1 from Finland to Ely and then west and south to Virginia. Cadotte drove to Silver Bay, hoping to get a break on Cassie Bandleson's past.

Highway 1, from Finland to Ely, was a curvy road bordered by the North woods on both sides. Mancoat got car sick on the lazy bends of the roads and had to relinquish the driving duties to Hodges. As Mancoat napped in the passenger seat, Hodges wracked his brain to think of reasons why Hecimovich would possibly register under a different name than his own. They knew Hecimovich had been a science teacher, but why would an upstanding citizen do what he apparently did? He shook his head when nothing approaching a good reason came to him.

Mancoat woke when he felt the vehicle slow.

"Ely?" he asked.

"Yes. I'll stop for gas at the Holiday, and get a cup of coffee, as long as we're there."

"Grab me one too," Mancoat said. "I'll fill up the car."

Hodges pulled up next to a pump and went into the station. He took his time. His muscles were stiff and he walked like the slightly out of shape sixty year old he was. No one greeted him as he entered and searched for the coffee. After a brief hunt, he found it and filled two large cups with the darkest brew available. He killed a little time waiting for Mancoat to fill the tank, and then paid for the gas and the coffee.

A minute later they were back on the road. The drive took another forty-five minutes. They entered the city from the northern edge. It was almost three pm., so they figured the timing would be perfect to track down Hecimovich and his fellow teachers.

Hodges spotted the older, two story building situated near downtown. He turned onto a side street and made his way to the school.

Buses and student vehicles slowly emerged from the parking lot as the duo entered. Hodges found a visitors' parking area and pulled into a spot. Several students loitered around the entrance doors, apparently waiting for their friends, while others nearly knocked Mancoat over as they piled out the door and down the front steps.

"No respect for adults," Mancoat muttered as he turned his head and watched them race to their cars.

Hodges agreed. He saw the same thing in Tasmania during his past two years there.

Hodges held the door for Mancoat. They entered the building, turned right, and followed signs to the office.

A middle-aged receptionist, busily entering data on her computer, peered over the top of her reading glasses as she noticed the strangers. "Hello, can I help you gentlemen with something?"

Mancoat opened his mouth to speak, but Hodge's beat him to it. "Yes, please, we've just arrived from Finland and..."

"We're looking to talk to anyone who knew Tom Hecimovich," Mancoat finished. He cracked a smile.

Hodges looked at him briefly before returning his gaze to the receptionist. "We're investigating his disappearance and are looking for any information that might help us determine what happened to him."

The woman looked confused. "Are you policemen?"

Hodges shook his head in the negative, and said, "No, we're friends of someone who disappeared in the same area and we're trying to establish if there were any connections between our friend and Mr. Hecimovich. We'd like to interview his friends, family and co-workers to help us gain knowledge and understanding of the situation."

The receptionist removed her reading glasses and placed them on her desk before she rose and told them she would let them speak to the principal.

Hodges and Mancoat followed her through a mini-maze of cubicles that ended at the office of Principal Gordon Lobbs.

Lobbs greeted them at the open doorway, shook their hands and gestured to a couple of chairs beside his metal desk. His computer terminal sat centrally on the desk, and two pictures of family and a stack of math curriculum papers sat next to it.

Lobbs began with a cheery smile and said, "So what can I do for you gentlemen today?"

After introducing themselves, Hodges launched into an explanation of why they came to Virginia. Mancoat interjected an occasional comment, and Lobbs listened politely.

When his guests were finished, Lobbs expressed his sympathy and described what the school had gone through with the disappearance and presumed death of Tom Hecimovich. "He was a great guy, and an even better teacher. His students, past and present, were shocked by the whole thing." Lobbs paused and gazed out the window toward the parking lot. "It was hard for the staff and student body to grasp the situation; not really knowing what happened to him." He paused a moment.

Hodges and Mancoat gave him time.

"As a school, as a community, we needed closure, so we had an all Virginia gathering at the high school auditorium and held a memorial for Tom. We must have had two thousand people there. Moving... it was so moving." He looked out the window again and this time, Hodges sensed Lobbs would not be continuing.

Hodges said, "We have a great deal of sympathy for the school's and the community's loss. We understand what you went through, and hope we can help with the closure part..."

"We have closure. We had a memorial. For us, it's settled. Tom will never come back and we're resigned to that. I'm not sure we really would want to open up any more thoughts or explanations of what may have happened. We've moved on."

"We understand, but the disappearance of our friend, Seth Tryton took place a little more recently, indeed, only two months ago. We're not resigned to anything in his case." Bending closer to Lobbs, Hodges said, "We think we have some information that may shed light, not only on Mr. Hecimovich's disappearance, but that of a young lady and our friend's disappearances as well. But we need some assistance from your community to flesh this out."

Lobb's curiosity peaked. "New information? What do you mean?"

Hodges detailed what they had found out about Hecimovich and Bandleson registering under different names at the North Star Motel and their determination that the North Star was at the nexus of all three disappearances.

"You've just pushed me down a road I really didn't want our school or little town to go. Tom registered under a different name? Why didn't the police tell us that?"

"They didn't know," Mancoat said.

"But how did you figure out that's what he and the woman who disappeared did?"

"Their vehicles were at the North Star, only under different names than their own."

Lobbs seemed bewildered. "What name did he register under?"

"Richard Gabrielson," Mancoat said.

"What did you say?"

Mancoat repeated the name.

"That's a name I haven't heard for a long, long time," Lobbs said.

Hodge's raised his eyebrows. "You've heard the name before?"

"Of course I have. That's the name of Tom's adoptive father."

"I'm confused," Hodges said.

"No need to be really. Tom was adopted when he was nine years old by Richard Gabrielson and his wife, Rebecca."

Mancoat interjected, "So Tom never went by Gabrielson's last name after the adoption?"

"No, he did. He was Tom Gabrielson until he turned twenty-five. At that time in his life, he was a very disenchanted man; disenchanted with himself, his adoptive parents, life in general, I think. He started looking for his birth parents. When he gained permission to contact them... well, he did. I guess they all hit it off to the point where he changed his last name to Hecimovich, his biological parents' name."

"How did his adoptive parents feel about that?" Hodges asked.

"Not real bad. To tell you the truth, I think by that time, with all the trouble they had had with Tom, they were glad to sever ties with him. I guess I might have been too. Tom had been a huge pain in the ass from day one for the Gabrielson family. Fighting, bad grades in school... alcohol, drugs in his mid-teens. He was a handful. Always angry—with a chip on his shoulder. But after he found his biological parents, everything changed. He went back to school and became a teacher. He turned his life around completely."

Mancoat shifted in his chair. "Are his biological parents around here?"

"No, they actually live in Thunder Bay. I can get you an address if you want. I don't think it would violate anyone's protocol or sensibilities."

Hodges flashed a grateful look before saying, "That would be helpful, Mr. Lobbs. In addition, we would like to speak with Tom's friends and co-workers. If it isn't too much trouble, would you make a list for us, including any contact information?"

"I'll have my secretary prepare a list for you." Lobbs signaled that he had to move on with other business, then stood and walked them to his secretary's desk and outlined what Hodges and Mancoat needed. "I'm sorry I can't spend more time with you, but I don't think I have anything more to add. I wish you luck in your research, and truly hope you find what you're looking for. And, in spite of what I said before about closure, if you do find out what happened to Tom, let me know."

Hodges and Mancoat said they would, shook hands with Lobbs, and then sat on a padded bench while they waited for the secretary to compile, type, and copy the list. When she finished, she directed them to Mark Seinfelt, another teacher, who had been close with Hecimovich, and whose room was closest to the office.

The two old men walked in silence through the hallway. They came to Seinfelt's open door and peered in. Seinfelt was bent over a table, sitting next to a student and giving him directions.

Hodges knocked.

Seinfelt looked up. "Yes... can I help you folks?"

Hodges took the lead, "We hope so, Mr. Seinfelt." After introducing themselves, Hodges and Mancoat explained the reason for their visit and what they hoped to accomplish.

Seinfelt dismissed his student. After he left, he said, "I'll do my best to help. Tom was a great teacher and an even better friend to me. This whole thing was a huge shock for all of us. I just don't know what I could provide you with that would help, but I'll answer any questions you have."

"First of all," Mancoat said, "Do you have any idea why Tom would use his adoptive father's name when he checked into a motel on the North Shore?"

Seinfelt gave a confused look. "He used Richard Gabrielson's name at a motel?"

"Yes."

"That's a hard one to figure out. He had severed pretty much all ties with his adoptive parents. Why he would be using the Gabrielson name is beyond me. He changed his name to his biological parents name in his mid-twenties. As far as I know, he couldn't stand his adoptive parents... and the feeling became mutual. In those days, Tom always seemed to have an anger inside him that the Gabrielson's just couldn't get at. I don't think it was their fault. It was just something about Tom."

"When he started searching for his biological parents, I warned him he might be opening a can of worms. Turned out, it was the best thing that ever happened to him. His life took a one-eighty once he met his real parents. He told me they gave him all the right answers to why they gave him up in the first place, and he just couldn't believe how relieved and grateful he was to them."

Mancoat put his elbows on the table. "Have you met his biological parents?"

"Yeah, they're great people! I could see, after Tom got over the jittery moments of actually meeting them, why it was so easy for him to accept what they said and form a real good relationship."

"You sound like you've been friends with Tom for a long time," Hodges said.

"I knew him since he came to Virginia. We were friends right away, but when he got into drugs, our friendship took a hit. But man, after he met his real folks, he got his life together, approached me, told me he'd changed, and we became friends again. He got his degree and started teaching. It's so hard to believe what happened. Do you think there's a chance he's alive?"

Mancoat opened his mouth, but was cut off by Hodges, who said, "To be honest, we don't know, but the lapse of time does lend doubt to the possibility. We can only hope."

Seinfelt sighed, "I miss him. I hope you find your friend alive, and find out what happened to Tom."

They said their goodbyes, and Mancoat and Hodges went on their way.

"Who's next?" Mancoat asked.

Hodges stared at the list. "Nancy Baldwin, science teacher, room number 216."

They walked through a convoluted hallway that descended and then rose to a higher level again.

"Must go under a street and come out in another building," Mancoat said.

"Apparently."

Hodges stopped to tuck his shirttail in his pants.

They continued through the poorly lit tunnel and then emerged into a brilliant, well illuminated building that housed the science section of the high school. Hodges and Mancoat admired the bright colors and large copies of famous works of art decorating the hallway walls.

"This is quite impressive, wouldn't you say so, Earl?"

Mancoat nodded his head and stopped in front of a six foot tall, photograph of Albert Einstein sitting in his Princeton University office.

"God, I wish I had a head of hair like that," Mancoat said as he stopped to gaze at the photo. He ran his fingers through his longish, thinning gray hair.

Hodges halted for a moment and then tugged at Mancoat's arm.

Nancy Baldwin was forty-six years old, but looked more advanced in her years. Her hair was pulled back and then piled on top of her head in a haphazard fashion. She wore a pencil skirt cut to just below her knees, and black, round toe shoes that could have passed for her mother's.

Her greeting surprised the two men. "Gentlemen," she said in a younger, cheerful sounding voice. "The office secretary let me know you may be stopping by." She rounded her desk and walked to where they had entered her room with her hand outstretched.

Hodges shook her hand first and Mancoat politely followed.

"You have a beautiful school here, Ms. Baldwin," Hodges said.

"Why thank you, teachers had a lot of input on how we wanted things arranged and designed, from the lab kits to the Albert Einstein photos in the hallways. Please, help yourselves to seats. I'm all set for you." Baldwin sat on the corner of her desk while Mancoat and Hodges occupied sturdy chairs at one of the dozen tables in the lab.

CHAPTER 11

Sheila Cadotte drove back to Highway 61 and then down a few miles to Silver Bay, a shrunken mining town, whose best years were forty years in the past. The 'downtown' area was a collection of businesses situated in a squared off horseshoe shape the size of a city block.

The only cafe in town, The Northwood's Family Grille, rested in the middle of the configuration. Cadotte knew from covering Bandleson's disappearance, that this was where she had worked.

Her scarf got caught in the car door when she slammed it, jerking her back and causing a few choice words to escape from her mouth. Cadotte opened the door, freed the scarf, took it off completely, and then threw it on the passenger seat in front. She slammed the door again and power walked to the restaurant entrance.

Cadotte sat at a small table and ordered a mocha latte. The restaurant had remodeled since she last visited. She looked around, admiring the wood-trimmed interior with new chairs. It had a nice, clean, woodsy feel to it.

The waitress returned with her latte and a smile. "Here you go, can I interest you in a slice of pie with that? We have blueberry on special today."

Cadotte looked at her name tag. "I don't think so, Linda, but I'm doing a follow-up story about the missing woman from town here, Cassie Bandleson. I know she worked here before she disappeared. Did you know her?"

Linda hesitated, but then said, "I didn't know Cassie very well, but Becky Jaakola did. I think the police talked to her before."

"Would you tell me where I can find her?"

"Well, she's not easy to find right now. She moved out in the country a ways. Ummm, I can get directions from the boss man here if you'll give me a few minutes. I see I have some other customers." A family of four had ambled into the restaurant and sat down across the room from Sheila.

"Sure thing, I can wait. Take your time." She burned her lips when she took a sip of the latte and watched Linda greet the family and then retreat to the kitchen. She returned with water glasses and menus.

"Be right with ya," Linda said as she returned to the kitchen. Three minutes later, she came back and laid a piece of paper with scribbled directions to Becky Jaakola's house.

Cadotte studied the directions and sipped her scorching latte. There would be no GPS assistance this time. No address was written on the paper, just scribbled directions saying turn here and there, and onto some county road Cadotte had never heard of before. I'll be lucky to find this, she thought. *Hell, I'll be lucky to find my way back.*

She took longer to finish her latte than she thought possible. Normally, she wouldn't have stayed and finished, but as the drink cooled, and her taste buds recovered, she thought it was the most wonderful latte she had ever had.

Cadotte thanked the waitress and walked to her Lexus. When she started the engine she noticed an older gentleman had pulled up in a pickup truck. She stepped out of her vehicle and approached the gentleman to ask him for more detailed directions.

The gentleman, who wasn't as elderly as she first thought, looked at the paper, chuckled, and then asked for a pen. He used the window glass on his truck as a writing table, and labeled each road she would be turning onto with a number.

"That should do it. I'm surprised they didn't label anything for you. I've lived here my entire life, and it's easy for me. You probably got some transplant to give you those directions. You shouldn't have any problems finding the place now, or back either." He raised a hand to tip his hat, but knocked the fedora from his head instead.

"Damn, I do that more often than I should. Serves me right for trying to act gallant."

She thanked the guy, but couldn't shake the feeling she knew him from somewhere. She paused for a moment while she tried to place him, but when nothing came to mind, she gave up and slipped into the Lexus.

The stranger's directions and labels were spot on, and she found Jaakola's house within half an hour. The house turned out to be a nicely landscaped, split-level home situated at the end of a five-hundred-foot gravel driveway bordered by mature spruce trees.

Cadotte parked near the attached garage and got out of the car. She approached the front door. No one answered the doorbell, or her heavy knocks. Still on the porch, she stepped backwards and looked around the front. The siding was done in cedar shakes, which had never been treated so they had turned a mottled gray. She decided it was an attractive look as she moved from the porch and looked around the side and back of the home.

She crossed into the back yard and was astounded by the beauty of it. Tall ferns along with native grasses were arranged in a tiered system lined with what she judged to be oak beams. Cadotte weaved her way around the layered gardens, taking care not to disturb anything.

"Can I help you?" It was a rough voice that sounded as if it was scarred from years of smoking.

Cadotte wheeled around and saw an older woman, half her body protruding from an upstairs window that had the screen removed.

"Um, I'm looking for Becky Jaakola." And then she added with an apology-laden tone in her voice, "I rang the doorbell and knocked."

"Didn't hear ya, I was running the washing machine. Come around to the back door and step in. I'll meet you there."

Cadotte gathered her thoughts and walked to the back door. She opened the screen door and stepped inside to a combination dining/kitchen area. She was surprised by the chaos inside. Dirty dishes covered the sink and counter. A dish towel was on the floor along with scattered bits of some kind of breakfast cereal she didn't recognize. The yard had been so beautifully arranged that she expected the inside to match.

"So Miss, what can I do for you?" Jaakola held out her hand.

Cadotte shook it and introduced herself.

"Miss Cadotte, can I interest you in a cup of tea? I make my own." She said it with such an invitational tone that Cadotte couldn't refuse. Jaakola directed her to a chair in the dining area while she cleared a space on the kitchen counter and prepared two cups of her mint tea.

"This is delicious," Cadotte said after her first taste.

"Thank you."

Jaakola then gestured to the back yard. "I have everything I need in this little patch of territory to make anything I like. And I do."

"Your backyard is amazing. I've seen very few gardens that can match what you've done here." Cadotte took another sip of tea and wondered why the old woman's eye for beauty and orderliness hadn't translated into a well-kept interior space.

Jaakola noticed Cadotte's facial expression change. "I see you noticed."

"Um... noticed what?" Cadotte crossed her legs and leaned forward.

"It's okay. I saw your eyes searching around in here. It's a mess, and you're wondering how a person can be so damn good at making the yard look nice and so damn bad at making the inside look good." Jaakola laughed a hearty, hoarse laugh.

"No... no, I wasn't thinking..." She placed her cup on the table and began to explain, but Jaakola stopped her.

"Relax, relax. I'm not faulting you at all. I'm not interested in housekeeping, and I really don't give a rat's ass on how the inside of a house looks, but get me out in the yard and I'm a demon for order and beauty. I don't know why, but I've always been much more comfortable outside than in. I've never been trained in landscaping, but I've read books and I know what looks beautiful."

"I was blown away by the front of your yard, but the gardens in back are, are... breathtaking."

Jaakola's eyes grew misty and she placed a hand on top of Cadotte's. "That was awful nice of you to say, Miss... Hell, I forgot your name already."

"Cadotte, but please, call me Sheila."

"Would you like to take a tour of my gardens?"

"I'd love to."

Jaakola lead Cadotte to the back yard and pointed out plants and flowers, giving the common name and the Latin for each. "These are my favorites... Canada wild ginger, common blue violets, wild geranium, and true Solomon's seal, or as it is scientifically named, Polygonatum biflorum," she said, proudly giving the Latin classification. Jaakola carried on for more than an hour.

Later they retreated to the dining room where Cadotte asked about Cassie Bandleson.

Jaakola raised and lowered the teabag in her cup of water several times, and then sighed.

"Cassie was a sweet girl, but..." She stopped.

"But... what?"

Jaakola sniffed. "But she was troubled. She *needed* a family. She told me that. I told her she could always count me as family. She just smiled, said she appreciated that, but I knew it wasn't enough for her." She fiddled with her teabag again.

"Do you think that might have had something to do with her disappearance?"

Shaking her head, Jaakola said, "I don't know for sure... maybe. I just know she was always searching for something... someone, anyone that might be part of her family. A month before she disappeared she told me she'd been doing some research into genealogy." Her hands waved dismissively. "I didn't think anything about it. She knew who her parents were."

"You're saying she wanted to find other relatives?"

"Probably... yes, I think so. You see, Cassie's parents were killed in a car accident when she was about nine. There were no known relatives so she was put in foster homes. I told her, 'Cassie, you don't want to go down this road. You don't know what can of crap you're gonna open up.' I tried to be that friend, you know, who talks sense into you, but she listened politely, and then did just exactly what she wanted to do anyway."

Jaakola sipped her tea and looked at Cadotte. "I don't know what she found, but it consumed her for the last month she was with us."

Cadotte, for once in her life, didn't know what to say.

CHAPTER 12

Sixteen months earlier

C assie checked into the North Star Motel at 5 pm. This was where she was supposed to have met Richard Gabrielson, two months ago. At least, that was the name he had given her. She knew his real name was Tom Hecimovich.

She knew he had been at the motel because he had called and said he would be ready to meet her the following morning. He never showed.

Now, two months later, she checked in under a different name. She wasn't quite sure why, but she felt vaguely embarrassed about her search and didn't want her friends to know anything about it. Her friends would ask questions, and she wasn't ready to answer them. After experiencing two months of shock and frustration when she heard the news of his disappearance and the baffled authorities, she had decided to try and find out what happened to Tom Hecimovich.

Cassie thought this might be a logical place to start. She had nothing else.

Nyla Borchard had been clueless. During Cassie's subtle probe of Borchard's knowledge, she knew nothing about Gabrielson/ Hecimovich or where he had gone during his brief stay, other than to mention the canoe on top of his Rav4.

Clueless.

That was exactly how Cassie now felt. She had spent a day interviewing others in the immediate area, seeking out any information that could help her find out what had happened to Hecimovich. She had no illusions about finding him, or discovering what happened, but she wanted to try.

Cassie had first contacted Tom after his name had been given to her by a local social worker who knew him and about his experience. Their correspondence had culminated in the meeting scheduled to take place two months earlier. During their conversations, a natural and enthusiastic bond had occurred. She thought he could have been the key to opening the mystery of her own family. But he was gone, maybe dead, and her hope of finding him had faded.

She stayed in her room at the motel that evening and ate no dinner. After a night of little sleep, she rose and ate three waffles, two containers of yogurt, and an orange. After scarfing it down, Cassie checked out and drove north on 61.

She stopped when she remembered the trailhead just off Highway 61. *I need some time to think, and fresh air.* Turning her car onto the county road, she headed to the trailhead. She had her backpack in the trunk for occasions such as this. Taking a quick two-hour hike always freshened her mind and spirits.

Cassie bounced out of the driver's seat and snatched her pack from the trunk, along with a couple bottles of water, four energy bars, and a banana taken from the motel. She strapped it on as she ascended the trail.

A cooling breeze caressed her face as she came to an overlook of the forest and Lake Superior a mile away. She never tired of this. Walking on the Superior Hiking Trail was one of the diversions that took her mind off her incomplete life; a life without relatives. She had no known bloodline. It saddened and frightened her.

Was her whole family dead? Or was Tom Hecimovich right? He said there had to be someone, and he knew how to find out. Tom had found his biological parents, and they were wonderful. They changed his life forever. She wanted the same thing, a life-altering event. She needed a change in her life. Cassie had friends, but as she had discovered, friends were transitory, here today and gone tomorrow.

Family is there forever.

She knew she had to have family somewhere, and Tom had promised to help her find them. She couldn't grasp how important he had become to her. If only... if only Tom hadn't vanished.

Why?

A switch went off in her head, and for the moment, she swept all thoughts of Tom and family away.

Just be... live in the moment. Look at the world around me. She watched a nuthatch work its way down the trunk of a tree, beak first. A gray squirrel scurried across the path in front of her, almost running over her toes in the process. Cassie laughed. *Live in the moment, enjoy what I have right now.*

After an hour of hiking, she came to the next trailhead and decided to walk farther. She thought she was the only person on this section of the trail.

At the next viewing point, she looked toward Lake Superior. Fog enveloped the lake, threatening to attack the shore and penetrate the forest where she hiked. Cassie had no desire to hike in the soupy mixture drifting toward her. She turned and started back. The fog moved quickly, enveloping everything around her. She was thankful for the clearly defined trail, but even so, the pace of her hike quickened.

"Hellooo," came a call from in front of her.

Maybe someone was in trouble, lost or frightened. "Hello," she called back, but her fear made her feel ashamed.

They called back and forth, eventually meeting near a feeder trail.

"I'm sorry if I scared you in this soup, but I was concerned when I noticed the fog drifting in from the lake," said Karonen.

Cassie flashed a puzzled look.

"How did you know I was up here?"

"Sorry, I should have explained that. I had just gotten off the trail where you parked and was sitting in my car when I saw you climb up the path like you really meant business. You seemed so intent on moving that you probably never saw me."

Cassie shook her head a little.

"I didn't see anybody, and you're right, I was intent on getting up the trail. So you followed me up here?"

"Not quite, I drove to where I knew this spur was and hiked up here, hoping to find you." He paused, sensing that he was frightening her. "Look, I knew the forecast called for fog, and I was just concerned that you might get lost, fall down, or get hurt. I didn't know if you were a novice or experienced hiker and just... I have a daughter and... well, I wouldn't want my daughter out, alone, in this stuff." He looked at her sheepishly, hoping his explanation would convince her and loosen her skepticism.

Cassie wanted to believe him. The old man looked harmless enough, and he sounded sincere.

"Well, thanks for your concern, but I've hiked this trail before." She looked around. "Although, never in fog like this."

"No pressure here, but my car is at the end of this spur. You could hike down with me and I'll give you a ride back to your car, and you could be on your way again. I wouldn't wish walking the next three miles in this fog on anyone, much less a young woman like yourself."

She bit her lip, hesitating.

"I would feel much better if you came with me," he said, playing his position for all it was worth.

Cassie didn't feel comfortable saying what she said next, but she didn't want to hurt the old man by acting afraid of him. She looked around again. The fog had grown denser, shrouding everything; even making the old man's face difficult to read. "It's a kind offer. I'll take you up on it."

Karonen smiled, and said, "Good, I think we should get going before we can't even see each other."

They both laughed.

She was impressed by the old man's nimbleness as he led the way down the narrow spur until it opened onto the gravel road. Karonen gestured toward the truck, which was barely visible. "Your carriage awaits."

A tight laugh escaped her, and she walked toward the pickup.

Karonen readied himself.

When Cassie was twenty feet from the truck, she slowed, and a chill blanketed her. Something inside of her, instinct, fear, distrust... something... cried out, *run, run!*

She broke for the trail, her breathing quickened as she bolted, but it was too late.

Karonen seized her, locking his arms around her in a bear hug, and pinning her arms at her side.

She screamed, but no one heard her.

He dragged her toward his truck.

She screamed, and struggled, and kicked at his shins, causing him to loosen his grip momentarily, but he recovered quickly.

With a Herculean effort, she broke his hold and tried to run, but tripped and fell to the ground. She screamed louder, and then felt the sharp pain of 55,000 volts surging through her body, which stiffened like a board. When the pain stopped, her body relaxed and she curled into a fetal position.

Karonen put the Taser in his pocket and dragged her to the truck, opened the tailgate, and reached inside.

Cassie's senses began to return and she tried to stand and run again. She didn't make it.

Karonen held the rag soaked in chloroform over her nose and mouth. She lost consciousness and didn't wake until she was locked inside a cell.

Where am I? Disoriented, she had no idea. She only knew she was a captive, housed in what seemed to be a cave.

She moved her arms and legs. Every muscle in her body smarted. As her vision improved and the haziness gave way, she looked around. Cassie lay on a well-made bed with a pink comforter. She raised herself to an elbow and inspected her surroundings. Paintings and photos hung on the rock walls. A chandelier dangled from the ceiling, and rag rugs covered wooden planks that had been spiked into the dirt and rock floor.

For the first time, she noticed music, a classical piece. Cassie had never been a fan of classical music, but recognized a familiar melody she had first heard while watching a TV commercial.

She moved her legs again and felt the clamp around her ankle. A chain attached to the clamp, extended across the room, and was tethered to a wooden plank bolted into the floor.

Above the cell door, she noticed a mounted video camera, which tracked her movements as she ambled away from the bed to where the chain was fastened to the floor. She dropped to her knees and pulled and jerked. The bolt didn't yield. Bending down, Cassie positioned her face close, examining it thoroughly. She tried to unscrew it. *It's a bolt dummy, not a screw!* In frustration, she slapped her hand on the wooden planks.

She sat upright and stared at the clamp on her ankle. Prying it with her fingers didn't work. She looked around the room, searching for something she could use to smash and break it. Seeing nothing, she stood and walked to the farthest boundaries of her chain. There were shelves on the walls, brimming with knickknacks and photographs. Nothing looked substantial enough to break the clamp on her ankle.

She thought of the underside of the bed; the springs could be used. *Maybe I can take one off and use it to pry or smash the clamp.* Cassie moved to the bed and looked under the box. The bottom of the box spring was covered with fabric; easy to tear so she could get at it. Another idea occurred to her. *The legs of the bed... I can take a leg off and use that to break the clamp. Even if it works, though, I still have the problem of getting out of this cage.*

She rose to her feet and then sat on the edge of the bed, feeling powerless.

Cassie stared at the floor. She was confused and frightened. *Who is this man and what does he want with me?*

"Cassie!"

She jumped when she heard her name called.

Karonen stood on the other side of the cell door. He held a tray with a pitcher, a sandwich, and an apple. They stared at each other for several moments, and then his free hand moved to the bars and opened the gate.

It's not locked!

She watched as Karonen entered the cell and placed the tray on a wooden table.

"I have some refreshments for you," he said.

"Why did you do this to me, and what do you want?" Her tone surprised her. It was calm and even.

She heard him suck his breath in as if he was going to speak, but he said nothing. Karonen turned and left the cell, walking at a pace that suggested he didn't want to communicate anymore.

"Wait, come back! Who are you?" And then she couldn't contain the rage she felt and she screamed, "Where am I, and what do you want?"

The soft, padding sound of shoes on a dirt floor was her only answer. When the sound of his footsteps faded, she felt very alone. The paradox was that she also felt safer.

Constrained by the chain, she stood and trudged to the table. She sat in the only chair and probed the sandwich with a finger. A thin layer of mayonnaise coated one slice of bread. Thin cut ham was folded over itself several times to produce a thick band of meat smothered in *Dijon mustard?* Lettuce was crammed between the ham and bread. She removed the top slice and inspected further. *If he wanted me dead, I'd be dead now. It's gotta be safe to eat this.* She replaced the bread, held the sandwich with both hands, and bit into it, grimacing as if it was going to hurt.

She chewed gingerly with her mouth open. Cassie grasped the pitcher and looked inside. Water, she thought. She poured a glass full, sampled a taste, approved, and slurped half of it down. She looked around as she chewed and drank.

Plans, I have to make plans. She jerked on her chain. The clamp bit into her skin. *I've gotta get this damn thing off!* She finished the sandwich and retreated to the bed where she tore a chunk of cloth covering the box spring and worked on dislodging one of the springs.

Karonen watched the video feed of Cassie from his bedroom. He admired her resolution. She worked with passion as she ripped the material covering the springs and took hold of a spring and tried to wrench it from the box. He was determined not to interfere with her, believing he had acted hastily when he told the fisherman of his plans. That man had gone insane, and Karonen had been lucky to escape the situation uninjured. Of course, it had been regrettable that the fisherman had died in the process, but Karonen worked assiduously to come to terms with that.

He would watch, feed her, but communicate little.

Give her time to adjust to the situation, then I can gradually win her cooperation. Yes, that's the winning strategy. She must want to cooperate.

When Karonen had first observed her at the motel, he knew she was alone and possibly a suitable target. Surprised he hadn't thought of it earlier, it was now obvious to him that a woman might be the optimum candidate for bringing his daughter back. Methodist would relate to another woman.

Karonen had followed Cassie around the community, intrigued by her interest in others. He wondered what she was doing; apparently interviewing people and asking questions. He was curious, but he would have to exercise patience and rein in his inquisitiveness. It was far more important for him to co-opt Cassie than discover her agenda.

A day later, he realized that he had probably missed his chance to abduct her when she checked out of the motel in the morning, but he had followed her anyway. He had almost given up his plan when she turned off the highway and stopped at the trailhead. She was so intent on grabbing her gear and hiking the path that she didn't appear to notice him slow his truck as he passed by.

Karonen was acquainted with the spur located after the next trailhead and hoped to intercept her at that point, but it all hinged on how far she hiked. Lucky for him, everything worked to his advantage, including the fog. He hadn't the slightest idea it was predicted or would arrive when it did.

After making contact, the most difficult element of the abduction had been the physical struggle. He would have to find a better way of achieving any further kidnappings, if any, in the future. Hopefully, she was the one who would accomplish what he wanted and there would be no need for that.

In the meantime, Karonen would observe. He would let her sit, try to escape if she must, maybe even help her do it, just to see her heart, her spirit. He wanted, no... he needed her spirit if she was to succeed in bringing Methodist back to him.

CHAPTER 13

B aldwin didn't wait for Hodges or Mancoat to ask a question, but jumped into a monologue. "Tom Hecimovich had a lot of people fooled around here. He wasn't the good guy he pretended to be. You know about the drug thing, I suppose?"

Hodges and Mancoat nodded.

"You probably think it was all in his past. It wasn't. Oh yeah, Hecimovich was loved by the kids, but for the wrong reason. He used drugs and, in fact, supplied some of the kids with theirs." She paused and scanned their faces for a reaction. She saw their skeptical looks.

"That doesn't quite jive with what the principal and Mark Seinfelt told us," Mancoat said. Hodges remained silent.

Baldwin scoffed. "Mark Seinfelt? He's a dipshit who knew about everything. He was Tom's best friend, and enabler."

Hodges peered at her. "Please... explain what you mean when you say, enabler?"

Baldwin got up from her desk. "I mean enabler, as in not wanting to admit what Tom was doing. You see, on the surface, Tom's story was an inspiring one, one the community wanted to believe. Mark knew about the continued drug use, and kept it under the radar."

"Excuse me for asking, but were you the only one to suspect this, or were there others?" Hodges asked.

"I'm sure there were others who suspected, but didn't want to admit the truth... I'm sure of that."

"How did you know the truth?"

She took a deep breath. "I've waited long enough to tell this,

I guess." She took a deep breath. "I had a relationship with Tom. We kept it quiet, which is a trick in a small town like this, but we were very discreet." Baldwin put a heavy emphasis on the word 'discreet'.

"So you observed his use of drugs and the selling of drugs to students?"

"I saw him use drugs. Oxycontin, pot, cocaine... I'm ashamed that I joined him sometimes, but I never actually saw him sell to students. Ask Mark about that."

"Did you tell the police about this after his disappearance?" Hodges asked.

Her lips pursed and she scrutinized several tiny gouges in the desktop. "No, I never did."

Mancoat dived in, "Why the hell are you telling us now, then?"

"Opportunity... and... guilt. The principal rang my room and let me know you may be stopping here. He explained your situation. I didn't think I could go through another interview and continue the lie. I enabled the whole thing to go on too long, and I know I damaged kids..." She wiped a tear from her eye. "I did it because I cared for him, and I was foolish. I'm forty-six years old, single, living in a place where there aren't many available men. I was selfish..."

Desperate, thought Mancoat.

Hodges turned the conversation back to Hecimovich. "Ms. Baldwin, it might help us determine what happened to Tom, and our friend, if we knew why he registered at the North Star Motel under the name Richard Gabrielson. Do you think it had anything to do with a drug buy?"

Baldwin wiped her tears away, grabbed a tissue and blew her nose.

Her voice quivered. "It's possible. He had a contact in Duluth and maybe decided to meet him near where he wanted to fish. That was the only real thing about Tom. He loved to fish and hunt." A look of enlightenment crossed on her face. "He might have used his adoptive father's name whenever he made a drug deal. Kind of a fuck you thing to the people who raised him."

Hodges and Mancoat tried to hide their surprise that the plain-looking science teacher used the f-bomb.

Baldwin noticed anyway. "I guess I'm not the person you, or the rest of this town, thought I was." She walked to a window and stared.

"You wouldn't happen to know the names of his contacts would you?" Mancoat asked.

"Ask Mark. He'll know." A sad, disinterested monotone colored her voice

Hodges walked to the window and stood beside her. He leaned close and said softly, "Thank you for telling us everything. It helps us better understand the situation." He fiddled with his hat for a moment. "We're not going to share the personal information you gave us. Trust me on that."

She gave him an appreciative look before returning her gaze to the campus green.

Hodges and Mancoat left the room and returned to see Mark Seinfelt. His room was locked. They stopped in the office and asked for his home address, which the secretary had no problem providing.

It took them six minutes to drive to Seinfelt's house; an older, two-story with a single dormer on the upper floor. A newer Subaru Tribeca was parked in the driveway. They assumed it was Seinfelt's.

"Not a bad vehicle for a teacher in a small town, heh?" Mancoat commented.

Hodges grunted and kept walking, ignoring the implication of drug money... for the moment.

Three knocks later, Seinfelt came to the door and asked them in. They followed him to the living room and sat on newer furniture. Hodges noticed it was solid and expensive looking. Mancoat raised his eyebrows when he caught Hodge's eye.

"Can I get you guys a beer, wine, coffee?"

They answered at the same time.

Mancoat said, "A beer."

Hodges said, "Coffee."

"Be back in a minute." Seinfelt disappeared and returned a couple minutes later with a can of Michelob Golden Light, and a cup of coffee.

Mancoat grimaced when he saw the beer. *Warm piss.*

Hodges accepted the coffee and sampled it immediately.

"Keurig machine." Seinfelt said. Neither Mancoat nor Hodges responded. "That's how I brewed it so quickly. One of the best investments I ever made." Hodges and Mancoat disappointed him when they just nodded their heads. "I just thought you'd be curious about how fast I brewed the coffee."

Hodges ignored the comment and said, "Tell us about Tom's drug use."

Seinfelt clasped his hands in front him and paused. "That was a long time ago; a dark part of his life that..."

Hodges interrupted. "Come on, Mr. Seinfelt... we know he never quit using, and we know you helped keep that fact from the adult community and school officials, correct?"

Seinfelt smiled nervously. "That... that is not true." His voice quivered. "I don't know where you got that, but it's a bunch of crap! Tom never used drugs after he found his biological parents and..."

"Mr. Seinfelt, we have proof." Hodges let the words sink in. "Now, we are not interested in making anything out of this fact, reporting these facts, or letting the police know about your connection to the whole thing, but we are interested in knowing if there was a connection between Tom's disappearance and a possible drug buy at the North Star Motel."

Seinfelt's eyes flicked back and forth between Mancoat and Hodges as he considered Hodges' words.

Mancoat tipped his beer and downed a mouthful of his Michelob, grimacing in the process. Hodges sipped his coffee and watched Seinfelt.

After a long pause, Seinfelt said, "Nancy told you that, didn't she?"

Hodges nodded.

"Well, that puts a whole different spin on this." He placed his beer on the table next to him. "Yeah, he still used drugs, sold them to kids too, and yeah, he often used Richard Gabrielson's name when he arranged for pickups. He thought it was kind of funny, actually." Seinfelt looked at his feet. His right leg ticked up and down as if he were keeping time to a very fast song.

Both Hodges and Mancoat noticed the nervous movement.

Hodges took another sip of his coffee and then set it down. "So, he used his adoptive father's name when he bought drugs because he thought it was funny and wanted to somehow hurt them? Nice guy! Give us the name of his contacts."

"I don't know them."

Mancoat finished his beer. "From the looks of this house, and all the toys you have... you know."

"Hey look, I could call some buddies and have your asses kicked out of this house in five minutes." He gave them a threatening look.

Hodges didn't melt. "Please, Mr. Seinfelt, that was very disappointing. This is not our first rodeo, and we know you'll do nothing of the sort. There are too many questionable actions in your past... and present, I might add. Give us some names, or we'll report your activities to the appropriate authorities."

The weasel caved.

"You promise you won't give this to the police?"

"We won't if you give us what we want. We're not interested in you and your little sideline business," Hodges lied.

Seinfelt stared meekly at Hodges. "Okay, as long as I have your word as a gentlemen." Seinfelt left the room briefly and returned with a slip of paper with two names and telephone numbers.

Hodges took the paper, looked at it, and showed Mancoat.

"Thank you, Hodges said."

They got up to leave. Mancoat turned, shot Seinfelt a look, and said, "You'll understand if we don't shake your hand, right?"

"Not a problem," Seinfelt said.

When they were outside, and safely out of Seinfelt's hearing, Mancoat said, "What an asshole! We're not really going to keep this secret, are we?"

Hodges opened the driver's side door, "Of course not. Mr. Seinfelt will be dealt with in the end."

Mancoat smiled as he got in the car, and said, "Where to now?"

Hodges looked at the numbers again. "These look like Duluth area codes, so I suggest we return there and make a couple of calls."

CHAPTER 14

Cassie's fingers ached. She'd been working for an hour trying to detach a spring from the box under the bed. Several minor, but annoying cuts laced her thumb, forefinger, and backs of her hands; plus her muscles were sore. She took a break. *Rome was not built in a day*.

She stood and walked around the room, reconnoitering and testing the limits of her chain. There was no doubt that this man had gone to extraordinary lengths to arrange a comfortable room for her, but why? She decided to press him when he returned, which didn't happen until the following day.

The difficulty of judging the lapse of time with no daylight or evening to guide her made the estimate an issue. Her disorientation made elementary perceptions difficult. She lay on the bed and fell asleep.

Her eyes sprang open when she heard the clank of the cell door as it unlatched. Karonen entered with another tray of food, which he placed on the table. He picked up the other tray with its empty plate and glass before he turned to walk away.

She watched and called to him when he began to leave, "Wait, I'd like some answers."

Karonen's body stiffened, but he didn't turn around. He had already decided not to engage her yet, so he walked away despite her continued pleas for him to answer questions. He left the cell door open and unlatched as he returned to his house.

Frustrated, but controlling her anger, Cassie moved to the table, sat down, and ate the food he brought. Like the first meal, this one was excellent. He even provided a glass of red wine. She sniffed, then touched it to her lips. She was no connoisseur. It tasted horrible. The wine was very dry, not sweet, like she was used to. But, it was alcohol, and she decided she would finish it.

Wine glass in hand, Cassie wandered to the bookcase and browsed the shelves. The only title she recognized was *Little Women*. She plucked it from the shelf, returned to the bed, and read a few pages. Her eyes closed, and once more, her thoughts went to escape. Soon, she downed the wine and started working on the spring again. This time, she wrapped her hands in the torn cloth she had removed from the underside of the box spring and tugged, pushed, and pulled. After an hour or more of laboring, she gave up and collapsed on the bed again. The spring was looser now than when she started. She was sure of it.

The same scenario presented itself again and again as the uncounted hours went by.

Karonen delivered meals and drink. He never explained what he wanted her for, or why he wouldn't communicate with her.

Cassie pulled and jerked as hard as she could. To her relief, the spring came loose. She grasped it, immediately inserting the narrowest end into the opening of the clamp on her leg.

Fascinated, Karonen watched the video feed, and cheered for her to break it open. His cheers were rewarded. On Cassie's fifth attempt, the clamp clicked open and she was free.

Her breathing was labored and her eyes were wild with excitement. *I did it!* She licked her dry lips and pulled her sweater on. The video camera whirred as it followed her across the room. She threw the chair at it, knocking it from its perch. Expecting Karonen to appear soon, Cassie passed through the open barred door and went the opposite way he had always gone when he retreated from her cell. Dim light illuminated the rock hallway as she fled upward.

Karonen knew that if she kept on the pathway she had chosen, Cassie would emerge from the rocky shaft on the eastern side near the top of the hill, behind his house. She could flee in any direction, but he surmised she would continue downhill and eventually intersect the county road leading to Finland. He waited several minutes, giving her time to make her way through and emerge near the apex of the hill.

Cassie's ankle burned as she ran as fast as she dared. Ten minutes after she dashed from her cell, she noticed a narrowing of the shaft and a steeper pathway. Another minute, and she came to the end, capped by what looked like a submarine hatch with a circular handle.

She grabbed hold of the handle and tried turning it. The handle wouldn't budge. She tried the other way, and she barely moved it. Summoning all her strength, she grabbed it again and jerked as hard as she could. The handle released. Cassie opened the hatch and emerged into the night.

Karonen peeked in on Methodist. He stood in the doorway watching the rise and fall of her chest as she breathed in and out. He walked to her and re-checked the flow of the IV. It seemed to be running well. Satisfied that she was fine, he left her, slipped the keys from the hook near his refrigerator, and jumped into his F-150.

Excitement filled his brain. *She is worthy. She has spirit*.

Karonen thought he knew where she would end up. He sat for several more minutes, letting his eyes adjust to the dark before starting the truck. He drove out of his driveway, turned left onto the county road, and followed it several hundred yards as it circled around the bluff behind his house. It was dark, and he didn't want to give himself away, so he proceeded without headlights, keeping a watchful eye for any movements.

A deer stood in the middle of the gravel roadway and watched him approach. Karonen advanced, but slowed to a near halt, hoping to nudge the deer out of his way. The deer's ears perked up and it stomped off, demonstrating its fear and annoyance with the large organism daring to approach it.

Five minutes later, he stopped his truck, opened the front windows, and turned the radio on loud enough for someone within a hundred yards to hear. Then he waited.

He loved jazz. Art Tatum had been one of his favorites. The nearly blind vocalist and consummate pianist had developed a style of his own, playing with a swinging pulse and improvisational abilities that were beyond his era.

Karonen lost track of time, bobbing his head in time with the music, until he felt the call of nature. He opened the door to relieve himself, finishing off with several shakes, when he heard a faint scream. He scrambled to tuck himself back into his pants, dribbling on himself as he did so, and rushed toward the sound.

He could hear the sound of her crashing through the brush, making more and more desperate cries as she tried to escape. And then he heard her footfalls on the gravel. Karonen knew he would have to push himself faster as he lurched onto the same gravel road and chased her. Sweat trickled from his forehead and into his eyes. He cleared it away with his forearm and gained on her, shining his flashlight toward the sound.

She screamed again when the beam from his flashlight encased her; she turned and flailed her arms to ward him off. He didn't know what else to do, so he swung the flashlight, hit her and knocked her down.

Cassie started to get up, so he swung the flashlight again. The adrenalin in his body drove him to a level he hadn't felt since overcoming the fisherman in his cell. Karonen cursed himself when he saw that the blow he had delivered had knocked her unconscious.

He dragged her body a hundred feet before he decided it would be easier to drive the truck to her. Tired as he was, he sprinted to the truck and drove it to where she lay. He took care not to injure her further and hoisted her inside.

Karonen feared that Cassie would not recover, cursing himself time and again as he drove back to his house and placed her in her cell. He cried and paced the room where she lay, until he noticed her first stirrings. His heart skipped with joy. He left the room, confident that she would recover.

Hours later, she opened her eyes and was able to focus. She almost jumped out of the bed when she saw Karonen.

They stood and faced each other in silence for several moments.

"How do you feel?" Karonen asked in a sympathetic tone.

"How do you think I feel, asshole?"

Karonen cringed. "I know you must feel that way about me, and I don't blame you right now, but please, if you are willing and patient, I will tell you everything."

"And if I'm not willing or patient, you'll let me go?"

"I can't do that."

Cassie sat down on the edge of the bed. "Then I have no choice, do I?"

"Regrettably, you are correct."

Another long silence filled the air as Karonen struggled to tell her what he wanted from her. She sat and stared into him, trying to pierce his heart and make him die.

Finally, Cassie glanced at the underside of the bed. "I see you fixed it so I can't get to any more springs."

"Uh, yes, I attached a three-quarter inch thick sheet of plywood to the bottom so we don't have a repeat."

More silence.

Karonen motioned with his eyes. "Do you mind if I sit near your table and tell you my story?"

Refusing to think of it as her table, Cassie flicked her head to the side. "It's your table, not mine. Do what you want."

Karonen sat in the chair, lightly tapping his knuckles on the table for several seconds until he finally decided how to proceed. He was brief. "My daughter, Methodist, had an accident, too many prescription pills, and she ended up unconscious. I've been trying to awaken her." He paused.

Cassie shifted her eyes to the picture on the wall and then back to Karonen.

His eyes followed hers. "Yes, that's her. I've done my best to help her... to bring her back, but it hasn't worked. I need help."

"There are hospitals, doctors, nurses, specialists..." Cassie said in a dry tone. "Why me?"

"I've watched you. You have pride... spirit, a will to live that I think Methodist would respond to, and you're a woman."

Cassie didn't speak for a while, but stared at the picture of the young woman. "I asked you who she was before. Why didn't you tell me then?"

Karonen stared at Cassie. "I wasn't ready, and I wasn't sure you could be trusted."

Cassie whirled around and glared at him. "Trusted? What the hell do you mean by that?"

Karonen looked embarrassed, shifted his gaze away, and then said in a quiet voice, "I mean that I wasn't sure you were the one who could do it—bring her back to me."

"And now you're sure because you determined that I have spirit," she said in a deriding way.

"Yes!" The tone of his voice brimmed with confidence.

The clanging sound of the chain being dragged across the rock and wood floor accompanied her as she walked slowly around the room, trying to compose a plan.

"And, what's in it for me, if she wakes up and I bring her back to you? Will you let me go? And if you let me go, what if I go to the police and turn you in?"

His face was resolute. "I don't care what happens to me after she's awake and well. I only care about getting her back. I'll drive you to the police myself, if you want." He clasped his hands together and tightened his body. "I just want what every parent wants for his child. I want her to have a life and to be happy. I want her innocent face to shine like when she was a child and she would come running to me with her arms out wanting me to pick her up and hug her." Tears streaked his face, but his gaze was direct and intense. "Can you understand that?"

Cassie stopped pacing, hesitated, and then said. "Yes, I understand. I'll help you."

Karonen's face glowed and his eyes widened. "Thank you. Thank you so much."

"What do you want me to do, and when do you want me to start?"

He rose to his feet enthusiastically.

"Now, right now. I'll take you to see her, but first I... I'm sorry, but I must make sure you don't try to get away. It will be a little uncomfortable, but... until I'm sure you're committed to helping her and won't try to leave, it's a precaution I must insist on."

He left the room briefly and returned holding a neck clamp that looked like a dog's shock collar.

Cassie stepped back and tried to swallow, but her mouth was dry. She pursed her lips and pressed her tongue to the roof of her mouth, trying to gather moisture. Finally, she forced a minuscule amount of saliva down her throat before she spoke. "I'm ready."

Karonen approached warily, but then stopped and backed away.

Cassie looked confused. "What's wrong?"

"Please walk to the end of your chain."

She had almost forgotten about the chain on her ankle.

He attached the collar around her neck and activated it. He also placed handcuffs on her wrists before he unlocked the ankle clamp.

She made no aggressive moves.

"Forgive me, but I'm going to demonstrate what this collar can do if you resist or try to escape."

Cassie steeled herself.

The pain was brief, but excruciating, dropping her to her knees.

"I'm so sorry, but I wanted you to feel it so you don't try anything. It will never happen again as long as you remain compliant."

It took a few moments for her breathing to return to normal. Cassie put a hand to her throat and rubbed it as she stood. "It's okay. I understand."

"All right. I'll take you to her."

They turned left after leaving the cell and followed the serpentine shaft. Cassie felt both hopeless and curious. They came to the opening to Karonen's house, where he pulled a lever and opened the door to the living room. When they were through the opening, he closed the bookcase, led her through another doorway and down a short hallway.

Freshly oiled hinges eased the opening of Methodist's door. Karonen motioned Cassie inside. He followed close behind. The dim light forced Cassie to move haltingly toward the bed. She could detect a shape under the covers that moved up and down to the whirring sound of a ventilator. She heard the oxygen being forced into Methodist's lungs and then released, as the inexorable whirring rose and fell.

Cassie's eyes adjusted to the dim light and she noticed an IV tube attached to Methodist's left arm. She watched the slow drip, drip as it made its way through the tube and into the young woman's arm.

Karonen encouraged her to move closer to Methodist.

When Cassie did, she was surprised to see the woman's eyes were open and her pupils were twitching minutely from side to side. Cassie inhaled a deep breath and touched the young woman's forehead with the back of her hand. As she did so, Methodist blinked.

Startled, Cassie jerked her hand back.

Karonen leaned forward, eyes intense. "She moved, my god, she moved."

Cassie opened her mouth, but no words came out.

Karonen looked at Cassie. A broad smile stretched across his face and he said, "I knew it. I knew you would do it." He squeezed Cassie's shoulder and patted her lightly on the back.

Cassie recovered, but there was wonder in her voice. "She moved her eyes when I touched her."

Karonen removed the ventilator mask from Methodist's face and turned the machine off.

Surprised, Cassie looked on. The woman continued breathing, though shallower and more labored.

"It's all right," he said to Cassie. "I've done this before. The ventilator only assists her. It makes her breathing easier." He hung the tube around a hook on the IV stand and returned his gaze to Methodist. "Talk to her," he said to Cassie.

"What do I say?"

"Tell her who you are, what you've done, where you're from—everything you can think of. She'll hear you. I'm sure of it." He touched Methodist's forearm near the IV.

Cassie spoke, telling Methodist everything about her life. The words flowed from her lips.

Karonen listened to her story, assured he had chosen the right person to awaken Methodist. His interest intensified when she mentioned a man she had arranged to meet at the North Star motel to help her find her family. She explained how he had disappeared before meeting her.

Karonen noted the timeline and thought the man she described was the fisherman he had abducted and killed. The anguish he felt at that time returned and he ended the session with Methodist, explaining that she was tiring and needed to rest.

Cassie was disappointed with the interruption. Relieving herself of the pain in her life had been a cathartic experience; one that she had no idea would be so consoling. She said goodbye to Methodist and was escorted to her cell where Karonen removed the shock collar and left.

Every morning following breakfast, for the next thirty days, Karonen attached the collar around Cassie's neck and escorted her to Methodist's bedside. Cassie talked about losing her parents and growing up in foster homes. She spoke of the depths of her pain, and the void it had left in her life. She spoke of the difficulty of finding any living relatives and the hopes she had of establishing family relationships. And every time she mentioned Tom Hecimovich, Karonen hung his head and looked away.

Karonen stayed and listened to everything. At times, without showing it, he found himself weeping inside for Cassie, empathizing with her situation and hoping everything would end well for all three people in the room.

At the beginning of Cassie's fourth month in therapy, a significant event took place. Cassie sat on the side of the bed near the ventilator, which Karonen switched on more and more frequently. The young woman could only breathe for short stints without the aid of the machine. Her condition was deteriorating. Both of them observed it, and both had become more concerned.

Cassie paused while reading *Sense and Sensibility*. The whirring of the ventilator had stopped. She yelled at Karonen who dozed nearby.

He awoke with a start and cried, "What are you doing, you'll disturb her!"

"The ventilator... it stopped working," Cassie shouted.

"What did you do? You shut it off," he screamed, and flew to the plug in. He feverishly plugged, replugged, and turned switches off and on, to no avail. They watched her chest.

It didn't rise or fall. Methodist remained motionless.

Karonen began mouth-to-mouth resuscitation as Cassie looked on, not knowing what to do. He pumped Methodist's chest five times and blew a deep breath into her mouth. Karonen kept up CPR for nearly an hour. And finally, exhausted, he stopped. He cried and threw his arms around Methodist.

Tears in her eyes, Cassie approached him. "Mr. Karonen, I'm sorry, she's gone... there's nothing we can do now." She placed a hand on his shoulder. It took a moment, but he wheeled around and slapped her hand away from him.

"No, no, no," yelled Karonen. He glared at Cassie. "You did this." He snatched the collar's remote and activated it.

Cassie screamed and fell to the floor.

Karonen jolted her again. Her body stiffened and she blacked out.

She awoke in her cell. The collar had been removed, but the ankle clamp restrained her. It was tighter than before, biting into her skin.

Karonen stood next to the bed where she lay.

"You failed me. You failed Methodist. I thought you would be the one, but you failed both of us. I wanted to be here when you woke up to tell you that I'm not sorry for what I did to you, and to let you know that you have been released... from your... mission."

Cassie shuddered. "But, I didn't do anything, it wasn't my fault. It just happened. It must have been a power surge or an outage that caused the machine to quit." Tears flowed from her eyes. "I didn't do anything. I called you! You were sleeping and I let you know something was wrong. You can't think I did anything to Methodist. You can't!"

His face was made of stone.

Cassie felt his hardened gaze for several moments until he turned and walked away.

Karonen closed and locked the cell door when he left. He brought her food and drink for the next month. Several times she tried to engage him in conversation, pleading with him to forgive her.

On his most recent visit, she requested that he loosen the clamp on her ankle where a pus-filled abscess had formed. She was worried.

Karonen glanced at the area on her ankle and returned the next day with Neosporin. He removed the clamp, cleaned the wound, and then applied the anti-septic. "I'll leave the clamp off your ankle... until it heals."

Cassie looked up from her bed. "Thank you, Mr. Karonen, but Methodist..."

"Methodist is fine for now."

Cassie shook her head, not comprehending. "Fine? I thought she..." She searched for a softer word to describe death. "I thought she... passed."

Karonen smiled.

"No, she is with us. I am still taking care of her."

"Then I can start therapy with her again," Cassie said hopefully.

His smile disappeared. "No, I've decided to go another direction."

"But... what will I do?"

He seemed to look past her. "You shouldn't worry about that. I'll take care of you." He left her, and locked the cell.

Cassie slunk back and curled into a fetal position on the bed.

CHAPTER 15

Hodges and Mancoat drove back to Duluth where they contacted Cadotte. Hodges explained to her what they had discovered, but didn't share the names and numbers Seinfelt had given them. That fact did not escape Mancoat. "Why didn't you tell her everything, Jasper?"

"We don't need to show all our cards yet. We'll make contact with the first name on the list and see where it leads. If it goes nowhere, we'll contact the second name and take it from there."

Mancoat started to disagree, but reconsidered and left shaking his head.

The following morning, they ate breakfast at the Lake Avenue Cafe, feasting on pancakes, sausage, eggs, and a several cups of coffee. From there, they went back to their suite and called the first number. After three rings a drowsy, hoarse sounding male voice answered.

"I need Oxycontin," Mancoat said in the most desperate sounding tone he could muster.

A voice cut through the phone. "Old man, you probably need a lot more than that. You know what I need?"

"How much?"

"Not how much. I need to know how you got my number," the guy on the other end said.

Stumped, Mancoat wasn't prepared for the question. He paused too long and the voice hung up.

Mancoat put the phone down.

"What did he say?" Hodges asked.

"He asked how I got his number. I didn't know what to say." He shrugged his shoulders and looked at Hodges. "I don't think we're cut out for this kind of investigating. We don't know what the hell we're doing and have no experience, at least with drugs."

Hodges strode across the suite and gazed out the window. "Let's go downstairs and use the hotel computer to do a Google search on how to buy drugs. We'll prepare ourselves for whoever it is we speak to next."

Mancoat looked at Hodges with incredulity. "Are you kidding me? We're going to use the hotel computer to look up how to buy drugs? You know they monitor those things. We'll probably be picked up in an hour by the police."

"It's a simple internet search, Earl. It won't take long and we're not going to be picked up by the police, but to make you feel better, we'll delete the record of our search when we're finished." He raised his eyebrows as if he was asking Mancoat, "Okay"?

Mancoat shrugged his shoulders, acquiesced, and accompanied Hodges downstairs where Hodges swiftly accessed the information they needed, and then deleted their search, satisfying Earl.

Their new plan required Hodges to make the call. He did, and the same male answered.

"Tom Hecimovich gave me your name and number," Hodges answered when the question came. The man's tone of voice changed.

"Have you seen Tom? It's been a long time. Where is he?"

"Tom is fine, but very nervous right now. He's in the area, but unwilling to come out of hiding at this point," Hodges said.

"I wanna talk to him."

"That won't be possible. He won't talk to you or anyone else until his, uh, situation is cleared up."

"Whaddaya mean, his situation?"

"He owes some money... to me."

"You're holding him?"

"You could say that."

"Then I wanna talk to him."

"Listen, we can do business with you or we can go to someone else. You can make a lot of money and be happy, or we can go to one of your competitors. We called you because Tom used you as his contact and said you could be trusted. Can you?"

The voice hesitated before asking, "What do you need and how much?"

"We need 2,000 Oxycontin and I am willing to pay $40 per," Hodges said.

The voice quickly did the math, and, again, hesitated. "I don't have that many, but I can get it. It'll cost you $50 a pill."

"We'll pay $40. Take it or leave it."

Unwilling to risk the deal going south, the dealer hesitated, this time a little longer, before he said, "Okay."

Hodges said, "Time is of the essence. When?"

"Tonight, I'll make some calls, and I'm sure I can have it by then."

"Where and when?" Hodges asked.

"You'll have the $80,000?"

"All of it," Hodges answered.

"Nine-thirty. Go to Lester River Bridge, number 5772." The phone clicked off.

Still holding his phone, Hodges turned to face Earl. "We have a date."

"You sure about this, Jasper? We don't have $80,000 and what do we do if this guy has friends and they pull a gun?"

"That's why we acquire a handgun and take the dirt bag into our custody."

Mancoat couldn't believe what he was hearing. "Listen, Jasper, I'm all for a little adventure and daring, but shit, this sounds fucking crazy!"

"You forget, Earl. I have skills. Don't worry, but we're going to need a facility to take the gentlemen so we can interrogate him. I'll leave it up to you to find an appropriate venue."

Mancoat looked flabbergasted—and protested.

Hodges assured Mancoat that he could do it and that he had better stop wasting time arguing and research convenient locations to carry out the plan.

Mancoat relented and busied himself with his task.

Later that afternoon, Earl pulled out a map he had purchased in Canal Park, and circled a spot that appeared to be within a mile of where the meeting would take place. They hopped into their car and drove to a small brick building that was boarded up. They worked on loosening the boards enough so they could easily remove them later, but still maintain the appearance of being shuttered.

On any given week the Duluth News Tribune published ads for sporting goods in its classifieds, including used guns. Private firearms sales between individuals don't need background checks or any kind of paperwork. Mancoat purchased a small handgun that day and then they spent the remainder of the early evening eating and playing gin rummy.

Nine pm arrived and they drove to the Lester River Bridge and waited in a parking area on the eastern side of the arched bridge.

Nine-thirty passed and no one showed. They began to think they had been had, but a few minutes later headlights approached from the other side of the bridge. The vehicle slowly crossed the two hundred foot span.

"We'd better flash our lights," Mancoat urged.

Hodges ignored him.

Soon they were swathed in light from the oncoming vehicle's headlamps. It pulled up to the space in front of their car and stopped. The lights flicked off.

Hodges opened his door, revealing himself in the dome light. Mancoat did the same, and they stepped out.

Mancoat moved to Hodges' side of the car where they both stood and waited for the occupants to reveal themselves. It turned out to be a single occupant.

As the man opened his door he was exposed by the dome light. Bald, tattoos on his neck, and piercings on his lower lip helped distinguish him from what they would have considered to be a "normal" visitor to the bridge. He clutched a plastic bag when he emerged from the vehicle and walked the short distance separating them. He stopped eight feet away.

The man gestured to a bench overlooking the Lester River. It was located twenty-feet to their left. In unison, they walked over to it.

He spoke. "I have it. Show me the money."

Hodges held the briefcase he bought at Duluth Pack earlier. He placed it on the bench. The dealer alarmed them at first when he reached inside his jacket. But they relaxed when he pulled out a tiny flashlight and flicked it on. He reached down, unlatched the briefcase and raised the lid, shining the light inside to reveal the contents.

Hodges withdrew the small caliber automatic pistol and pointed it at the dealer who backed away a step with his hands raised.

"Shoulda known you weren't for real. Stick me up for this?" He held the bag high. "You want it, you're gonna have to swim for it." He wound up like he was going to throw it in the river.

"We don't want it," Hodges said.

The dealer stopped, confused. "What the hell do you want?"

"Information. Tell us what you know about Tom Hecimovich and the last time you saw or talked to him," Hodges said.

"So this really does have something to do with Tom, huh? I was beginning to think it was just bullshit."

Hodges gestured with the gun. "Just tell us about Tom, asshole."

Mancoat and Hodges heard the unmistakable noise of a pump-action shotgun being readied for firing behind them.

"How dumb you fellas think I am that I'd come out here without backup. That sound you heard was Freddy—with a sawed-off, twelve gauge shotgun. He's fixin' to blow a hole the size of Rhode Island in you two." The moonlight reflected in his eyes and gave an otherworldly look to an already strange looking human being.

Hodges showed no emotion, but Mancoat trembled. "It would appear that we have a standoff," Hodges said.

"A Mexican standoff, I'd say. Ain't that somethin'? Freddy, keep your gun on 'em till we figure out what we're gonna do." He stood by the bench, keeping his eyes on Mancoat and Hodges.

"We have a conundrum," Hodges said. "May I propose a solution?"

"Got a few solutions myself, but you go first. I'm curious." The dealer flipped the briefcase off the bench and sat down.

Hodges kept the pistol trained on him. "All right, why doesn't... Freddy, come into view and we both lower our weapons, then, like civilized men, we can converse. Since we brought you out here on false pretenses we will reimburse you an appropriate amount of cash after you answer our questions. In the end, everyone goes their separate ways."

The dealer rubbed his lower back. "Sorry, I got a bad disc. The doctor says I might need surgery at some point, but all I got is Obamacare, high deductibles, copays, you know the story. Anyway, I digress. What kind of reimbursement you talking about?"

"It depends on the information you provide," Hodges said.

Mancoat tried not to fidget.

"About Tom,"said the dealer.

"Yes, everything you know would be appreciated," said Hodges.

"Freddy. Get over here!" Freddy turned out to be female. In the partial light of the moon, she looked about thirty, fine figure with short, black hair.

"Okay with you if we lower the guns on three?"

Hodges nodded.

"Okay, one... two... three." Freddy and Hodges slowly lowered their weapons.

"Now, Tom was a unique individual. I liked him, but he was a little messed up," the dealer said.

Like you're not, Mancoat thought.

The dealer shifted his weight, and then went on. "I've known him for a long time, and I suspect he may not be with us anymore. I don't think you guys know Tom. You got my number from some-body else, or maybe you got into his paperwork and found my number. I don't know. Personally, I think Tom's dead. Doesn't make any difference anymore. He was a small piece of my business. One thing, you want to know is that he always used the name Richard Gabrielson when he bought from me—kind of a kick at his adoptive parents, I guess."

"So what do you think happened to him?"

"I don't have the slightest idea. I hadn't seen him for months before he disappeared, got offed, or whatever."

"So you didn't have anything to do with his disappearance?" Hodges asked.

The dealer looked hurt. "That's a big negatory. Tom was okay, and we had a mutually beneficial relationship, but you learn to move on. Anyway, I'd check with his adoptive parents. Maybe they finally got tired of his bullshit and offed him."

"I think they're dead," Hodges said.

"Well, I don't have a clue, then. Now, about that compensation..."

"It's not much information you've given us," Hodges said.

"Gotta be worth something, after all you dragged me out here with the lure of big money, and I have expenses, and I did pull a few favors to get the stuff. Now I have a bit of an oversupply, so I think a grand should accommodate me."

Hodges nodded at Mancoat who reached into his wallet, unfolded ten, one hundred dollar bills, and handed him the money. The dealer accepted the cash, gave a hundred to Freddy and the rest went in his pocket.

"Hope you find what you're looking for," Freddy said as she and the dealer returned to their car.

Mancoat kicked at the dirt. "Well, that was a waste of time... and money."

"At least we confirmed that Tom Hecimovich was not the innocent, upstanding person most of his coworkers and community thought he was."

"But it hasn't helped a damn in finding Seth," Mancoat said.

Hodges couldn't disagree. He retrieved the briefcase, disappointed. He tilted his hat, and got into the car. "Tomorrow we'll check in with Sheila and find out if she's discovered anything new. This appears to be a dead end."

Mancoat woke up to the sound of intense knocking on their hotel door. He looked at the bedside clock and moaned, six-thirty

---

am. The knocking became more frenzied as he rolled out of bed and pulled on his pants and a shirt.

Before he could get to the door, Hodges had opened it and ushered Sheila Cadotte into the suite.

She was gesturing and talking a mile a minute, none of which Mancoat could understand. "Jasper and Earl, you gotta see this again. I think I found the guy in the video," Cadotte said.

She flew to the table, opened her computer, and ran the video feed from the Suites again. Soon, they all watched as the shorter man wearing Seth's fedora appeared at the front desk, spoke to the woman and then left.

Hodges sat back. "All right, we saw the video, now what do you have?"

Cadotte closed the computer, smiled, and said, "I saw him!"

"You saw him," Mancoat said skeptically.

Hodges tilted his head forward, "Tell us..."

She recounted her trip to Silver Bay and her encounter with an older man in the parking lot of the only business center in town. The kicker, she added, was that he wore a fedora exactly like the one worn by the imposter in the video.

When she finished telling them the story, Mancoat stated condescendingly, "Sheila, there's gotta be a million of those fedora's around."

"Earl," Cadotte cocked her head, "I know that, but when I talked to the guy, he gave me directions, so I got a good look at him, height, build, color, length of his hair, and the way he stood. At the time, I thought, this guy looks familiar. I've seen him before, but I didn't remember where, until last night when I looked at the video again. It's him! I tell you it was him!"

Hodges spoke first. "It's possible. You may have come up with the lead we've been looking for." He patted her shoulder. "Providence arrives in the most mysterious of ways. When we recognize the act, we are most fortunate, indeed."

Mancoat was not convinced something beneficial had happened, but after last night's debacle, he was willing to go along with just about anything. "Okay, so how do we find this guy?"

Cadotte answered, "Or do we tell the police we ID'd him and let them handle it?"

"I think, for now, we should do a little more research," Hodges said. "And I suggest we begin where Sheila met him." He looked at Cadotte for affirmation.

"Sounds like a plan," she said.

"Earl, are you game?" Hodges asked.

Mancoat agreed, and then excused himself to take a shower and dress.

Half an hour later, they were on the road to the Northwoods Family Grill. Another half hour and they pulled into the parking lot that served the cafe and surrounding businesses.

"It was just over there," Cadotte said, pointing at a parking area fifty feet away. "That's where he got out of his car and we talked."

Barely acknowledging what she had pointed out, Mancoat said, "I'll head on in to the cafe and get us a table."

Cadotte pivoted, "Right behind you, Earl."

Hodges fell in line.

Mancoat entered first. The restaurant was more stylish than he had thought it would be. The place was busy, but an unoccupied table was available; he strode to it and sat down. The other two joined him, ordered coffee, and then perused the menu. When the waitress returned, Cadotte struck up a conversation about the previous day, asking her if she remembered an older gentlemen who had come into the restaurant just after she'd left.

"Honey, we get a lot of old men in here every day. Now I do remember that I sent you to see Becky Jaakola. Did you ever find her? I know the directions I gave you were a little discombobulated, so I'd get it if you didn't."

"Yes, I did, but I needed a little help with them so I talked to an older gentleman in the parking lot who cleared up everything for me. He was a nice fella, wore a fedora..."

"Oh! Now, I know who you mean, Peter Karonen. He comes in here a couple times a week for the specials. He's a good guy—lives by Finland and takes care of his daughter. She had a terrible accident a few years ago—prescription drug overdose—Oxycodone, I think."

Cadotte held herself in control, though her insides were bursting with excitement. Hodges and Mancoat sipped their coffees.

"You said the older man's name is Peter Karonen?" Cadotte stifled a nervous laugh. "You wouldn't be able to give me directions to his house would you? No offense to you, but he saved my day. My editor would have flayed me if I didn't get that interview with Ms. Jaakola."

"After your last experience with my directions, you want more?" The waitress chuckled. "Tell ya what, I'll look up his address and write it down, then you'd have better luck GPSing it. Sound okay?"

"That'd be wonderful! Thank you so much."

When the waitress left, Hodges said in a low tone, "Well done, Sheila. You ever thought of a career in law enforcement? You certainly know how to get information in a nonthreatening manner."

Cadotte feigned humility, "Every good reporter knows how to do what I did. It's an everyday part of the job."

Their breakfasts arrived along with the address. They didn't linger when they'd finished. They paid the bill and hurried back to Cadotte's Lexus. After punching the address into her cell, she placed it on the dash and followed the directions toward Karonen's house.

They followed the directions on faith for a fair distance. Mancoat expressed his distrust of GPS devices as they switched from one gravel drive to another, finally turning into what appeared to be a long driveway up a significant incline. A two-story house sided with cedar shakes stood in front of them. It seemed like it was built into the 400-foot tall hill behind it.

Hodges didn't notice any vehicles parked in the driveway, although a dilapidated, detached garage sat near the house and could have hidden one.

"Well, shall we?" Hodges motioned toward the house. They vacated the Lexus and walked to the front door.

Cadotte took the lead and knocked three times. Mancoat started whistling the old Tony Orlando and Dawn song, *Knock Three Times*. Hodges motioned him to stop. They waited a respectful amount of time. No one answered. She knocked three more times, but this time, significantly louder.

Still no answer.

Mancoat stepped away from the porch, scanned the yard, and then walked to one side of the home. Hodges walked to the other side and looked around back, noticing the house was built into the hill. *Interesting design*, he thought. Mancoat noticed the same thing. Cadotte stayed at the front door.

Cadotte started to walk away, but suddenly, the door opened and Karonen stood looking at her from the opening. "I'm sorry, I was in my daughter's room reading to her, and didn't hear anything until I finished." He looked in surprise from one side to the other as Mancoat and Hodges converged on the porch from opposite sides of the house. He stammered a little, "Forgive me, I don't get many visitors out here. I'm pretty isolated. Is there something I can help you with?"

"We apologize for disturbing you, sir, but we're lost and need some guidance. We're looking for Lax Lake, and somehow ended up here," Hodges lied.

"You really aren't that far off," Karonen said. "You need to turn right out of my driveway, follow the gravel road for, oh, about two miles until you come to the first intersecting blacktop. Turn right again and that will take you right past the lake."

"That's twice you've helped me, sir. I was in the parking lot in Silver Bay the other day where you gave me directions to Becky Jaakola's house."

Karonen gave her a puzzled look, but then smiled in recognition and slapped his hands together. "I recognize you now! Yes, of course, someone had written awful directions, and you were having trouble figuring them out. You just needed a little clarification." He performed an exaggerated bow. "I'm always happy to assist a beautiful woman in her time of need." He pivoted, but caught himself in mid-turn. "I'd invite you into the house for drinks, but the place is a mess, and I wouldn't want you to see it like that." He shook his head and uttered something unintelligible.

Mancoat said quickly, "That wouldn't bother us. Jasper and I are not the greatest housekeepers so it would probably be an upgrade from what we're used to."

Karonen lifted an eyebrow when he looked at the men. "Are... you two partners?"

"Yeah," Mancoat responded before getting the drift of what Karonen was asking.

"Uh, I mean, no, no, not partners in that sense. We don't live together, we're separate, uh, we both like the opposite sex." Digging himself in deeper, Mancoat continued, "We're partners in the respect that we sometimes work together, uh, like Cagney and Lacy, Abbott and Costello... Bogart and Bacall." He added emphasis when he repeated the line, "We work together."

Hodges took a breath and rolled his eyes. Cadotte, embarrassed, looked away.

Karonen's jaw was open and his brow was furrowed as he tried to process Mancoat's explanation.

Several moments passed before Cadotte finally said, "Well, we should be leaving. Thank you again for being my savior and helping us find our way."

She shook Karonen's hand and they left.

"What the hell was all that bullshit, Bogart and Bacall, Abbott and Costello?" Cadotte asked.

"I was stuck. I kept on talking when I should have shut the hell up, okay?"

Tired of the back and forth, Hodges shushed them. "The question is, what do we do from here?"

CHAPTER 16

C assie marked another day on her homemade wall calendar. She judged her days by Karonen's arrival with breakfast; usually muffins, fruit, and coffee. Adding her marks, she came up with 395 days. He never asked her to read or speak with Methodist, which made her wonder. When would Karonen tire of taking care of her? During the last month of her visit, as Karonen called it, he had seemed happier, even though he didn't speak with her often or stay for more than the time it took him to deposit her breakfast tray and pick it up later.

While depression had affected her for the past year in captivity, it was alleviated when Karonen ran a TV cable to her cell, allowing her to at least keep up with the news. That's how she learned of Seth Tryton's disappearance during the past month. She asked Karonen about it, but he ignored the question, causing her suspicions to rise. If Karonen had abducted another person and replaced her, she had to know. Somehow, she knew she had to find out for sure, and make contact. The only question was how she could do it.

Karonen never left her cell unlocked anymore. He hadn't since her escape and recapture more than a year earlier, but he did allow her to roam untethered within her cell. The video camera still worked, tracking her every move. She knew, if Tryton was here in another cell, it wasn't close. She had called and rapped the cell bars with the table chair. There had never been an answer. If she was to find out for sure, she had to escape somehow, and search the caverns. There had to be connecting tunnels. He was possibly imprisoned in one of those.

She felt her best chance for escape was somehow attacking

and overcoming Karonen, but he always insisted she stay at the far end of the cell when he arrived with her breakfast and when he returned later to retrieve it. Getting close to him was problematic. She identified three possibilities for escape: Karonen slipped up and left the cell unlocked, she picked the lock, or she dug her way out.

Cassie plotted for a long time, but none of the options ever seemed manageable until she finally worked a leg of the chair loose and used it as a chipping tool. If he knew about her success, Karonen never let on that he knew what she had done, or was doing. For the past week, while Karonen appeared to ignore her, she discovered she was able to direct the video camera away from the area she had chosen to dig into the wall, allowing her to chip and scrape at the rock and dirt for long periods of time. She made slow progress, but knew if she continued working at it she would be able to carve a hole large enough for her to wriggle through.

Whenever she finished digging, she slid the small bookcase in front of the dug out area in the wall and scattered the loosened rock and dirt around her prison. It was a time consuming procedure to empty and replace the books from the shelves. Fortunately, Karonen was a creature of habit and visited only at select times, allowing her to avoid discovery.

Seth Tryton woke up early, 7:35 am according to the battery powered wall clock Karonen had given him. Karonen had also been provided him with a TV cable and an old tube set. The items were amenities that Tryton had requested. Karonen had been pleased with him so he was happy to bring them to Tryton's cell.

Karonen always delivered his breakfast at 8:30 am. An hour later, he would return, attach the shock collar and take Seth for his daily ritual of reading to Methodist's corpse. When he finished with Methodist, he was returned to his cell, where Karonen would remove the collar, collect the tray, and leave.

Today, after finishing his breakfast and watching the news, Tryton watched Karonen enter. He didn't carry the shock collar, so Tryton assumed he was not going to read today.

"Do you notice anything different today?"

Tryton studied him for a moment. "I see you didn't come with the shock collar."

Karonen walked closer to where Tryton lay on the bed. "I didn't bring it because it won't be needed."

Just as I thought: no talking to the corpse today.

"I believe now that I can trust you, Seth." He let the words dangle.

Tryton remained silent for several moments, finally managing to say thank you with every bit of sincerity he could muster. He had worked hard to convince Karonen during his two months of captivity that he wanted to help him and that he was committed to reviving Methodist. What he had to do to satisfy the delusion of this sick man was repugnant. But the absolute worst component of the ordeal was the odor, the revolting stench of Methodist's rotting corpse, which Karonen seemed immune to.

Tryton had devised an argument to help him avoid as much of the disgusting stink as possible. He convinced Karonen that Methodist was at risk of contracting an infection from Seth. Embracing Seth's idea, Karonen bought the most efficient facemask he could find for Tryton to wear whenever he was in contact with Methodist. The mask helped dissipate most of the odor, but still allowed some of it to invade his olfactory receptors. It made his loathsome job, if not pleasant, at least palatable.

"So, shall we begin? It is the dawn of a new day, Seth." Karonen reached out to shake Tryton's hand. Tryton reciprocated, and they both flexed strong, bonding grips.

Karonen beamed. Tryton managed a passable smile.

"Please, lead the way," Karonen said as he waved an arm toward the door.

Tryton stood and walked slowly to the hallway, pausing at the entrance to his cell and breathing deeply. He looked back inside.

"It feels good, doesn't it?" Karonen said

"Yes... it does."

Karonen grasped Tryton's shoulder. "It's only the beginning,

Seth. As you prove yourself, I'll give you even more freedom. I feel that our friendship is growing stronger and stronger, don't you?"

Tryton didn't hesitate, "Yes, I do, Peter, and I'll continue to prove myself to you. You'll see."

Karonen smiled. "Come, let's not keep Methodist waiting." He took the lead, walking with the confidence that Seth would follow him without attacking.

Tryton stooped over as they walked; a natural consequence of getting older.

He noted, as he had many times, connecting hallways with what he assumed held cells where others may have been detained to perform the same duties he now performed. Only a couple of the other tunnels were lit, which always peaked his curiosity. He resolved, if he were able to gain a larger measure of freedom, to explore them and find out what they concealed, if anything.

For a few unsure moments, Seth considered slamming Karonen into the rock wall, but he knew the younger man was in better shape and stronger. He knew he would need a weapon and a better opportunity to make it work. He decided to bide his time. *Play it out, generate more trust.* That was what he would do for now.

Karonen spoke with excitement and more loudly than Seth had ever known him to do. The nonstop, loud talking made the winding trip through the tunnels seem shorter. It occurred to him that if there was someone else alive in one of the lit tunnels, he might gain a measure of hope if he heard another voice besides Karonen's. He resolved to find out if he were given the opportunity so he offered an occasional loud response.

Just as Karonen exited the tunnel into the living room, he heard loud knocking on the front door. He stopped and motioned Tryton to be quiet.

Seth waited in the tunnel.

Karonen caught a glimpse of someone passing by the window of the living room and stepped back inside the tunnel.

"What is it?" whispered Tryton.

Karonen didn't answer immediately, but peeked his head out

of the tunnel again. "I'm sorry, Seth, but I have to take you back to your cell. Please, go back with me now."

His heart told him to yell and try and push by Karonen, but his mind told him he wasn't strong enough. *Karonen will never trust me again if I fail.*

Tryton stepped back, then turned and hurried to his cell, which Karonen locked with apologies.

Ten minutes later, Karonen returned. "It was just some people who were lost. I gave them directions to Lax Lake and they left." Karonen then became remorseful. "I'm sorry I treated you the way I did. I trust you... but, obviously, we still have some work to do in that department. Forgive me, please."

Tryton looked at him with an exaggerated expression of forgiveness. "I understand. I hope that when I didn't yell out or try to escape that I passed another test."

Karonen's mood became more cheerful, "Yes, yes, Seth, you gained more trust."

Tryton smiled, and the two of them walked back through the tunnel and into Methodist's room. After donning the facemask, Tryton, although his voice was slightly muffled, read another passage from *Mansfield Park*. Karonen left the room for a long period of time. When he returned he checked the IV tube and dried some of the liquid that had leaked onto the bed with a towel. He replaced the IV, adjusting the drip rate to a slower speed.

"Ah, that should take care of that!" Karonen said. "Now, I have a surprise for you. Come with me." He led him to the kitchen where he had set the table for two and piled soft buns with loads of pulled pork. It was a step up from the nominal, informal dinners he had provided Tryton for much of the past two months. Cloth napkins were folded and hot coffee was brewing in a pot.

Tryton, salivating, looked at the sandwiches with bugged eyes. "And, we're eating here... together?" he said with feigned amazement.

Looking pleased with himself, Karonen replied, "Yes. You proved yourself to me, and this is your reward."

Tryton pulled a chair out from the table and sat down.

Karonen did the same. The smile on his face did not wear off. They began to eat. It was almost as if Tryton were not a prisoner and Karonen was not his captor. They spoke of politics, football, and women. Laughter punctuated their easy conversation.

Tryton found himself enjoying Karonen's company and thought, in another time, Karonen would fit in with the cabal of old men back in Rose Creek, drinking at the local Muni and ogling the waitress. The dichotomy of the situation irritated him.

I'm a captive! I was abducted and am being held against my will by a crazy person...but he doesn't seem crazy now. How can it be? He didn't know.

Sweat dripped off Cassie as she chipped and dug with a furious passion. Nearly out of breath, she stopped, and squinted at the section she had hollowed out several inches. She repositioned herself, kneeling in the rock and dirt she had had deposited on the floor. A shooting pain flared through her knee, which made her stand up. She dug a triangular shaped pebble out of her knee. The pain softened immediately.

She stood, exhausted, wet with sweat, and wracked by residual pain in her knees, hands, arms, and shoulders. It was getting late and she expected Karonen to make his appearance in half an hour, so she spread the debris from her diggings around the floor of the cell and pulled the bookcase in front of the hole. She refilled the shelves with books and changed her clothes, hanging her wet laundry out to dry on the far side of her cell. Karonen had never paid any attention to the wet clothes she'd hung out before. He seemed obsessed with something, or someone else now. She was grateful for that.

Cassie had not heard Karonen and Tryton talking as they walked back to the other cell. She was too preoccupied with taking care of her own needs.

Twenty minutes later, Karonen appeared, on schedule, bringing a tray with a small amount of pulled pork and baked beans.

After unlocking the door, he entered and set the tray on the table. Uncharacteristically, he stopped for a moment and cocked his head to look at the video camera.

Oh my God, I forgot to reset it.

He stared at it for a few moments and then moved from side to side. The camera failed to move with him. Karonen studied it like an engineer. Finally, he placed his hands on the camera and gently moved it. The mount it was on emitted a scraping, metallic sound as it was loosened from where Cassie had stuck it in place with a sliver of wood.

Karonen didn't notice the sliver drop to the floor.

Cassie said nothing.

Karonen stepped laterally to test the movement. The camera advanced with each step. He grunted his approval, and after locking the cell door, he left without saying a word to her.

She breathed a sigh of relief, settled herself at the table, and ate her evening meal. She planned to be more careful next time and not let herself be so rushed that she'd forget to reset the camera.

Tonight she would rest, watch some TV, and regain her strength.

Tryton lay on his bed, considering his attitude toward Karonen. He was confused by the pleasant communication he and Karonen had experienced earlier. The conflicting, baffling thoughts circling his brain bewildered him. He had heard of individuals being kidnapped and then brainwashed by their captors to the point where they became allies. Tryton had always dismissed such experiences as hogwash. But now, he wasn't so sure. He was definitely at the point where he sympathized with Karonen and didn't want to see him get hurt.

Small twinges of remorse encroached upon his mind when he thought of escape.

This is crazy. I'm crazy! Peter kidnapped me and held me prisoner. He needs to be in a loony bin... An afterthought hit him. *But I'll make sure it's a good place where he can be helped.* He placed his hands against the sides of his head and pressed hard. *What is happening to me?*

He straightened up in an abrupt motion. Tryton switched his gaze to the cell door. It was unlocked and open. The light on the video camera still blinked and moved when he did. *I guess he still doesn't totally trust me.* He decided to take a chance that Karonen wasn't constantly watching the video feed. Tryton got up and walked to the open door and peered down the lighted tunnel. He took a measured step out of the cell, and then another, and another. Soon he was exploring a connected tunnel.

His labored gait carried little sound as he slowly made his way; an uneasiness plagued every step he took. Placing a hand on the tunnel wall to steady himself, he traveled a couple hundred feet. He could see a widening, and maybe, a bend in the hallway ahead. Tryton slowed. He thought he heard a scraping noise. Timorousness struck him and he noticed sweat beads forming on his forehead, but he continued. The scraping became louder as he approached the bend. He could see that the opening widened and the light was brighter.

Tryton stopped his advance and listened. He heard heavy breathing accompanying the scraping. Someone was working hard. His heart pounded as he stuck his head around the corner to see what or who was making the noise. He saw another cell like his. The barred door was shut and padlocked. The scraping noise was very near so he ventured around the corner of the tunnel and into the larger opening. A length of rock wall stretched for ten feet before being interrupted by the door. Another ten feet of rock wall adjoined it on the other side.

"Shit," Cassie said in a low voice. The chair leg had broken. In frustration and anger, she threw it down. It landed on the wooden section of flooring. She had instantly regretted her action.

Tryton heard her voice and the clattering of the chair leg. He crept to the cell door, looked in, and saw Cassie. "Hey," he said in the quietest voice he could.

Cassie jumped to her feet, and took several steps back.

Tryton looked around, making sure Karonen wasn't anywhere in view, and then he looked back at Cassie. "I can help you. Just... talk quiet."

Cassie hurried to the bars. "Who are you? Can you get me out of here?" Her voice, though quiet, was a bit shrill.

He was calmer than he thought he could be. "My name is Seth Tryton. Peter drugged me a couple months ago and brought me here." He shook his head. "He's not a well man. He, he's..." He looked at her. "He's very sick, very sick." He rambled on about the corpse and reading to her.

"Stop. Methodist is dead?" She grasped the bars of the cell.

"Yes, she's been dead for quite a while by the looks of her. There's hardly anything left to her." Tryton was anxious and in a hurry to get back to his cell. "I've got to get back before he finds out I'm gone. I'm sorry, but I'll come back when I can." He stepped away from the cell, but she grabbed one of his wrists.

"Wait, don't leave me. You're the first person, other than Karonen that I've seen for over a year."

He stopped. "You've been here that long? Oh, my god, I'll come back. I promise." He put his hand on hers and squeezed. "I promise. I won't leave you here."

Cassie was incredulous. "Wait, how come you're free? Why aren't you locked up if you're a prisoner?"

"I got him to trust me, and he left my door open tonight. But I've got to get back before he finds out I'm gone." He pulled away.

"You promise?" Her tone was desperate.

He nodded his head and hurried back toward his cell.

Cassie picked up the largest piece of the broken chair leg and began hacking at the wall again. She knew she couldn't rely on anyone else.

CHAPTER 17

Cadotte drove the few miles back to Finland where they stopped at the West Branch Bar and Grill. Mancoat rushed in first, claiming he had a powerful thirst that needed to be satisfied. Hodges and Cadotte took their time. When they stepped into the bar, Mancoat already had his paws around a glass of rum and coke.

"What do we do now? I'm sure that's him," Cadotte said.

Mancoat sloshed down the remainder of his drink and raised his finger to the bartender, signaling another of the same. When the bartender brought Mancoat's drink, he asked what he could get Cadotte and Hodges.

"Water for me, please," said Hodges.

"Get me a Summer Shandy, if you've got it," Cadotte said.

"Come on Jasper, have a real drink. I'm sure they've got wine here," Mancoat encouraged as he tipped his glass.

Hodges ignored him. "I need to get in the house."

"What we need is the police now," Cadotte said. "We've done everything we can, and now it's up to the police."

"I'll second that," Mancoat held his glass up and took another swig.

Hodges persisted. "We'll split up. Sheila, you get ahold of Lieutenant Johnson while Earl and I pay another visit to Karonen's."

"Absolutely not," Cadotte interrupted, loudly enough for the bartender to lift his head in their direction and stare. She recovered and added in a quiet voice, "No, no, we leave this to the police now. There's no sense in you two endangering yourselves, or messing up a search of Karonen's house."

Mancoat gulped another mouthful of rum and coke. "I tend to agree with her, Jasper."

"Sheila, I came all the way from Tasmania to find out what happened to Seth. I'm not going to sit on my derriere and let someone else do the work for me. Earl, we can do this," Hodges' eyes blazed.

Earl relented when he recognized the hardened look. "OK. OK. You got a plan?"

Cadotte shifted her position. "Now wait. Before you go spouting off about this plan, know for the record that I am totally opposed to it."

"Wait till you hear it, Sheila," Hodges said.

He explained everything, and when he finished, Cadotte acknowledged that it might work—and that she would go along with it. They finished their drinks and returned to the entrance of Karonen's driveway. Cadotte dropped Hodges off and watched him sneak up the drive. Cadotte and Mancoat drove back to Duluth where Mancoat hopped in his car and started back to Karonen's.

Hodges padded up the driveway, keeping a low profile and staying close to the trees. He snuck along an edge of the yard running through the trees, and checked the garage. The truck wasn't in the garage nor in the driveway. Not knowing when Karonen would return, Hodges moved without hesitation to the front door. He picked the lock and ushered himself inside. He noticed the odor, but he didn't think much of it. Exploring the house, he looked for any hidden doors or signs of Tryton.

He peeked inside Karonen's bedroom and observed nothing unusual and then proceeded down the hallway to another room, which was locked. Using his handy lock pick set, he dispatched it with ease and opened the door. The stench hit him hard. He placed a handkerchief over his nose and stepped inside Methodist's bedroom. After flicking on the light, he saw a bed with the shell of a rotted human, hooked up to an IV system. He quickly shut and relocked the door.

Hodges found a cushioned chair near the bookcase in the study and sat down to wait. He didn't have to wait long. Only eight minutes later, the front door opened and Karonen walked in the house with two bottles of red wine, which, after throwing off his coat, he placed on the kitchen counter, opened one and poured himself a glass. He then walked into the living room where Hodges waited.

Karonen made it halfway through the room before he noticed Hodges sitting in his favorite chair holding a small automatic weapon.

"Please join me, Peter. May I address you as Peter, and not Mr. Karonen?"

Karonen didn't answer. He stood in the middle of the room like a statue.

"You were here earlier. Are you here to rob me?"

"Oh good man, no. I am here to find a friend of mine, Seth Tryton. You are going to tell me where he is."

Karonen's body wavered a little. "May I sit down? I feel a little faint."

"You certainly may." Waving the pistol, Hodges motioned him to a nearby chair.

After sitting and recovering his wits, Karonen took a sip of wine. "Excuse me, I'm used to a glass of wine at this time of the day and like to maintain my daily rituals." Raising an eyebrow, Karonen said, "Where are my manners? Would you like a glass? I have plenty."

"What kind do you have?"

"It's a very good Petite Sirah from Sonoma Valley. I buy a case every other month... member of a wine club. It's one of the few things I find worthy of spending money on."

"Very kind of you to offer when I'm pointing a gun at you." Hodges considered the offer. "I do believe I'll take you up on that. I really haven't had an acceptable Petite Sirah this entire trip."

Karonen smiled. "Splendid, I'll just place this on the table and return with a glass for you." He got up to leave.

"Just a moment. I'll accompany you." Hodges rose and followed Karonen.

When they entered the kitchen, Karonen turned to his right

and grabbed a glass hanging from a rack underneath the cupboard. He poured a glass. Thinking his body had shielded the container of roofies from Hodges, Karonen slipped one of the pills into the glass and deftly slipped the bottle into his vest pocket.

Hodges stepped closer to Karonen. "Now, let me see the bottle you're concealing."

Karonen sighed, retrieved the bottle, stepped to the side and handed it to Hodges. "Can't blame a man for trying," he said.

Keeping the pistol on Karonen, Hodges studied the pills. "I would guess flunitrazipam, a club drug, or what some people use for a date rape drug. Am I correct?"

"You are correct, Mr.... Can you tell me your name?"

"Call me Jasper. You know, I don't mean to be rude, but I think I'll pour myself a drink. May I?"

"Certainly."

Karonen handed him another glass. After filling the glass, Hodges said, "And now, shall we sit down and have a chat?"

"I am at your command... Jasper."

They moved back into the living room, sat down, and sipped their wine. Hodges looked around the room, noting the photos and famous paintings hanging on the walls. "You have some wonderful paintings, The Starry Night, Girl with a Pearl Earring, American Gothic. It's quite the eclectic collection."

"Thank you, but they're all prints as you most likely know."

Hodges nodded.

"They're still beautiful, don't you think?"

Hodges took a sip of his wine. "They are beautiful. I used to have quite an assemblage when I was married." He gazed across the room at a Rene Magritte print. "Ah, I see, The Son of Man. Did you know he painted it as a self-portrait?"

"I do. You know it is so good to converse with a person who knows his art."

Hodges sipped his wine and seemed to get lost in the painting before he said, "You have good taste."

"Thank you. Art has never been an expertise of mine, but I have a layman's interest in it. My specific pedagogy concerns the northern environment. The trees, the bushes, flowers, plants. I spent many years working for the DNR educating the general populace about their environment."

Karonen noticed Hodges was not paying attention to him and had rested the pistol on his thigh. Karonen thought he could rush Hodges and turn the situation around, and so rose slowly from his chair.

Hodges took hold of the gun again when he noticed Karonen's movement.

"As you know, Peter, I didn't come to discuss your artwork or the environment. Seth Tryton. Where is he? We know you impersonated him and parked his car in the Canal Park area, but why? What did you do with him?" Hodges took another sip of the Petite Sirah.

Wine in one hand, Karonen relaxed back into his chair. "You're obviously a good friend of Seth's. I want you to know that I've become a good friend of his as well." He put his wine on the end table nearest him.

"I doubt that very much. First off, he'd never forgive you for kidnapping him and bringing him here."

"How do you know I brought him here against his will?" Karonen, displaying a nervous habit, intertwined his fingers and moved them one at a time in sequence, again and again.

Hodges studied Karonen, who was smiling a sickening, self-confident smile, and decided that he really did not like this man. "I'll tell you why, because Seth, for all his faults, and he has many, would not allow you to drive his car or take his fedora. I see it's still hanging on the rack in your entryway."

Chuckling lightly, Karonen nodded his agreement. "You're partially correct. Seth did come here willingly. I took the measure of his character right away and lured him here with the promise of fine whiskey or beer. He chose whiskey. I was able to drug him and enlist him in an act of mercy." Karonen was excited now and just warming up.

"The whisky, I can see," said Hodges. "But an act of mercy? I have a harder time accepting that."

"Look at the photo behind you."

"All right, but please move to my left so I can keep an eye on you," Hodges said.

Karonen did as he was told, and Hodges stood up, turned a little to his left, and gazed at a photograph of Methodist in her early twenties.

"That's my daughter, Methodist. She's been in a catatonic state for more than ten years. I brought Seth to my home so he could help me wake her. Seth has rewarded me in so many ways, not the least of which is, I believe, the imminent recovery of Methodist."

Thinking of the mostly rotted corpse in the locked bedroom, Hodges cocked his head to the side like an Australian sheep dog.

"How did it happen? The catatonic state."

"An accidental overdose of drugs. It was... was... devastating to me." He began to cry. Karonen recovered his composure after only a few moments.

"So Seth has been helping you. How?"

Karonen's excitement returned. "He reads to her and tells her about his life." He waved his arms and pointed at the hundreds of novels lining the bookshelves. "Seth has been a godsend. Methodist has made so much progress since he arrived that I don't know how I could thank him."

"You could start by letting him go."

Stammering, Karonen said, "I... I... I don't think he wants to leave. He has demonstrated to me how committed he is to making sure Methodist makes a full recovery." He wrung his hands and paced the living room and began jabbering to himself.

Hodges watched him like a hawk.

Realizing he might be dealing with a nutcase of the first order, Hodges changed his tactics and said in a pleasant manner, "Perhaps you should take me to Seth now and he and I can have a chat."

"Yes, yes, I'll take you."

Hodges lowered his wine glass and placed it on the bookcase.

"You might want to move that," Karonen said.

Hodges retrieved the glass and put it on the table opposite Karonen's.

Karonen motioned for Hodges to move to the side and grabbed hold of a book and pulled. The bookcase moved outward.

Lucas Johnson answered on the first ring. "Sheila, I've been trying to get a hold of you, where've you been?"

She explained the situation, detailing what Hodges and Mancoat were up to.

Johnson listened and then said, "Now, I have something to tell you. He's not Jasper Green. He's Gerald Hodges. Ring a bell?"

When she didn't answer right away, Johnson filled her in.

"He's the guy who killed all those people in southern Minnesota a few years ago, maybe his two wives before that in England. Remember now?"

Cadotte knew it had been one of the biggest stories in Minnesota. Her mouth hung open. With a hitch in her voice she answered. "My God, I do remember. I never made the connection."

"Well, little wonder. He somehow vanished and now turns back up in northern Minnesota. How 'bout that? Mancoat and Tryton are, or were, buddies of his. We don't know whether Mancoat contacted Hodges, or vice versa, but we do know he flew to Australia and Tasmania and came back with Hodges. We can't prove that exactly, yet, but it seems a good bet. Hodges must have been real tight with those guys to risk coming back here."

"Anyway, I'm wasting time. I'll see if the Lake County Sheriff's Department will coordinate with us and ask if they'll let us help with the bust at Karonen's house. Maybe we'll kill two birds with one stone here. Wrap up a local mystery and arrest one of the most wanted criminals Minnesota's ever had. The most ironic part of this is Hodges will have helped us break this case."

Cadotte said, "Yeah, too bad it won't give him a break in his own case, huh?"

"Who'd a thought?" Johnson said. "One last thing. How's it feel to have come so close to the most famous killer Minnesota has ever had?"

"Lucky... I feel lucky," she said.

"Well, gotta go. You did good, Sheila." Johnson hung up, plucked his coat off the back of his chair and hurried to his rendezvous with destiny.

Cadotte suppressed the sick feeling roiling in her gut and called Mancoat.

CHAPTER 18

"They're on their way. You have about forty minutes." Cadotte hung up. She wondered if she had done the right thing. Hodges had confided in her just hours before at the restaurant in Finland. He had left out the teeny tiny part about killing *several* people, though. For some odd reason, she still trusted him. He said he had changed; that he was a better person now. She believed him, although it was a mystery to her, why. But, she thought she had gotten to know the man, and her gut had said he was a man who would do the right thing despite his past.

Mancoat kept the cell in his hand and punched in the Trac phone number for Hodges. It rang three times before he answered.

"Jasper, Sheila says you have forty minutes."

"All right, have the car ready." Hodges answered and then hung up.

Hodges walked through the tunnel with Karonen leading the way. He was surprised by the reception within the cave. It had been strong and clear.

It didn't take long before they came to the first widening in the tunnel. An open, empty cell greeted them. Karonen seemed stunned.

"I... I don't know where he is." Still using the term he preferred when describing Seth's cell, he said, "This is his room. Perhaps he took a walk."

Leery of Karonen's grasp of reality or proclivity to strike out, Hodges kept a respectful distance from him. "We have to find him, Peter. Where could he have gone?"

Turning in a tight circle, Karonen appeared confused, but

eventually stalked from the cell entrance and walked through the lighted tunnel toward the next cell. As they walked, they heard voices ahead and a scraping noise.

"He's with Cassie," Karonen said surprised.

"Cassie Bandleson? She's alive?" Hodges asked.

"Yes, yes. I've kept her for a long time. She's near."

They entered the widened tunnel where Cassie's cell was found. Tryton had a shovel and was digging at the outer wall while Cassie chipped away from the inside.

"Seth," Karonen called in anger. He ran to him and tried to wrest the shovel from his hands. Tryton fought back with the diminished strength of a frail, seventy-three year old man who had been physically working for hours. During the struggle, Tryton didn't notice who stood behind Karonen. It wasn't until Hodges stepped forward that he knew he was there.

Tryton blinked when he looked at Hodges.

"Gerry? What the hell?"

"Don't say anything, Seth, I've got to get you out of here now. There's no time."

Tryton looked around. "But we can't leave Cassie."

Hodges turned to Karonen. "Open it."

Karonen ignored Hodges. "Seth, I thought we were friends; that you were going to keep helping me... helping Methodist. She's doing so well with you. You can't leave now. You can't."

Seth took hold of Karonen's shoulders. "Peter, I... I don't know how to say this, but I'm going to leave and get help for you and Methodist."

Karonen shook himself loose from Seth's grip.

"No... No."

"Peter, the key! Give me the key to the cell," Hodges said again.

Karonen fumbled in his pants pocket and withdrew the key.

"Here, take Cassie, but Seth... you must stay with me and Methodist."

Hodges opened the cell and Cassie plastered him with a quick embrace.

"Seth, the police are coming. I have to go... quickly."

Cassie looked confused.

Tryton looked as if he were torn between Hodges and Karonen.

"Gerry, I don't know how you found me or where you've been, but I thank you from the bottom of my heart for saving me." He looked into Hodges eyes. "And I know you have to get the hell out of here before the police come, so go... go. I'll deal with Peter and the police."

"Are you sure you'll be all right?" Hodges' eyes shifted to Karonen, who sat against the rock wall with his face buried in his hands.

Seth followed his gaze and said, "Yes, just go!"

Cassie plucked the backpack from her cell and followed Hodges back inside the house.

Mancoat had left and police cars were pulling up the driveway.

"Thank God, the police are here," she said and started for the door.

"Unfortunately, that's not a good thing for me," Hodges said and moved in front of the door before he peered out the window. He quickly checked the Trac phone and saw that Mancoat had left a message. "We must have been too deep in the cave for a signal."

"Please, Ms. Bandleson, you don't know me from the man who delivers Mr. Karonen's mail, but I can't let the police find me. I'll go to prison for the rest of my life. Please delay, distract them to give me time to get away from here."

His tone told her everything she had to know. Her own eyes switched from his to the police gathering outside and back again.

"You're right, I don't know you from Adam, but I know you freed me and your friend. I can help, but I'm not going outside." She locked the door and quickly rummaged through the refrigerator, throwing food items and water bottles into her backpack.

"Quick, this way." She grabbed the pack and hurried back to the tunnel entrance. Hodges followed as fast as he could. He closed the bookcase door and they ran through the tunnel.

"Gerry, get the hell out of here," yelled Seth as they nearly ran into him.

"We're trying," shouted Cassie as they scurried past.

"It would help if you delayed the police out front and say you never saw me," Hodges yelled as they quickly ran out of sight.

Seth guided Karonen, who jabbered aloud and fiddled with his shirt collar as they made their way out of the tunnel and into the house. Tryton shut the cave entrance door, sat the non-functioning Karonen down in the living room, and went to the kitchen door. He peered out the window and saw armed police flanking the perimeter of the house and three more approaching the door.

Tryton unlocked the door and opened it a few inches. The lead cop noticed, putting his arm up in the air, halting the others.

"We're unarmed in here. I'm Seth Tryton. I know you've been looking for me. Come in." He opened the door all the way and showed himself. He held his arms high.

The officers advanced, but with caution. When they reached Seth, he was patted down and they entered the house.

"Where are the others?" Lieutenant Johnson asked.

"Peter Karonen is in the living room. I'll take you to him."

"That won't be necessary," Johnson said. He motioned two officers to search the house. They found Karonen sitting in a chair, staring at the framed photograph of Methodist that he had removed from the wall.

"Karonen's back here, and the house is clear," Officer Chester said to Johnson

Johnson turned to Tryton. "Where's Gerald Hodges?"

Tryton looked flummoxed. "Gerald Hodges? Gerry? I haven't seen him for more than three years. Why are you asking for Gerry?"

"Gerry, as you call him, has been gallivanting across northern Minnesota for the past week. I took a little drive with him myself up to the Superior Hiking Trail. He was looking for you."

"Damn... I could use a drink. That's amazing. I haven't seen him at all. Why would he risk his neck coming back here looking for me?"

Johnson shook his head, but suddenly thought of the other two who had disappeared.

"You ever see Cassie Bandleson or Tom Hecimovich here?"

"I never saw nobody, but I'm really glad you guys showed up when you did. Peter here is getting screwier and screwier, if you know what I mean."

"Was Mr. Karonen holding you against your will?" Johnson asked.

Tryton hesitated. "Well, uh, at first he was, but I started helping him after a while. You see..."

"Lieutenant, we've found something." He led Johnson back to Methodist's room. Several minutes later, Johnson and the officer returned to where Tryton stood, rummaging through the refrigerator.

Johnson took a deep breath, and then asked Tryton, "What the hell's going on here?"

Tryton placed a hunk of venison sausage in his mouth. "You mean the rotted corpse in the locked bedroom?"

Johnson tapped one foot on the floor and crossed his arms. The glare was answer enough.

Tryton launched into a brief response, leaving out the part about how Gerald Hodges freed him and the subsequent hasty getaway with Cassie Bandleson.

Cassie and Hodges fled as fast as their legs could carry them through winding tunnels until Cassie froze mid-stride.

Hodges followed suit, and then asked, "What's wrong?"

They stood in front of a split in the tunnel.

Cassie looked like she was wracking her brain for an answer. "I don't remember if I went left or right, here."

"Focus. Study it," Hodges barked as he stole a glance backward and listened for sounds of anyone following them.

Cassie gave the tunnels her most intense look. "I think I went to the right before."

Hodges glanced over his shoulder again. "Think!"

"Yeah, I think so."

Hodges grabbed the pack, strapped it on and then said, "We have to go. Let's take it."

Cassie led the way and dashed through the opening to the right with Hodges behind her. Almost immediately, they noticed a definite incline and a narrowing of the tunnel walls.

"This is it. I'm sure of it," Cassie said. "We've still got a ways to go, but this will take us out near the top of the hill in back of Karonen's house."

Hodges got closer to her. "Where do we go from there?"

"I think we can make it to the Superior Hiking Trail from there. It's gotta be close, and I'm really familiar with that." She paused for a few moments and then added. "The opening has a funky door... kind of like a submarine hatch. I think that might be hard to open. Karonen might have done something to it after he recaptured me."

"How did you escape from your cell?"

Cassie panted. She was getting tired. "Karonen left my cell door unlocked. He did it on purpose. To test me, he said."

Karonen noticed her fatigue. "Save your breath. Don't tell me anymore now. Hopefully, we'll have time to talk when we get to the trail... if we get to the trail."

They slowed to a fast walk as the incline got steeper and the roof of the tunnel became more truncated. Hodges slammed his head into a rock jutting from the ceiling, and got knocked back a step.

Cassie stopped to help him. "Are you all right?" She grabbed him by an arm.

"I didn't see that coming." He touched his head where it had smashed into the rock. Hodges felt the warmth of blood on his fingers. "I'll be bloody more careful from now on, I'll tell you that. No pun intended."

Cassie groaned. "Okay, duck your head here, you don't want to hit it again." She guided him forward, leading him by the hand.

The light in the tunnel dimmed and their progress slowed. Ten minutes after Hodges' accident Cassie let out a quiet whoop.

"I see it. We're here."

She let go of Hodges' hand and darted to the hatch and tried to open it. Again, as before when she escaped, it wouldn't budge.

Hodges took off the backpack and laid it to the side. He ducked his way to the door and grabbed hold of the wheel, putting his weight into it.

The wheel didn't move.

Both of them stopped to gather their strength and inspect the wheel to determine if Karonen had done anything to ensure it wouldn't open. They saw nothing to keep the wheel from being opened.

"Wait, wait," Hodges said. "Let's try something different." He left and returned a few moments later with a three-foot hunk of two-by-four, and lodged it between the spokes of the wheel. "I noticed this further back. We can use it as a lever and get this damn thing open." He added, "I hope."

At first, Hodges strained so hard Cassie thought he would have a heart attack. She joined him; pushing in short, staccato like bursts. The wheel emitted a protesting screech. The hatch popped.

They clamored through the opening, almost forgetting the backpack, which Hodges scuttled back to retrieve. He brought the two-by-four chunk and wedged it in the exterior wheel hatch, effectively blocking it from anyone following them from the tunnel. He put on the pack and watched Cassie orient herself to their surroundings.

"This was a little different in the dark, but when I got out before, I went down that way—where you run into a gravel road that can't be far from Karonen's house."

It was twilight, and she had a better view of the hills, valleys, and forest now than before. Her eyes searched for a spot where she thought they could intersect the Superior Hiking Trail.

Hodges followed her up the incline, in the opposite direction from where she had gone during her escape attempt the year before.

He asked her, "Will the Superior Trail take me all the way to Canada?"

Cassie stopped. "That's where you need to go? That far?"

He hesitated. "Yes, but I don't need you to get me there, just point the way and I'll go on my own."

She dropped her head and let a tiny laugh escape. "It's not just getting you started and saying, 'go that way.' It's a little more complicated than that. There are crossing trails, and even though there are signs for this hike or that hike, it can get confusing. If you don't mind a guide, I'll get you to Canada." She waited for his response.

Hodges bit his lip and tried to decide what to tell her about himself. He thought this might be the right time to see if his transformation from unforgiving murderer to caring, honest human being would bear fruit. "Cassie, before you go any further with me, I have to tell you something. You can decide to help me or to walk down this hill, find the police, and tell them where I am, after I tell you. I wouldn't stop you, and I wouldn't blame you."

His voice got quieter, and more emotional. "In my defense, I can only say that I'm a different man than I was." He hesitated, looked at the ground. "Without getting into the details," he paused for several moments and then reconsidered how much he would tell her, "I hurt some people a few years ago and I'm ashamed of what I did." He stopped.

"What did you do?"

His chin touched his chest and he couldn't bring himself to look at her.

He struggled. "I can't say, except...." His voice trailed off. For a minute, Hodges thought she would do what he said she might: walk down the hill, find the police, and tell them where to find him. He wouldn't blame her.

She thought about it. Many questions pummeled her brain at the same time. But one stuck out. *Did he kill someone?* She started thinking. *What the hell have I gotten myself into? From the frying pan into the fire. At least Karonen hadn't killed anyone that I know of.* She remained standing, not saying anything for a long enough time that finally, Hodges raised his eyes from the ground to her face.

And then he waited.

Her voice shook. "I won't ask what you did. All I know is you saved me." She stopped, gathered her incomplete, contested thoughts, and then continued. "Why can't anything be simple? Peter Karonen kidnapped me and your friend. And yet, I don't think he's a terrible man. He's a man who loved... loves his daughter. He loved her so much he couldn't give her up for dead, even after she was dead. And then he took people he thought could help him bring her back. People could argue over how bad that is. People could admire his love for his daughter."

Cassie stopped talking and gazed outward to the forest. "I can't easily forgive Karonen for what he did."

She moved a little farther away from him.

He dared to look at her. What he saw gave him heart. The cold expression on her face masked eyes that, to him, seemed to hold sympathy, maybe empathy... and trust in him as a man whom she would help. He started to speak, but she interrupted him.

"You saved my life. That doesn't make up for what you did before, whatever that was, but it doesn't hurt. I'll take you as far as I can," she said in a monotone. "Then we're even."

CHAPTER 19

"You never saw Gerald Hodges here?" Johnson shouted and slammed his fist on the kitchen table. His face was red and his hands trembled. "What about Earl Mancoat?"

Tryton paused from clearing out the refrigerator to fill his stomach, and looked up at Johnson.

"Earl's here, too?"

Johnson shook his head like a puppy shaking a stuffed animal. "This dumb act is wearing thin. We know they were both here. Karonen shanghaied you, and Hodges and Mancoat figured out that he brought you here, or at least they suspected it." Johnson sprang from his chair and paced across the kitchen and turned back on Tryton. "Look, you can cooperate or not, but any way you look at it, we're gonna find your buddies." He glared at Tryton.

His mouth full, Tryton looked back at Johnson and mumbled, "If you're hungry, this stuff is really good."

Johnson flipped his hand out as if he was slapping a fly out of the air. "Jesus, this is unbelievable."

One of the officers entered the kitchen.

"Lieutenant, we've searched the perimeter and no one else is around."

"No one around," steamed Johnson. "Well, they can't be that far away. Get up in the hills and start looking." The officer started to leave. "Wait, let me talk to Sheriff Morton. We're going to have to organize a search of the area and watch the roads for Mancoat's car. They're around, and by god, we're going to find them."

Sheriff Morton, who had been searching around the perimeter of the house, stepped inside. After a short conversation with Johnson, he agreed, got on the phone and called for help from the Bureau of Criminal Apprehension.

Johnson dug his phone out of his pocket and called Cadotte. She answered on the second ring.

His voice was loud and blunt. "Sheila, we got Karonen, and Tryton is here and alive, but there's no sign of the Bandleson woman or the other guy that disappeared. As far as Mancoat and Hodges, they're not here either. Then he got nasty. "You telling me everything?"

Cadotte made her voice sound offended and huffy, "You're asking me that, after I gave you the tip to find them? You're an ungrateful son-of-a-bitch!"

"What am I supposed to think, Sheila? You told us they'd be here, and they're not. Maybe you got close to this Hodges guy and he persuaded you to help him."

She acted incredulous. "Lucas, listen to yourself, you're not making any sense. Why would I tell you where to find them and then help Hodges get away? Don't you think I know he murdered four people? I know about him."

Johnson started to cool down and regained control of himself. He paced the kitchen with his ear to the phone.

Cadotte did her own pacing as she waited for his response.

Johnson exhaled long and hard. "You're right, Sheila. This Hodges thing, we were so close. I thought we had him... Sorry I blew up at you." There was another pause. "At least we found Tryton. We made some progress."

Cadotte breathed an inaudible sigh of relief and acted magnanimous. "It's okay, Lucas. I can understand how frustrated you must be. But, for real, nothing on the other two missing people?"

"Not yet, at least, but I have a definite feeling Tryton knows more than he's saying. He acts pretty uninterested in the whole situation, and when we asked about Hodges and Mancoat... Let's just say, his reaction was unconvincing."

Cadotte fiddled with her hair as she passed by a mirror. "What can I do, Lucas? I feel awful that you didn't find Hodges and Mancoat," she lied.

Johnson turned around when he was tapped on the shoulder. "Uh, nothing for now, Sheila, sorry, gotta go." He shoved the phone in his pocket and turned to the officer. "Whaddaya got?"

"You have to see this," said the officer.

Johnson followed him back to the living room where he stared at the bookcase opening.

He smiled at the officer. "Well, well, well, looks like we have an opening in the case."

The officer cringed.

"Sorry, I couldn't resist," Johnson said. He walked to the opening where another policeman was speaking to Karonen.

Karonen was wringing his hands and speaking gibberish.

"What's going on?" Johnson asked.

The officer stepped away from Karonen, gently taking hold of Johnson's arm and guiding him out of the doorway as he did so. "I thought I saw movement when I looked out the window and when I looked back in here, that thing is open and Karonen was heading down a tunnel. I went in and brought him back here and he started spouting all kinds of crap I couldn't understand."

Johnson and the officer talked and didn't notice that Karonen had moved quickly into the tunnel and closed the door, until it was too late.

Johnson ran to the bookcase and screamed, "Get this damn thing open. Now." He and the officers pulled on the edge of the framework, but it wouldn't budge. Johnson pulled books off the shelves hoping to find the key to opening the door. The other officers followed suit. Soon the floor was littered with books. Only the top row of books remained.

Johnson pulled each book off of the shelf. He could tell something was different when he grabbed the ninth volume, *The Decline and Fall of the Roman Empire*. When he pulled, it resisted. He pulled harder and heard a click. He pulled the bookcase outward, sweeping the books on the floor to the side.

Johnson looked gratified. "That gentlemen, is how you open a case." He stepped inside, expecting Karonen to be long gone, but was surprised to find him sitting on a small ledge... crying. Before he went over to him, Johnson eyed the tunnel and blurted out, "Why the hell is this here, and who the hell would have made it?"

The other two officers hurried to Karonen, grabbed him by his arms and escorted him into the living room where he cried without inhibition.

"I think we need to take him to the psych ward," Johnson said. "Maloney, Karonen's not going to do us any good here, in fact, he's only going to get in our way. Take another officer and get him downtown where he can be locked up until we figure out what to do with him." He pointed to two more officers who had entered the room to check out all the noise. "You two come with me."

Johnson led them into the tunnel and followed it wherever it led. They made their way slowly, watching for anything that might trip them up. The further they progressed, the more the lights in the tunnel dimmed. The lieutenant began to doubt the wisdom of exploring the passageways without proper equipment or a spelunker to guide them, but he and the officers continued on.

When his doubts got the best of him and he was considering turning back, the narrow tunnel widened and they stepped into the first chamber that housed a cell. The cell door was open. Johnson walked in. "I'll be damned."

He thought the room could have been featured in some avantgarde magazine advertising interesting hotel spots that would appeal to adventuresome couples. The two officers looked on in disbelief.

An officer's spoke. "Lieutenant, do you suppose this is where he kept Tryton?"

Johnson picked up a pillow that was on the floor and tossed it on the unmade bed. "I don't know, but one of you go back to the kitchen and bring him up here. I wanna hear what he has to say about it."

One of the officers left and returned five minutes later with Tryton.

"Tell me about these quarters, Mr. Tryton," Johnson said.

"Not much to tell. This is where I stayed while I helped him with his daughter."

"Yeah, his daughter; what's her name again?"

"Methodist," Tryton said.

"I'm trying to get this straight, Mr. Tryton. You helped him with his dead, rotting daughter, Methodist?"

Tryton sighed. "It's complicated."

Johnson's head bobbed up and down. "Yeah, sounds like it. Why don't we sit down, and you can tell me all about it?" He patted the bed and motioned Tryton to come over beside him. "Let's start at the beginning," Johnson said.

Cognizant that the longer he could keep the police occupied, the better it would be for Hodges, Tryton said, "It's gonna take a while."

In Johnson's view, things seemed to be going his way now. His men were out looking for Hodges so there wasn't anything more he could do on that front. He spread his arms out wide in a classic invitation for Seth to open up and tell all. "I've got all night, Mr. Tryton. Tell me about your grand adventure."

Tryton sat on the bed beside Lieutenant Johnson and described how he had met Peter Karonen, been drugged, imprisoned, and eventually enlisted in Karonen's plan to revive his daughter.

"But it had to be obvious to you that his daughter was dead for a long time before you started working with her."

"Yes, yes, it was. I smelled her first, so of course I knew she was dead. The first time he brought me into her room it was like man, this is crazy... Karonen's crazy. He had me talk to her, read to her, tell about my life. After a few weeks of that, well... Peter and me, we just started getting along, and we became, like, friends. I bet this is hard to understand." He gave Johnson an unsure look. "And I know I sound a little crazy myself, but you don't know what it's like, and I can't explain it. It just became natural. I read to her, talked to her, and most of the time Peter was there or nearby. I saw myself in a different way. I saw Peter in a different way..." He stopped.

Johnson scratched the back of his neck and considered Tryton's confessional.

"Sounds like Stockholm syndrome—the victim starts to identify with the kidnapper," said one of the officers. Johnson signaled him to shut up.

"Go on, Mr. Tryton, tell us more."

Eager to string this out as long as he could, Tryton continued. "One day, not very long ago, Peter started trusting me more and more. He unlocked my cell door and I could come and go as I wanted. Oh, don't get me wrong. I thought about getting the hell outta here but... something always stopped me. Every time I started to think about getting away, I couldn't stop thinking of how I'd let Peter down if I left."

He looked at Johnson. "I already said it must sound crazy, but it's the truth. Peter is sick, no doubt about that, but I started seeing him as a human being in need of support. The guy loved his daughter so much that he couldn't let go... even after she died. So my thinking now is that we do what's right for Peter and not just treat him like some kind of monster, because he isn't one."

Johnson clasped his hands over his crossed knees and rocked back and forth. He tried to imagine the circumstances Tryton described, and had to admit he could see how it all happened. But then, the cop in him, the skeptical, non-believing cop, started to throw a monkey wrench into it. *Kidnapped man forced by deranged kidnapper to help revive a rotted corpse.* He didn't like what he heard. He couldn't imagine, on his worst day, doing what Tryton said he'd done, especially the part about becoming friends with Karonen and understanding him. "You sure this is what you want to tell us, Mr. Tryton?" Johnson looked straight at him when he asked.

"It's what happened, Lieutenant. It doesn't matter if it's what I want to tell you or not. It's the truth."

"The whole truth? Didn't leave anything out?"

Tryton looked away. He faltered just enough for Johnson to notice. "I, uh, told you the way it happened."

Johnson rose up from the bed and ambled across the room with his hands in his pockets.

"Let's see what else is in this tunnel. You can be our guide, Mr. Tryton."

Tryton hesitated. "There's not much more that I know of. I never did any exploring."

"Nonetheless, let's take a walk and see what we can see, okay?"

Tryton accompanied Johnson and another officer away from the cell and toward Cassie's chamber. The lights in the tunnel flickered as they progressed.

"You got a flashlight handy?" Johnson asked the officer.

"No, but I've got a flashlight app on my phone. I think you do too, Lieutenant."

Johnson cursed his technological challenges. He didn't know how to work the damn phone except for talking. "Show me, quick. I don't want to be caught in the dark."

The officer showed him, and they continued until there was another widening in the tunnel and Cassie's empty cell appeared. Johnson shot Tryton a glance. "Never saw this, Mr. Tryton?"

Tryton feigned ignorance of the cell and its contents.

Johnson walked into it and knew immediately it had been recently occupied. He noted the ruffled blanket on top of the bed. "My, my, somebody's been sleeping in that bed. And I don't think it was Papa Bear."

"It looks like somebody tried to dig their way outta here, Lieutenant." The officer stood by the concave depression in the wall and shined his phone light where Cassie had worked for the past month.

Johnson stepped over, examined it, and stepped out of the cell to opposite side of the depression. "Looks like someone worked from this side to help out." He glanced at Tryton who squirmed. "So, you still want to claim you saw no one else in this cave, Mr. Tryton?"

Tryton remained silent.

Johnson reverted to Tryton's first name using a mocking tone. "Cat got your tongue, Seth?"

Tryton stood his ground and didn't speak.

"Okay. It's gonna be that way, huh? Keep this up and you're gonna find out about obstruction of justice and all sorts of charges you haven't yet imagined. It's obvious you know more than you're saying." His tone softened just a touch as he reverted to classic cop speak. "Just go easy on yourself and tell us."

Tryton caved. "The woman you're looking for, she was here. I helped her out, but it was Gerry who really saved us. You'll consider that if you catch him, right?"

Johnson's tone shifted along with his feet. "I can't promise anything, Mr. Tryton. Gerald Hodges is wanted for murdering at least four people, maybe more, but if he helped you get away from Karonen he did a good thing. He'll still have to pay for what he did to those four people."

Tryton paced the inside of the cell while he debated with himself. "Cassie said there was a way out of here... up the tunnel quite a ways and then out the top of the hill. They probably went that way." He felt ashamed of himself and sat heavily on edge of the bed.

"You did the right thing, Mr. Tryton. It'll be better for Mr. Hodges and you. You'll see. So, why did Ms. Bandleson go with him?"

"She doesn't know anything about Gerry. She only knows he helped her, saved her life, and she wants to help him."

Looking curious, Johnson asked, "So how can she help him now?"

Then Tryton lied. "I don't know."

Johnson didn't ask any more questions. He rounded up two more officers, one of whom escorted Tryton to a squad car for transportation back to the station and the other to accompany him and the third officer through the tunnels. The three trudged through the tunnel, but split up when they came to where it divided. Johnson and one officer followed the right pathway. It took them twenty minutes to get to the end where they tried to open the hatch door with no success.

"It's either stuck or they wedged it shut from the other end. Shit." Johnson kicked at the hatch. "This slows us down. Okay, let's check with Laramie, see if he could get out of the other tunnel."

They started back down and soon ran into Laramie.

"Dead end, Lieutenant."

"Not much better here," Johnson said. "They must have wedged the hatch. We'll check with the searchers outside, see if they found any sign of Hodges and Bandleson."

Twenty minutes later, Johnson and the others emerged from the house and called to the officers searching the hillside. The one in charge reported no sign of anyone or the hatch.

"Keep looking," Johnson barked. And then he added, "It's gotta be near the top of the hill. Look for some sort of hatch. It might be covered by bushes."

Johnson started muttering to himself, *This is where somebody in the movies always calls in the dogs.*

Laramie walked up to Johnson. "It's gonna be dark in an hour and we're gonna need lights and it might be a good idea to bring in the K-9 unit, Lieutenant."

"Sounds like a plan," said Johnson. And then, an afterthought struck him. "Hey, we need some topographical maps of the area and a local who knows the territory."

"I'm on it," Laramie shouted as he jogged to his squad car and the radio.

Sam Moller pushed past the partially opened doorway to Cadotte's desk.

"My God, you helped find Tryton, and he's alive." He paced back and forth in front of her desk.

Cadotte's fingers whirred across the keys on her computer.

"Tell me you're writing this up now, Sheila."

She stopped and gave him an, *are you kidding me look*, and said, "Of course I am," and reverted to typing.

Moller, nearly jumping up and down in his excitement, said, "And Gerald Hodges was the guy helping you and the police? This is a newspaperman's dream. When did you know it was him? I mean you had to be shocked as hell to find out the man you'd been working with so closely the past few days was a serial killer."

Cadotte stopped typing. "Sam, are you going to let me write this story or not? I can't be interrupted every time I get a sentence down." The look she threw him was enough to make him apologize and retreat.

As he passed out of the office, he grabbed the knob and shut the door. Before the door closed he gave her a thumbs up and slipped away.

Cadotte paused, wondering how she was ever going to explain her role in the breaking of the case. She knew she couldn't admit that Hodges told her who he really was in the restaurant where they discussed his plan. Nor could she admit her role in letting him know the police knew who he was and were going to arrest him.

For good or bad, she had made a split-second decision in the restaurant. After getting to know the old guy, it had been difficult to reconcile the news stories of Hodges then with what she knew of him now. She placed her elbows on the desk and rested her chin in her hands.

She didn't feel guilty, well, maybe just a little, but Cadotte decided she could live with what she had done. For now, she'd write her story and let the saga play out. She started typing again, but paused when she thought of Earl Mancoat. Earl might be in some trouble for sneaking Hodges back into the country and concealing him from the authorities. He would have some explaining to do. She felt sorry for him.

CHAPTER 20

They pushed as fast as they could through the brush and rocks. The dark was beginning to close in around them, and they wanted to put as much distance as they could between them and Karonen's place before it became too difficult to see. Cassie thought it was a good thing the fall season had begun; the mosquitoes would be sluggish, and more importantly, fewer in number. She didn't relish the thought of spending days and nights in the wilderness with no shelter, or unable to build a fire.

If they were lucky, it would take them ten days to hike the ninety miles to the Canadian border where Hodges could slip across, and hopefully, be picked up by one of his friends. She surmised that was his plan.

Hodges stumbled and fell. It surprised her when he jumped to his feet and motioned her to keep going before she could offer help. Without a word, she moved on.

The terrain was rough, making the footing difficult. Up and down they travelled, slashing their way through thick, tangled undergrowth. Although Hodges kept up with her, she knew he would not be able to sustain the pace she had established and worried about him experiencing some sort of catastrophic event.

Cassie didn't know what she would say if, and when, the authorities caught them. She hadn't thought that far ahead. The only possibility she thought of would be to say that Hodges forced her to guide him across the countryside until they reached Canada. *Yes, that's the plan.*

Behind her, Hodges made a sort of burping noise. She turned around. He stood, leaning on a large triangular shaped rock. Unable to speak, he breathed deeply, holding up a finger to indicate he needed a minute of rest. She had to admit she could use the rest as well. She moved to the rock and leaned against it. She figured they had covered a couple miles and could afford a rest.

Cassie breathed in the cooling air and suddenly realized how wonderful it felt to be out of the cell, out of the cave, and away from Karonen and his daughter. She opened her mouth and drank in the air, and just at that moment, a mosquito slipped in. She spit and lashed her tongue to get the tiny creature out. At first, Hodges was concerned, but his concern quickly turned to laughter as he realized she was trying to eject a recalcitrant mosquito from her mouth.

"Ms. Bandleson, I'm sorry. You were just so funny." Smiling, he eyed her to see if she accepted his apology.

She made sure the mosquito was gone first, and then said, "Apology accepted, Mr. Hodges." She broke down and started laughing as she thought of how she must have looked and sounded.

They both laughed for several moments. Then, almost perfectly synchronized, they stopped. If you could feel silence, they did.

Cassie gathered herself. "We'd better get going." She picked up the backpack and slung it onto her shoulders. She looked back, but Hodges hadn't moved. "You coming?"

A few chuckles emerged, and then he nodded his head and followed.

Their pace slowed as darkness fell. Although their eyes had adjusted and could actually discern objects quite well, there was still the danger of tripping over a rock jutting from the soil, a tangled bush, or an out of control root system. They moved carefully. Cassie, her eyes straining, would stop often and look for signs of the trail she sought, all the while listening for the sounds of search teams and dogs.

Cassie was an experienced hiker and knew the area well. That was a good thing because they were now hiking cross-country, without the aid of a compass or a trail, in the wilderness. Hodges hadn't imagined this when he thought of coming back to Minnesota and searching for Seth. He hadn't thought it would be easy to find his friend, but this... well... this was another matter. The sound of the slap against his skin reached Cassie in an instant. She knew exactly what that meant--mosquito. She also heard something else, a rushing of water.

She slowed and tried to see what lay ahead. As they progressed, the sound became a roar, making it clear they would soon be facing one of the innumerable waterfalls along the route. This was good, she thought. When the Superior Hiking Trail had been planned and built by hundreds of volunteers, the idea was to access as many waterfalls and mountain lookouts as possible. The trail was probably near.

Hodges strained his eyes in anticipation of the falls. Five minutes later, they stood before a twenty-foot cataract spilling into a pool and flowing toward Lake Superior. Hodges noticed a sliver of moonlight glinting off Cassie's face. Her expression revealed concern and uncertainty.

He stood beside her. "So... where do we cross?"

Still looking at the falls, Cassie paused, "I don't know." They stared at the pounding, rushing cascade, which, if it had a personality, seemed like it wanted to batter their eardrums into mush. Cassie unslung the backpack. "I'm not confident in finding a way around this in the dark. I think we should try to make ourselves comfortable until we have more light, and then look for a way across it."

"Agreed," said Hodges.

Sustaining her role of a guide, mountain woman, or camper extraordinaire, Cassie scanned the immediate area for a flat area to rest. She found a suitable spot and Hodges joined her. The ground was hard, and slightly damp, so she pulled a sleeping bag from her pack, unzipped it and laid it on the ground.

"We can both lie on this," she said.

Hodges almost said, "as long as you're comfortable sleeping next to a serial killer," but thought better of it. He lay down and fastened the top button on his shirt, trying to seal in as much heat as possible.

Cassie, though exhausted, did not fall asleep. Her mind raced with visions of her imprisonment, and she now wrestled with second thoughts about helping Hodges. *What the hell am I doing? Can we make it to Canada?*

Hodges, graced with age and a mind that feared little, fell asleep after a few minutes. Fortunately for Cassie, he did not snore. Unfortunately for Hodges, dreams of past misdeeds tormented him. Still awake, Cassie watched him twitch and flail his right arm as if swinging a club. The motion was dampened by the vagaries of sleep and lack of muscular control. She wondered what dreams he dreamt.

Nightstick in hand, he stalked his target. The snow glistened in the moonlight and he tried to match his own crunch of boots on the snow and crumbling ice to hers. To his delight, he was successful. He hadn't considered his shadow alerting a drunken Laura Walters to his presence.

She stopped and turned to face him. The look on her face and what she said in recognition forced his hand and he delivered the first strike, followed by several other powerful, demented blows to her head. The blood splattered the sidewalk and snow covered portion of the front yard she fell on. He checked her pulse and found none.

"One down," he said to no one. Before leaving, he gazed in amazement that the book she had taken from the book club meeting did not fall from her hand. It still partially lay in her palm, the title face up. The reflection only delayed him for a moment and he knew he had to leave. Moving fast, he scurried three blocks away. He was careful not to leave a trail of blood or boot prints.

Soon he was home, removing the women's clothing he had donned earlier. He took the coat he had worn, taking meticulous care to eliminate all specs of blood he could find with bleach and then threw it into his washing machine with plenty of stain remover. He then changed to his lounging clothes.

Hodges prepared a ritualistic cup of green tea, sat at his kitchen table and sipped...and planned.

The same dream plagued him, over and over. The swinging of the nightstick, the sickening thud when it connected to the woman's skull, the ritualistic drinking of tea. All of it played on and on in his brain as if it were a continuous loop.

He woke with a start. The first spasms of light filtered through the leaves clinging to the trees. He turned to his left, fixed his gaze on Cassie's innocent face. *My God, how could I have killed those people?*

He answered himself. *You were a different person then.* It was a comforting thought, but one he knew was inadequate. Someday, he would pay for what he had done. He knew that. But, he also knew that he wanted to remain free to make up for what he did. He needed time.

Hodges lay for several more minutes, unaware that Cassie, after watching him twitch and mumble during the night, had only recently fallen asleep. He raised himself up on an elbow, reached out and gently tapped her shoulder. The deep sleep that clutched her seemed impenetrable, but he knew they should rise and move, so he tapped and then shook her shoulder.

Cassie opened her eyes.

Hodges spoke, "We should leave."

Cassie closed her eyes tightly before reopening them.

"Okay." She stretched her arms and legs, drew in a deep breath, and let out a long stream of air. "Okay," she repeated, and then sat up and looked around. They both got up and peed in separate places.

Cassie stuffed the sleeping bag into its sack and pounded it into the already full backpack, and Hodges marched in place in a feeble attempt to throw off the cold that had oozed into his body.

Another minute later, and Cassie led the search for a pathway around the falls.

The daylight allowed her to explore the area in a safer and more efficient way. Soon, she found a shallow place to cross the stream above and beyond the falls. It was an easy crossing. They sloshed their way through ankle deep water and progressed to the other side.

"I can't say I enjoyed getting wet back there. I was already cold and that just made it worse," Hodges said.

"We do what we have to do," Cassie said without emotion, and then turned her attention to finding a spur to the Superior Hiking Trail. They walked without speaking for twenty minutes. The rushing sound of the waterfalls had gradually faded, allowing bird songs and chattering squirrels to be heard.

The terrain rose and fell, presenting rocks, trees, brush, and roots as obstacles. At different times, they each tripped, but never fell. Although Cassie had tried to keep fit while in captivity, she concluded that her condition was inadequate. And Hodges? She didn't know how he was going to complete the journey. But, the old guy kept up.

Cassie stopped when she heard faint traffic noises.

Hodges sidled up along next to her and listened.

"This isn't good," Cassie said. "I thought we'd find the trail before we ran into a road." She

crawled ahead and listened. It didn't sound like a traffic jam. She heard the sound of vehicles moving. More disturbing, both heard voices shouting.

They snuck forward and descended a hundred feet.

The voices got louder.

Cassie took off her pack and laid it on the ground. They walked low to the ground as they slunk closer to the roadway.

Hodges spread some bushes apart to get a better look.

One squad car and a police wagon blocked a gravel road in front of them. Local vehicles were being stopped and checked. A young man, traveling with his wife and child, talked to the lead officer. He shook his head and Hodges heard him say he hadn't seen or heard anything unusual. The officer thanked him and let the family pass.

"We should parallel the road and cross it somewhere else," Cassie said. She gazed at the hill on the other side. "See that hill?" She pointed a half-mile on the other side. "That's gotta be where the trail runs."

"The question is, which way do we parallel the road? To our left or to the right?" Hodges asked.

"I think we should retreat a ways and cross where the police can't see us. Looks like the roadway curves to the left so we shouldn't have to go far to be out of sight."

He accepted her reasoning and knowledge of the area and nodded. "Lead the way."

They backtracked from their vantage point, retrieved the pack, and moved as quietly as they could, trying to keep the roadway within sight. Cassie had been right about the gravel road bending to the left. They moved a couple hundred yards from where they had seen the police vehicles before venturing closer to the road. Hodges and Cassie watched both ways for any movement before scurrying across and back into the bushes and trees on the other side.

They scrambled up a low ridge paralleling the road and slunk deeper into the forest. Cassie seemed to know where she was going now. She took powerful strides, not bothering to check on how Hodges was doing.

He was right behind her. Sweat gushed from every pore in Hodges body as he did his best to keep up with Cassie.

They kept a withering pace for the next two hours. Fear of being caught fueled them, driving them to a confluence of trails that would be their ultimate guide to Canada.

"I have to rest," Hodges panted and then settled onto a convenient boulder.

Cassie pulled up and looked behind and around them. She took off the pack, let it drop to the ground, and sat on it.

Between pants, Hodges asked, "How much farther to the Superior Trail, do you think?"

Cassie thought for a moment. "It can't be that far. You've noticed we're on a trail now?"

Hodges responded with an exhausted nod of his head.

"Deer trail," she said. "We're not far from Crosby Manitou State Park. It's very isolated, only backpackers go there because it's undeveloped, lots of waterfalls and steep trails. It's going to be tough." She gave him a sympathetic look.

"Don't worry about me. I can hold my own." He appeared to have gained a second wind.

Five minutes later, they continued upward. When they stopped at an opening on the hillside, they had gained enough altitude to see Lake Superior behind them. Hodges commented that it was surprising to see how far up the hills they had walked. "From here, it looks like we're a mile above the lake."

"Maybe 800 feet," Cassie corrected.

"And we're not at the top, yet," Hodges said.

Cassie motioned him on with a flip of her head. "We should hit the Superior Hiking Trail at the top of the ridge line." They trudged on, and soon made their connection. She pointed to a small wood rectangular sign.

Hodges squinted to read it, "Superior Hiking Trail." He turned to Cassie. "We made it." He sounded convinced that it would all be downhill from here.

"We've got a long ways to go, Mr. Hodges. Don't think we've got this licked yet. Come on, let's keep moving." He followed her down the trail that made the deer path look like a super highway.

They tramped the tree-lined ridge and looked out over openings to see valleys, rivers, and lakes, including the most spectacular views of Lake Superior. Hodges no longer oozed the weariness he had earlier. The beauty of the hike evaporated the tiredness in his muscles.

The ridgeline descended and ascended, sometimes involving switchbacks up steep areas, which took its toll on both of them. Their pace slowed at the steepest points and then quickened when they moved downhill.

When they ascended to the highest point of the latest ridge, Cassie paused. "We should eat something."

Hodges walked up next to her, helped peel the pack off her back and broke out a couple of bananas and bottles of water. They ate slowly, savoring every bite.

Cassie took long swigs of water between bites of banana.

Scavenging through the pack, Hodges examined the other food Cassie had hastily thrown in before they left Karonen's place.

"We'd better conserve what we have. I don't know where we'll find more food along the way," Cassie said.

"Merely taking inventory," Hodges said. "Nine energy bars, four bags of peanuts, three apples, two chocolate candy bars, three bottles of water, and one chunk of pepper jack cheese. You're correct, Cassie. This won't last long."

"The water won't be a problem. If you look in one of the side compartments of the backpack, you'll find a water filter. Quite useful when you're backpacking." Cassie smiled.

Hodges fiddled with the side pocket, found the water filter and examined it. "Looks like it should work," he said, and then returned it to the pack. He suddenly noticed the twilight. They had trekked all day, up and down hills, across streams, avoided police, and admired beautiful vistas of Lake Superior.

Cassie looked across the valley and to the east where the darkening horizon melted into Lake Superior. "We should look for shelter and settle down for the night." She pointed to clouds that roiled in the distance.

Hodges nodded. "There must be caves along the way we could take advantage of."

Cassie shook her head. "As far as I know, the rock in northern Minnesota is some of the hardest in North America. We're not gonna find any caves. There might be some outcroppings we could huddle under though. Either way, I think we'd be better off building some kind of structure, and soon, cause that sure looks like rain to me." She nodded toward the eastern horizon where dark sheets of rain could now be seen shredding the sky.

Hodges followed her gaze. "I see what you mean." He picked up the pack and slung it over his shoulders. They padded down the trail. Cassie scampered ahead. A few minutes later, lightening split the clouds and thunder cracked. Hodges thought he could almost hear the rain beating down on the water a mile away.

As desperate for shelter as she seemed, Cassie stayed calm until the first gusts of wind struck them. They knew the rain wasn't far behind.

Against the howling wind, Hodges yelled, "There, that looks like a cave." He pointed. A hundred yards forward and below stood a diabase structure that receded into the hillside.

Cassie had to admit, it looked like the opening of a cave. They hurried to reach it before the rain hit them. Thunder clapped and the wind bayed. They scampered off the trail and through a thin hedge of brush.

The cave turned out to be a nice overhanging ledge they could crawl under to stay dry. It retreated into the hillside eight or ten feet under the ledge. Hodges threw off the pack, depositing it deep under the overhang, and then scuttled to the hillside where he broke off dead sections of brush. Cassie joined him, and they had soon lined the outside edge of the ledge for additional protection. When they finished, they jammed themselves inside and pulled the undergrowth close around.

"Makes for a cozy little structure, eh?" Hodges said, slapping his hands together to generate heat. The temperature had dropped significantly with the rain.

"Here," Cassie said as she dug inside the pack and dragged the sleeping bag out. She unzipped it and pulled it over both of them. The rain intensified. Wind howled, lightning flashed, and thunder clapped around them.

The storm lasted an hour. The clouds thinned, revealing a blue sky dampened by the encroaching night.

Cassie and Hodges breathed easier.

They sat, scrutinizing what shaped up to be a perfect sky graced with scintillating patches of dim starlight. As darkness advanced, the starlight brightened, providing a theater of dazzling radiance Hodges had never before witnessed.

He pulled the sleeping bag tighter across his chest, and said, "It's magnificent, isn't it?"

Cassie kept her gaze on the sky. "It is. I've hiked this trail a lot over the last few years, but I've never seen it more beautiful than right now."

They didn't say much for the next hour. They just sat.

Cassie felt warm, safe, and content. Huddled close, both managed to fall asleep for several hours.

He tapped her shoulder several times before Cassie woke up.

"Hey, hey, careful," she said as she pulled away.

Hodges breath came in spurts. She thought he might be having a heart attack and pulled his face closer to hers. "Are you okay?"

Hodges stared at her without speaking.

"Are you okay?" she asked again.

"Yes, yes, I am," he said. There was plenty of headroom under the ledge, and he used every bit of it as he sat straight up.

"Did you have a nightmare? I noticed you thrashing around." She said it with a hesitancy that made clear she felt uncomfortable prying into his thoughts.

"No nightmare. It was an epiphany."

She flashed him a look of confusion.

Hodges said, "Tom Hecimovich was another person who vanished. You knew that, didn't you?"

Cassie hesitated, but looked straight at him. "I did."

"Did you see him while you were held captive?"

Cassie looked clueless. "No, he was never there. It was just me, and then your friend."

"But, you never knew Seth was there until he'd been there a month. Is it possible that Hecimovich was there, and you just weren't aware?"

"I... suppose," she admitted.

"My friends and I determined that there had to be some sort of connection between the three of you. The common thread was that you all had stayed at the North Star Motel, which just happens to be in the center of where we believe all the disappearances occurred. Did you know Mr. Hecimovich before he disappeared?" Hodges asked.

Cassie looked down and away from him, and then shared her connection to Hecimovich.

Hodges said, "I think he was the first abductee. Did you know Hecimovich was a drug dealer as well as a teacher?"

"No, no. I didn't. I had no idea!"

"I believe Hecimovich didn't fall out of his canoe and die in the lake or river. That never made sense to me."

"But people fall out of canoes and drown all the time," Cassie protested.

"His body, if by chance it did drift to the falls leading out of the lake, would have gotten hung up on something at the bottom of that falls, or in a pond further down the river, or at the bottom of one of the numerous other falls before it ended up in gichi-gami." He used the Ojibwa name for Lake Superior.

"So, you're saying, Karonen kidnapped him and forced him to try and revive his daughter—the

same as your friend and me?"

"No, I'm saying he grabbed him because Hecimovich provided the drugs to his daughter that caused her to end up in the vegetative state she was in."

"Revenge," Cassie said.

"Yes, and what happened to him next..." he nodded her way. "I'm only theorizing, but I think it's pretty safe to say that he's dead, just not the way the police thought he died. Karonen killed him. He must have. Somehow he found out Hecimovich sold her the drugs." He paused for several moments and then added, "I know about emotion, rage, and revenge."

She pulled the sleeping bag over her chin and shuddered.

Seeing the change in her demeanor, Hodges repeated, "I know about emotion and revenge, but trust me when I say, I'm not the same person who..." His voice trailed off and he peered at the sky. Hodges couldn't bring himself to say the murderous words to the innocent woman beside him. He turned his face to her again and pleaded, "Please... believe me."

Although she nodded her affirmation, she still was not sure, and he knew it.

To help reinforce his point, he dug the TracFone out of his pocket and offered it to her. She took it from him and turned it on. The battery indicator showed plenty of power. Two bars were visible. She could make a call if she wanted.

She turned it off and handed it back to Hodges. "I trust you, Mr. Hodges." Her head was downcast and she fiddled with her fingers.

"But?"

She answered slowly. "I need to know what you did, and why."

Hodges took a deep breath, let it out, and stared at the lake.

It seemed like forever to Cassie, but then he began, holding nothing back.

"I was a confused, sick man—a man who had become wrapped up in his own world of make believe—much like Peter Karonen. I understand him. I know how he could have become so engrossed in his love for another that he lost all objectivity and sense of what's right or what's wrong." He shook his head and grimaced.

Cassie thought he was going to cry. There was a long pause.

When he began again, his voice was cold steel. "I took a nightstick and smashed it into the heads of four people I thought had harmed... or refused to help a woman I loved." He didn't notice Cassie pulling the sleeping bag protectively closer. "I shot and killed a woman deputy because she murdered the woman I thought I loved."

He paused again—sat with his eyes closed. When he started talking, his eyes remained closed; the memory of it all seemed to crush him to the bone. "After I killed the deputy, I walked away, dropped to my knees and put the gun to my head. My finger curled around the trigger... and I pulled it halfway...God I wanted to kill myself then, but I stopped."

He opened his eyes and looked at her now. "In the crazy moments that my finger lingered on the trigger of that gun, I realized this was not who I was... who I wanted to be. The person who murdered those people was sick. I was not that man." He said it with force. "I knew my death wouldn't solve anything for me or anyone else."

He sniffed. "I knew, although I surely didn't deserve it, I knew that I had to somehow try to make up for what I had done." He looked away, not sure his confessional had accomplished anything, but certain that he felt better for the effort.

Cassie stayed silent, and looked out over the lake.

A little while later, he put the phone back into his pocket.

"As soon as it's light I'm going to call the man who has been helping me. I'm going to give him a job that I hope he's up for."

If it involved getting Hodges to Canada as soon as possible, Cassie was all for it. Now, more than ever, she wanted to be done. The level of trust that had been building inside her for Hodges was now diminished.

The sky was clear, except for a million speck of starlight, and the winds were calm. Sitting under the ledge, looking out over the lake that seemed motionless, Hodges and Cassie said no more. They both receded into their own thoughts and curled up separately under the sleeping bag.

Mancoat's neck and back ached like never before as he turned to his side. The car seat, even when fully reclined was not very comfortable. He thought he heard ringing and reached for the TracFone sitting on the dashboard. His arm stretched as far as it could, coming up short by the width of a nickel before he made a desperation grab at the phone.

"Got it," he said and then punched the answer button.

"Earl, you sound tired," came Hodges' familiar voice.

"You're damn right I'm tired. I've been camped out in my car for two nights avoiding the police and the highway patrol."

"I have a job for you."

Mancoat bolted upright, squinted the sleep away from his eyes, and protested, "A job? I'm hiding out. I can't pick you up like we planned." His eyes darted around the back lot he was parked in. "They're looking for me. How can I do a job?"

"Earl, you're a wanted man, not quite in the same category as me, but you aided and abetted me. You need some negotiating power when you turn yourself into the police."

Mancoat gulped.

"Are you ready to listen?"

Before responding, Mancoat nodded his head absently, and then said with a growl, "Yeah, I'm ready."

With Cassie listening in, Hodges continued, "Call Sheila Cadotte and have her pick you up. You two will pay our Duluth drug dealer another visit."

Mancoat groaned. He had little stomach for subjecting himself to the dealer and his sidekick, Freddy.

"See if he ever heard Hecimovich talk about any of his clients. I suspect Methodist Karonen was one of them. If you can establish that as a fact, we may have substantiated my theory that Peter Karonen found out about Tom, nabbed and murdered him. You can tell your story to the police and gain leverage in your negotiations to disassociate yourself from me and save yourself some jail time." Hodges waited for a response from Mancoat.

Mancoat tried to get comfortable as he listened. His anxious rubbing of the two-day growth of beard had almost worn away a patch of stubble the size of a quarter. "But what about you? What are you going to do?"

"Don't worry about me, Earl. I'll be fine."

There was a long silence on Mancoat's end. "Good luck, Gerry," he finally said, reverting back to Hodges' real name since the ruse was now up.

"Do it as soon as possible." Hodges hung up before Mancoat could say any more.

"Gerry, Gerry? Damn it." Mancoat clicked off and sat for several moments. He collected his thoughts and called Cadotte.

Mancoat's eyes twitched from one side to the other as the Lexus pulled into the back lot of the motel.

Cadotte swung the car around when she saw Earl open the driver's side door of his vehicle, step out, and hurry toward her. Her wheels emitted a low screeching squeal as the car made a sharp turn before skidding to a halt.

Mancoat swung into the front passenger seat and quickly slunk low, the top of his head rising just above the dash.

Cadotte's eyes flashed toward Mancoat. "You ready for this?"

"I'm not looking forward to it, but like Gerry said, it's the best chance I've got of getting some leverage and making a deal."

She drove south to Duluth.

"Stay down," Cadotte admonished Earl as she pulled into a Walmart parking lot on a hill in Duluth. When she had situated the Lexus between two campers parked half a block apart, Mancoat sat up and glanced around.

Digging a strip of paper from her purse, Cadotte stared at the numbers. She took a deep breath and made the call. Mancoat watched and listened, praying it would all work out and that they would gain the information needed to help save his skin. Still, it bothered him. He felt as if he were abandoning Gerald Hodges and committing a selfish act to keep himself out of jail.

Even after the unconscionable acts Hodges had committed three years ago, Earl wanted his friend to be safe. He wanted him to get out of the country and live the good life he knew he would. *First things first*, he told himself. We need to find out if Gerry was right about Hecimovich, Methodist, and Karonen. He pushed his thoughts away and tuned into Cadotte's conversation with the man on the other end of the phone call.

It was brief.

Cadotte said, "My name is Sheila Cadotte and I'm a reporter for the Duluth News Tribune. I'm hoping you can provide me with some information.".

Pause. A tingle of excitement flitted through Sheila's voice. "Um, we're looking for information about Tom Hecimovich and his clients."

Pause.

"Will you help us? We think he was murdered," Sheila said. Cadotte heard a slow exhalation on the other end of the line.

Pause. "Look, this is difficult over the phone. Can we meet?"

Cadotte listened, and then her excitement seemed to build, she said, "That's not a problem. Tell me where and when."

Cadotte wrote down directions to the bridge where Mancoat and Hodges had met the dealer and Freddy, and Mancoat signaled her that he knew the area.

"Okay, we'll be there at ten," she said.

Pause.

"Me and one of my associates." Trying to make it more palatable, she added, "He'll bring the money."

Cadotte clicked off.

"Same place me and Gerry met him. He's gonna bring his friend, Freddy, a shotgun wielding gal with lots of tattoos," Mancoat said.

Visibly nervous, Cadotte shoved the slip of paper with the phone number on it back into her purse, sat back, and whistled a short breath of air.

"Come on, we'll go back to my place until it's time to meet him."

Mancoat scrunched down in the seat again as she pulled out of the parking lot and drove to her house farther up the hill.

The clock read 9:45 p.m. Cadotte and Earl arrived at the Lester River Bridge numbered 5772 and parked in the same area Hodges and Mancoat had for the previous meeting. As before, the dealer approached from the other side of the bridge, walked across, and approached the Lexus.

Cadotte and Earl, exited, stood together near the driver's side and waited.

"I wanna see some bills before I say anything more."

Mancoat pulled out two, one hundred dollar bills, crossed the ten feet separating them and handed the bills over.

The dealer took the money and said, "So, what ya wanna know?"

"Did Tom sell drugs to a woman named Methodist Karonen?" Sheila asked.

He folded the bills neatly, placed them inside the breast pocket of his light jacket, and zippered it up. "I didn't know all of Tom's clients. That was his business, but I know that name. I dealt with her three or four times."

Sheila's thinking skills slipped. Being a reporter does not necessarily insulate a person from being caught flat-out unaware—and not know what to say. Neither she nor Mancoat had expected that answer. The whole time she had been thinking Tom Hecimovich had been Methodist's dealer.

She fumbled, "Uh, what did you sell her?"

His head bent to the left leaving one cheekbone higher than the other.

"Whatever she wanted. Mostly oxy."

Not thinking it through, Mancoat interjected, "Do ya know she ended up in the hospital in a catatonic state from that stuff?"

The moonlight shone down, illuminating his narrowed eyes and taut face as he spoke. "I don't keep track of nobody I do business with except when they call me again. I don't have nothin' ta do with how they use the stuff. That's their problem, however they end up." The tone was dull, uninterested, and unemotional. "I supply what they want. Can't be sentimental in this business."

Cadotte shivered when a cold breeze lay into her, although she couldn't tell if it was the breeze or his callous indifference that made her tremble.

"Did you know her father, Peter Karonen?" Cadotte asked.

He answered right away, "No." He turned and walked away.

Earl stood with his hands in his pockets while Cadotte watched the dealer fade away. She tried to digest the significance of what he had told them. Several moments passed before both of them got into the car and started the drive back to her place.

They arrived and sat in the living room; both of them cradled Leinenkugels in their hands.

"We'll have to tell Gerry he was wrong about Hecimovich," Earl said.

"So said the scumbag," Cadotte said.

"Why would he lie about that? If anything, he'd be getting himself into more trouble by admitting he was the one who sold the drugs to her that sent her into a vegetative state. The other thing that bothers me now is that we don't have anything to leverage my freedom with." Mancoat looked worried.

"Don't be so fast. We can still go to the police and tell them who the dealer is and that he admitted he sold her the drugs. And, although it removes a motive for Karonen killing Hecimovich, it still doesn't mean he didn't kidnap and kill him." She thought for a moment longer. Earl observed the wheels turning and let her think.

"If I could get some time with Karonen, I'll bet I could get it figured out," she said.

"From what you said in the car, he's a raving lunatic right now, doesn't know left from right, up from down, his ass from..."

"Yeah, yeah, I get the picture," Cadotte interrupted. "I hear you, but, I'd still like to try and get it out of him."

Mancoat twisted the beer bottle in his hands. "The shrinks have probably gotten a hold of him and tried. Maybe they already figured it out and we'll have nothing to give to the police." He took a long hard pull from the bottle, and then looked at Cadotte. "I think I'm probably already in the shit hole."

Cadotte sipped her beer. "Then we've got nothing to lose. Are you ready to see Lieutenant Johnson tomorrow?"

"Nothing else I can do, I guess. It all depends on Karonen now."

CHAPTER 21

Hodges snapped the cell phone off. He moved away the bushes he and Cassie had stacked at the edge of their shelter and crawled out from underneath the ledge. The sun was just cracking the horizon beyond the lake. He sat on the ledge, stretching his arms and shoulders above and then outward toward the lake, emitting a medium-sized groan.

"Do you think your friends will find the drug guy?"

Hodges stretched and said, "One never knows, but I have confidence in both of them. Earl will complain and act like a fool sometimes, but he is cleverer than most would think. Sheila Cadotte seems to be a good reporter who has already proven her wit to me." He looked down to the rocks and trees below, his legs dangling over the ledge. "And, I think I proved to her that I was worthy of her trust."

Cassie dug into the backpack. "How about a little breakfast? I've got a couple bars."

Hodges reached over as she handed him one. "Thanks."

They chewed on their bars and gazed out over Lake Superior.

"Where'd you grow up?" Cassie asked

Hodges chewed, swallowed, and then answered. "I grew up in a little town called Rose Creek, in southern Minnesota."

"I like the name of it," she said. "But you don't sound American." She looked at him sidewise.

Hodges winced.

"Sorry, I didn't mean that as an insult or anything."

"Oh, I don't take it that way," Hodges said. "I spent a good share of my life in England and just acquired the accent, I guess you would say. I did a lot of acting in the theater, and you don't act in theater in London without acquiring English speech patterns."

Cassie took another bite of her energy bar and squinted into the sun. If she had to guess the time, which she did, she would say it was around 7 a.m. "We should get going pretty soon."

"Please, before we go, tell me about yourself," Hodges urged.

She took her wrapper, crumpled it up and stuffed it into the backpack. "There's not a whole lot to tell. I was placed in foster homes after my parents were killed in an accident when I was nine. They couldn't find any relatives who would take me, so I don't know if I have living uncles, aunts, or cousins." She sighed. "It seems like I have to have somebody!"

Her expression turned bleak. "I tried to get help finding any family I could, because I just felt... alone. I needed a connection. A social worker steered me to Tom Hecimovich. We talked and he made me feel like there was hope. He had found his parents and told me we could find my relatives. He made me feel so much better about myself, and then... he disappeared." She paused and in a defeated voice, she added, "And you think he's dead."

A pained look broke across Hodges' face. "I'm sorry... about your family and the feeling you have about being alone in the world. I know how a person can feel that way, even when they're surrounded by people." He paused. "What about grandparents?"

"I never saw them."

He handed her his wrapper and she stuffed it into the pack. Without another word, they gathered their loose gear and clambered away from the overhang and back to the trail above.

They walked the trail for an hour before they heard the sound of a helicopter in the sky. Hodges and Cassie dashed from the opening on the trail and scrambled under the birch that pervaded the hillside. The chopper got louder and emerged over the hillside and the trail behind them. They watched as it slowly passed over the trees. It seemed like it was searching the pathway they had walked just a moment ago.

The chopper passed overhead and occasionally zigzagged back and forth as it flew.

"It's a good thing they haven't developed a hybrid chopper that doesn't make any noise when it flies," Cassie said.

Hodges looked at her as if she was serious.

She stared back and then said, "I was just joking."

Hodges' face remained a mask. "They probably have searchers on the ground. We'll have to watch for them."

Cassie nodded, following Hodges out of the trees and onto the trail. She didn't kid herself that she would be unhappy if they were found, but she had made up her mind that it wouldn't be because of her.

The chopper had long disappeared from view when Cassie assumed the lead. Hodges kept a watchful eye for any hikers. They covered several miles before an abrupt descent and bend occurred in the trail. Their pace slowed, and they became more watchful. Their senses jumped to alert when they approached the base of the hill where a parking lot was visible through the trees.

Hodges maneuvered himself in front of Cassie and leaned against a tree. Two cars were visible; neither one was a marked squad car. He moved around to get a better look at the other side of the parking lot to see where the connecting trailhead was. Cassie joined him and looked for people.

No other humans seemed to be around, but they waited, anyway, unsure if they should nonchalantly walk across the parking area to the trailhead or make a mad dash. The nonchalant method won out, and they descended the last few meters of the hill and walked across the parking area like any other pair of hikers out for a two-day walk.

Hodges and Cassie didn't say a word as they entered the parking lot, but stopped as soon as they heard voices and saw three figures exiting the trailhead and entering the lot.

Cassie held her breath and Hodges nudged her to start moving.

The voices belonged to a couple of kids and a lone adult. They broke into the parking lot and moved toward the larger vehicle, an SUV, without looking toward Cassie and Hodges.

As they got close, the adult, an athletic looking man in his late thirties glanced at them while loading his pack into the trunk of his SUV. "Hey, where ya headed?" he said with a cheery tone.

Cassie said, "Up near Little Marais. Where'd you and your kids come from?"

He laughed. "They're not my kids. They're my sister's twins. We were just out for a couple hours, so didn't go very far. Little Marais, though, you've got a ways to go today." He closed the trunk. "Well, have a good hike. I've gotta get these critters home."

Cassie said, "Thanks, we will."

She waved and Hodges tipped his hat. They walked the remaining fifty feet of the parking lot and started up the trail. Cassie breathed a little easier. She eyed him as they ascended the trail. Again, a nagging doubt hung around her brain like a millstone. He had confessed to her that he had killed four people. Somehow, she still had a hard time picturing this grandfather-like man as a murderer. *Maybe there were extenuating circumstances,* she told herself. She rationalized several scenarios where, if she had to, she could kill someone.

Cassie watched him.

Hodges seemed like he wanted to avoid saying anything while they trekked up the hillside. He seemed more distant than before and she wondered what he was thinking. This was definitely complicated, not simple at all, she thought.

When they reached the apex of the hill it flattened out. The walking got easier, and less rocky. After a mile, Hodges stopped, took off the pack, and laid it on the ground. He perched himself on a nearby log, removed his hat and traced the inside of it over and over.

She sat on the opposite end of the log and rested, not saying a word. After several minutes of tracing the inside of his hat, Hodges spoke.

"You could have said something back there. You could have gone back to your life, but you didn't. Why?"

"For one thing, I know you have a gun." She had been staring ahead, but she turned her head and looked at him. "I didn't want anybody to get hurt, especially children. Another thing... I don't have a life."

Hodges removed the weapon from his jacket pocket.

Cassie drew back and took a breath.

He held the gun in his hand and stared at it.

She just watched him; her fingers tensed, her legs and feet were sore, her mind was a mess. She watched. The only sounds she heard were her heart pumping and his thick breathing.

Hodges turned toward her with the gun in his right hand.

She slid her body farther away on the log until she had nowhere to go.

"Take this, I don't want it." He laid it on the log between them and moved several yards away.

Cassie hesitated and then picked up the gun. She had never used one before. She thought all she would have to do was point, and pull the trigger.

His back to her, Hodges said, "The weapon is de-cocked and a round is not chambered."

She looked at the weapon and noticed the trigger. It looked like it had already been pulled.

"How do I cock it?"

Hodges never turned around. "Grip the slide on top of the gun and pull it back."

Cassie looked at the gun and thought she knew what he was talking about. She placed her hand over the slide, gripped, and pulled. It didn't move.

"It won't move." Her voice sounded desperate.

"It will. Pull hard and fast, but please, point it downward." He turned around and looked at her. "We don't want any accidents."

Cassie pointed the gun at the ground, gripped the slide, and pulled backwards fast. She was surprised when it moved and a round chambered. She let her breath out.

Hodges spoke, "Keep the gun. I think you'll feel safer now."

She was unsure how to answer him. Finally she said, "How do I de-cock this thing so I won't fire it by accident?"

"Look at the trigger, beside it on the left side of the grip you will see a magazine release. Push in on that and the magazine will drop out." She did as he said and the magazine fell to the ground. "Now pull back on the slide again. The round you chambered will eject." She followed his directions and the round flew out and landed near the magazine. She picked the round and magazine off the ground, but hesitated, not really knowing what to do with them. She wanted the magazine in the automatic, but didn't want a round in the chamber.

"Please, would you put the magazine back in the gun for me?" She gave him a nervous smile. "I'm afraid I'll mess something up. Maybe shoot a foot off."

He took the gun when she offered it, replaced the round in the magazine and put it back in the gun. "If you need to use it, pull the slide back like I told you. It'll chamber a round and then you can point and pull the trigger. Understand?"

She nodded her head and he handed the gun back to her. She placed it in the side pocket of her backpack and strapped the pack on.

Hodges started walking the trail ahead of Cassie.

"Wait. I have one more question, Mr. Hodges."

He stopped and turned to face her.

Her hesitancy to speak her thoughts was obvious.

Hodges lifted an eyebrow to prod her.

"Why... why did you bring a gun with you? If you've changed like you say you have, why bring a weapon to Minnesota?"

He didn't hesitate. "My friend bought the gun in Duluth before we met the drug dealer. We, uh, Mr. Mancoat in particular, thought it would be the intelligent thing to do in order to ensure our safety. Given my experience in confrontational matters, I thought I should be the one to carry the weapon. Earl concurred." He waited several moments for any further questions.

"Would you have used it?" Cassie asked.

Again, Hodges didn't hesitate. "If our lives depended on it, particularly Earl's, yes, I would have." He stepped toward her, just one step, but enough to stiffen her.

"You have the weapon. I guarantee I will not be a cause for you to use it. My only remaining objectives are to get to Canada and make sure that Earl is not prosecuted for helping me."

"Okay," she said in a fake cheery tone. "We've got a long way to go."

They resumed their trek.

CHAPTER 22

adotte made the call to Lieutenant Johnson. At first, he denied her request to interview Karonen, telling her it would be a waste of time, but he relented when she told him she had pertinent information that might get through to him. When he asked what that pertinent information might be, she said she would share with him after the interview. He didn't like it, but given their historical working relationship, he gave her the benefit of the doubt and okayed the meeting.

Mancoat stayed out of sight at Cadotte's house. Karonen was being held in a private room at St. Luke's Hospital in Duluth. He was being temporarily cared for in the inpatient mental health unit. So far, police interviews with Karonen had yielded no discernible results.

Armed with her note pad and recorder, Cadotte stood in the open doorway of Karonen's room where she observed him. He sat on the edge of his bed, dressed in a hospital gown. His hands were clasped and he rocked back and forth. Incomprehensible gibberish dribbled from his mouth, along with a thin stream of spittle.

"He's been like this since his arrival," said the psychiatric nurse standing next to Cadotte. The nurse was a stout man with a short, black beard. "He hasn't been violent at all. In fact, he's been easily guided and cared for, but as far as saying anything that makes sense, besides his daughter's name, well..." His voice trailed off and he shook his head.

Cadotte approached the bed slowly. The nurse slid a high backed chair within five feet of Karonen, and then stood off to the side with his arms crossed. She eased into the chair opposite Karonen and watched. He acted like no one else was in the room. The gibberish continued along with the rocking.

She began talking in a gentle, soothing voice, "Mr. Karonen, my name is Sheila Cadotte, and I'm a reporter for the Duluth newspaper. I'm here to talk to you about your daughter, Methodist, and a man named Tom Hecimovich."

Karonen sprang to his feet in a flash and zipped around the bed, slamming himself into the Plexiglas window. The nurse, reacted in lightning fashion, rushed to the window and held Karonen by his shoulders. "Mr. Karonen, it's fine. It's fine," he said in a quiet voice. "We're going to sit back on the bed and relax."

Karonen trembled and struck out at the Plexiglas. After several punching motions, the nurse felt Karonen's shoulder muscles loosen. He guided him to the bed, rubbing his shoulders in a circular pattern and patting him on the back. The nurse stood beside him and maintained a physical connection. He gave a nod to the startled Cadotte, signaling her she could resume the interview.

A slightly discombobulated Cadotte, changed tactics and tried again. "Mr. Karonen, I know who gave the drugs to Methodist."

Whatever slight relationship Karonen had with reality seemed to take hold of him. The gibberish stopped. The rocking motion stopped. He swallowed and lifted his eyes toward Cadotte.

She said it again. "I know who gave the drugs to Methodist."

A pitiful expression came to Karonen and he said in a just audible voice, "Methodist."

Cadotte almost jumped to the ceiling.

The nurse nodded his head twice, encouraging her.

"Methodist," Karonen said again, but louder this time. "I miss her."

"I know, Mr. Karonen, lots of people miss her. She was a good person."

"Yes," he said and then nodded. "The drugs, she didn't try to kill herself." He looked at Cadotte. "It was an accident. She would never do that on purpose." His head hung low.

The nurse rubbed his shoulders.

Cadotte feared he would revert to his former non-communicative state, but his head turned up again and he asked, "Who gave her the drugs?"

"A man sold them to her. He lives in Duluth. I don't know his name, but I know how to find him," Cadotte said.

"Find him. Make him pay," Karonen said and then wiped his nose with his hand.

"I will—the police will, but we need your help on something." Before she said anymore, Cadotte motioned to the nurse that he could leave her alone with Karonen.

He shook his head no.

Cadotte decided he wasn't going anywhere, but she didn't want him telling anyone that Karonen was lucid... at least for a couple of hours.

"Okay, stay, but I don't want you to tell anyone that he's talking, okay?"

"I can't do that lady. It's my job. I've got to let the doctors know."

She dug out fifty bucks.

He looked at the money. "What's that for?"

"Time. You wait three hours, and it's yours."

He looked uncomfortable. Whispering, he said, "Make it a hundred and I could manage it."

Cadotte dug another fifty out of her purse. *Good thing I stopped at the bank earlier,* she thought. She returned her attention to Karonen. "Tell me about Tom."

Karonen lifted his eyes.

She feared he would lose it again. She said it softly, slowly, "Tom Hecimovich. Did you take him?"

Karonen groaned. "His name wasn't Tom Hecimovich. It was Richard Gabrielson."

"Yes," she said. "He used his step-father's name sometimes. His real name is Tom Hecimovich. Where is he?"

Karonen started crying, but didn't lose it totally.

Cadotte asked in a gentle voice, "Mr. Karonen, where is he?"

Silence for a moment, and then he mumbled, "Devil's Kettle. It was an accident when the fisherman died." He spoke in a stronger voice now. "He tried to hurt me, and we fought." Karonen gripped his hands and moved them as if he were wringing out a towel. "He didn't understand—I just needed his help."

"I know," said Cadotte. She took one of his hands in hers and held it.

Karonen relaxed. "I brought him back to my house. I had prepared a room in the cave. I tried to explain to him, but he... got mad." His voice sounded incredulous. "He grabbed me." He shook his head back and forth and closed his eyes as he relived the scene in his head. "I hit him and hit him, and I slammed his head to the floor... a lot. I reacted, just reacted. If he had hurt me badly, I wouldn't be able to care for Methodist." He looked at her and cried. Tears dripped onto his hospital gown and Cadotte's hand.

He started talking again. "I left the room and went back later. I thought maybe he was okay... but he wasn't. A couple of days later, I took him to the Devil's Kettle and pushed him in." His mouth twisted into a grimace and he shook his head. "He'll never be found."

Cadotte composed herself before she said, "Mr. Karonen, thank you for telling me what happened to Tom. His family will appreciate that."

Karonen closed his eyes and said softly, "Tell them it was an accident."

"I will," she said. She nodded at the nurse and left.

"Whaddaya got?"

Cadotte had barely opened the door to her place and Mancoat was in her face. She pushed him back, closed the door quickly, and took a breath. "Well, we know where Tom Hecimovich is."

"You're kidding, you got that out of him?" He clapped his hands and laughed, and then his demeanor changed. "The police don't know yet, right?"

"Not yet, I hope. You've got to get on the phone right away with Lieutenant Johnson and tell him what I found out. This is your leverage before he finds out another way."

"Whaddaya mean, another way?"

"Karonen is more grounded in reality now, and before he says anything to the police you've gotta put in your two cents."

Mancoat took his cell phone out of his pocket.

"Wait, first I'll give you everything you need to tell Johnson."

She recounted what Karonen had said, and then he called.

Soon, he was patched into Johnson's cell and repeated what Sheila had told him to say. Johnson said it would help him avoid the worst of the charges being considered against him, but cautioned that he would have to turn himself in now and agree to help them find Hodges.

He agreed.

CHAPTER 23

They walked until late morning without seeing another human being or helicopter. The day was unseasonably warm and stains of sweat dampened their shirts. Hodges stopped and sat on a large boulder off to the side and panted. The combination of age, heat, and unaccustomed exertion took its toll on his body. Cassie took the pack off and broke out their last water bottle. She tossed it to Hodges and watched him remove the cap and down three large gulps before he tossed it back. She took a few gulps and returned it to the pack.

"This'll last us a few more hours in this heat and that's it," Cassie said. She kept looking ahead, trying to make out what she was seeing.

Hodges noticed her staring and looked the same way. "I'm sure your eyes are better than mine. What do you see?"

"Hikers, coming this way."

"Let's move back into the trees so they don't see us," Hodges said and then stood up.

Cassie gathered the backpack and they moved into a hidden spot among the trees. It was an area where they could watch the hikers, and remain unseen.

"Do you think they're searchers?" Hodges asked.

"I can't see them well enough yet."

Fifteen minutes later, they got their answer. Three men and a woman, wearing DNR uniforms approached the rock where Cassie and Hodges had just rested.

The two slunk lower, and kept silent..

The group paused at the rock, a natural resting place at the pinnacle of the hill they had just ascended. Two of the group removed daypacks and broke out water bottles. An animated discussion erupted among the searchers, but neither Hodges nor Cassie could make it out. After a few minutes, they put their gear away and resumed their hike, treading the ground Hodges and Cassie had covered minutes before.

When they could no longer see or hear the group, Hodges and Cassie talked about what they should do next.

"I'll do whatever you suggest. You're the one who's familiar with the area," Hodges said.

"I hate to say this, but I think we should get off the trail and head inland for a hundred yards and try to parallel it. There's gonna be more searchers on the trail, for sure."

Hodges looked inland. Nothing but forest and hills lay before them. There was no trail that he could see to make the going easier, and getting lost seemed like a distinct possibility. He took his hat off and drew more rings around the inner space of it.

"Can you keep us on course?"

"I think so," she said.

He stood up. "Alright then, I'll follow you."

Cassie picked her way around a blackberry bush, but not before she had scraped a hand on the thorns protecting the non-existing berries. Most had been eaten long before by the birds and black bears that populated the Arrowhead Region of Minnesota. "Ouch," she said and immediately inspected her hand. Blood trickled from three little scrapes on the backside of her left hand. She wiped it with her shirtsleeve, and then pressed her shirt against the skin to stanch the blood.

"Are you okay?"

"Just scratches. I'll be more careful." She inspected the bush, looking for any berries the bears or birds had missed.

Hodges joined in the search.

"Ah ha." He reached deep within the bush, careful to avoid the tough thorns, and deftly plucked a handful of blackberries and brought them out to share.

Cassie's eyes widened when she saw the large, ripe berries. To her surprise, she felt herself salivate with anticipation of their sweet flavor.

Hodges counted out several and gave Cassie one more than he kept for himself. She smiled in appreciation and ate the berries one at a time, savoring each morsel of fruit. When finished, they looked around, found a few more and devoured them.

Red-black stains marked their hands. Cassie sucked on her fingertips.

Breaking with his elitist manners, Hodges did the same.

During their afternoon walk they heard another chopper, but never saw it. The canopy of leaves hid portions of the sky making their detection from above impossible. Cassie managed to find deer paths to walk, which made the trek easier, but it also took them off course as the paths wound their way in the patterns that deer took as they ate their way through the forest. She knew they had diverged from her chosen route, but following the deer trails presented an easier path to follow through the underbrush, and it was safer than sticking to the Superior Hiking Trail.

Waterfalls and rivers cut through the terrain of the North Shore in abundance, and it was likely they would encounter several more if they were lucky enough to reach the Canadian border. She knew more than most that they presented challenges and dangers.

Two years before, while hiking in the Tettegouche area, off-trail and by herself, she had slipped on a steep embankment and tumbled down the seventy-degree slope, twisting an ankle and breaking a wrist before ending up in rapids. The swift current carried her downstream for a hundred yards before she gained a handhold and pulled herself to shore. After that, it had been a wrenching hike back to her car and an hour drive to the hospital in Duluth for treatment. Hiking off-trail had not been a part of her activities since that accident.

She sneaked a peek at Hodges, who trailed her by twenty feet. He seemed to be holding up well, for an old guy. Once again, she found herself wondering about him, what he had done, and why.

She knew she should fear him, and she had, but now, not so much, and it bothered her a little. The guy admitted he had killed four people, and yet, here she was helping him escape to Canada, risking her own life in the process. She also thought of the gun in her pack. He gave it to her so she would trust him. Well... that worked.

"Miss Bandleson, we seem to be moving farther away from the main trail. I don't mean to be disrespectful, or doubt your skills, but do you think we should try to get a little closer to it?"

Cassie held an overhanging tree branch so when she let go it would not slap him in the face as he caught up to her. He arrived at her side and she let the branch snap back into place.

"You might be right, Mr. Hodges. These deer trails are easier to walk than plowing our way through the underbrush, but they do meander."

"Please call me, Gerry. I would feel better about that. It's a tad less formal that way."

"Okay, Gerry, but you have to call me, Cassie, then."

"Alright, Gerry and Cassie it is."

Hodges tipped his hat and followed her as she left the deer trail and veered to the east. The underbrush seemed sparser, which made sense, as the foliage above was denser, drowning out life-giving sunlight for plants to thrive on. They made their way easily in a northeasterly direction, hoping to get closer to the main trail and regain their bearings.

CHAPTER 24

Mancoat sat silent in a wooden, hardback chair in Lieutenant Johnson's office. Johnson sat behind his metal desk, facing him. Leaning backwards, he twirled a recently sharpened pencil; his right leg crossed over the left as he pondered everything Mancoat had told him.

"So, you say Peter Karonen killed Tom Hecimovich, and you know where he tossed his body."

Earl nodded.

"And you also say you know who gave his daughter Methodist the drugs that caused her vegetative state."

Mancoat nodded again.

"And you also say Tom Hecimovich was a small time drug dealer along with a fellow teacher in Virginia, named..." He fumbled through his notes. "Mark Seinfelt."

Mancoat nodded once more and said, "Yes, Lieutenant."

"And your proof for all this is... where?" Johnson tilted his head.

Mancoat hadn't thought of needing to offer any proof, but he pulled out the Duluth drug dealer's phone number and the address for Mark Seinfelt. He also gave the lieutenant, Nancy Baldwin's name and said she would corroborate the facts about Hecimovich and Seinfelt.

Johnson took the papers Mancoat offered and said, "But you haven't given me one bit of information about your friend, Gerald Hodges, whose crimes make the others seem like boy scouts. How come?"

"I'll be honest with you. Gerald Hodges is a friend."

Johnson rolled his eyes and leaned back even farther in his chair, threatening to tip it over. "Yeah, yeah, and this makes everything he did okay, because he's your friend, right?"

"No, it doesn't, but Gerry's a good man who did some terrible things. He's different now. He says he's only gonna do good things with the rest of his life. That's why he came back here to help find Seth... and he did find him." He glared at Johnson. "That's something you guys couldn't do. Plus he found those other people too."

Johnson squinted at Mancoat, not saying anything for several moments. Anger seemed to build inside of him until Mancoat thought he might explode. Suddenly, Johnson tipped his chair forward and slammed his feet onto the floor.

Mancoat jumped back in his chair, not sure what to expect next.

Johnson stood up, turned his back on him and looked out the window to the street. He tapped one foot on the floor, in slow, measured movements.

"Do you remember Wilt Chamberlain?" Johnson asked in a melancholic tone.

Mancoat frowned, not knowing where this was going.

"Of course I do. He was the greatest NBA player of all time."

Johnson turned around, "Second best of all time. Michael Jordan was the best."

"Your opinion," said Mancoat derisively.

"We could argue about that, but Wilt Chamberlain once said that he slept with 20,000 different women during his career. You remember that?"

"Who wouldn't remember that?" Mancoat said.

"You believe him?"

"Course not, it's impossible."

"Well, when I think of what you've told me today, I think the same thing about your story as his. Well, almost the same thing. Your story is possible, but as a cop, it sounds implausible."

Mancoat squirmed in his seat.

"You check out my sources and you'll find out how plausible it is. Check with Peter Karonen now and you'll find out he's back in the real world and singing." Mancoat smirked, just a little.

"Oh, I will, Mr. Mancoat, and in the meantime, you're going to be my guest."

It took Mancoat a split-second to stand and blurt out, "Now wait a damn minute. I gave you actionable intelligence that can be corroborated. You can't lock me up."

"I didn't say locked up. I distinctly recall that I said you will be my guest."

"Yeah, in a jail cell," Mancoat snarled.

"A very comfortable cell, I might say. If, and that's a huge if, your story and information check out, it'll all be taken into consideration and probably result in lesser charges filed against you, Mr. Mancoat. In the meantime, please accompany my associate, Mr. Wilkins to your accommodations." Wilkins had appeared in the doorway moments before Johnson motioned him in.

Johnson smiled as he watched Mancoat leave with Wilkins. He didn't doubt Mancoat's story as much as he had intimated, but he couldn't resist making him squirm a bit because of the entire charade with Hodges. He was pretty sure everything would check out as Mancoat had stated, but why not have a little fun in the meantime, put the screws to him, and make him reveal more about Hodges' plans and whereabouts. It couldn't hurt anyway, he thought. Also, he had just a smidgen of suspicion that Sheila Cadotte was more involved in this whole matter than she let on. He sauntered across the office floor and picked up the phone and dialed Cadotte's number.

She picked up on the second ring, "Cadotte," she said in a hurried voice.

Johnson could hear the sound of her fingers pounding the keyboard in the background.

"Sheila, how's it going?"

"Lieutenant Johnson, I didn't expect to hear from you. I'm about as crazy busy as you could get right now, getting my stories ready for tomorrow's edition. You know how bad it gets."

"Indeed I do, but I was hoping we could meet for a friendly drink later, and wrap up some loose ends regarding your story."

Cadotte ceased typing and a feeling of dread hit her. "Uh huh, sure, I'll be busy until say six." She looked at her watch. It read 4:15.

"Let's say 6:15 at Fuzzy's Place?"

She put on a cheery voice, "Sounds good, see you there." Cadotte reclined in her comfortable office chair, rubbed her temples, and said aloud, "What the hell is going on now?"

Johnson arrived early and ordered bourbon on the rocks. He'd barely gotten his wallet out of his pocket and the short glass was set in front of him.

"Three-fifty," the bartend said in a manner suggesting no small talk, hurry up and pay.

Johnson gave him an off-kilter look and said, "You're new, aren't you?"

The bartender swept up the five-dollar bill, said, "Yeah," and stormed to the other end of the bar to get change. Johnson watched him with disdain. The kid was young and not the usual friendly person he expected in Fuzzy's. He always liked this bar because of the staff. They had all been friendly as hell, but not this kid. He wondered what the hell was wrong with him.

The kid returned, dumped the change on the bar, and started to leave.

Johnson put his hand roughly on the kids forearm and held him tight.

"Hey, what gives?" The kid asked.

Johnson looked him up and down before responding. "Just wondering what got shoved up your ass this morning?"

"Wha... what?" The startled kid asked in a high-pitched voice.

"I mean, you're running around here like you got a corncob shoved up your ass and you're pretty damn impolite. So what gives?" With his other hand, Johnson held his police identification badge close enough to the kid's face for him to see it clearly. The kid glanced at the ID and immediately his attitude became deferential and apologetic.

"I'm sorry Lieutenant... Johnson, but... it's my first night and I'm trying to be really good at serving everyone right away... and give my boss a good night's work."

Johnson eased off on the grip he had on the kid's arm.

"Well, that's all well and good, uh..." he looked at the kid making it clear he wanted his name.

"It's Rick. Rick's my name."

"Well, Rick, I'm sure your employer would appreciate efficiency, *and* a friendly attitude from his bartenders. You get my drift?"

The kid went overboard with the deference now. "You bet, Lieutenant, sir. In fact, the next drink will be on the house..."

"No, that won't be necessary. I, like your other customers in here, would merely like a friendly attitude, a shoulder to cry on, and a receptive face to tell stories to. Know what I mean?"

The kid nodded his head up and down in a frenzy, "You bet I do, Lieutenant." He slapped the bar top lightly with the hand Johnson had released and said he would be the friendliest bartender Johnson had ever seen.

"Thanks, kid." Johnson smiled at him and tipped the bourbon to his lips. The kid retreated to the other end of the bar.

Five minutes later, Cadotte walked in. She spotted Johnson at the end of the bar, drifted over and tapped him on the shoulder. He had just brought the glass of bourbon to his lips, and spilled a slug of it over his chin when she tapped his shoulder.

"Oh, sorry about that, Lucas." Cadotte looked around for an empty table. She spied one in the corner, and said, "Let's grab a table. It's easier to talk."

Johnson wiped the liquid from his chin and the front of his shirt. "It's a good thing I'm off duty. It wouldn't be good if I went back to work with the smell of bourbon on my clothes."

Cadotte apologized again then made tracks for the table.

Johnson picked up his drink, caught the bartender's eye and signaled him to bring another bourbon on the rocks. They had just sat down when the now super friendly bartender arrived with Johnson's drink.

"Wow, that's what I call service," Cadotte said.

"What can I get for you, Miss?" The bar tend said it with an ingratiating tone.

"Get me a Leiny Dark."

The kid shot back to the bar and went to his taps.

"That is one friendly bartender, I'd say. A little sucky, but, I'll take it," Cadotte said.

Johnson sipped on his bourbon and studied her for several seconds.

Looking uncomfortable, Cadotte stared back at him. "What?" She finally asked.

The kid slid a tall glass of the dark beer across the table. "Anything else you two need right now?"

Johnson didn't look at the kid, but kept his eyes on Cadotte. "Nothing now, kid. I'll give you the signal when we need something. Just keep watch." He leaned over to Cadotte, and said, "We've known each other for several years now, right?"

"Yeah," Cadotte said.

"So why you lying to me? Why have you been lying to me the whole time Hodges has been here?"

Cadotte looked flustered and started to deny it.

Johnson put a hand in the air to stop her and leaned back in his chair. "Don't bother. No more shit from you." He pointed his finger at her. It trembled. Clearly, he was angry, and she knew he had every right to be. She wouldn't believe her attempted denial either.

"Now, we're gonna get right down to this, and you're gonna be straight with me." His eyes stayed on hers while his hand rested again on the table.

Still, she decided to reveal only what she had to. She knew she'd have to do it well, though.

She took a sip of the Leiny Dark and placed it down in front of her. Her elbows rested on the table.

"No bullshit," she began.

"Damn straight, no bullshit," he said in a stern tone.

"Okay. I got the information from Karonen and gave it to Mancoat."

"That, I know. You interviewed Karonen and got him to talk.

Now he's singing like a bird... yada, yada, yada. You've been keeping contact with Mancoat the whole time we've been looking for him, Hodges, and the girl, Bandleson. And you probably knew Hodges was Hodges, not Jasper Green like his passport says. You got more than that?"

She shook her head violently and pulled back from the table. "I never knew he was Hodges until..." *Wow,* she thought. *I caved on that quick enough. I'd never make it if I were water boarded.*

A broad smile spread across Johnson's face and he said, "Go on, until... when?"

Cadotte puckered her cheeks and looked down at her feet. She took a breath and decided she would tell him the truth now.

"I didn't know he was Hodges until just before we met to make a plan to get into Karonen's house. Hodges and Mancoat went to Karonen's house, and then I called you and told you they were there."

He gave her a skeptical look.

Her eyes flashed when she looked up at him. "It's the truth," she blurted.

Now it was Johnson's turn to pucker up while he sat in silence. He picked up his bourbon and brought it to his lips in a relaxed, loving way. He took a sip and savored the cool taste and feel of the bourbon as it slid down his throat. He rapped his fingers on the wooden surface of the table.

To Cadotte, the rapping sound seemed amplified and drowned out the din of conversation in the bar. She picked up her glass. Her hand trembled so bad that she almost dropped it.

Johnson seemed intense as he watched her. "You seem nervous, Sheila. Your hands are shaking." He nodded at her still trembling hand, trying to maintain a grip on the bottle.

She put it down, cocked her head, and crossed her arms. "Of course I'm nervous, you ass." She threw up her arms as if she was giving up everything, but she wasn't. Her voice was made of steel when she pointed at him and said, "I told you the truth. That was the first I knew he was Hodges and not Jasper Green, and..." she stated even more forcefully, "and... I did call you and tell you where he was."

He seemed to consider her statement again. After a few moments, he leaned toward her.

"How long did you wait to tell us?" He smirked.

Her body retreated into a shell, and her voice lost the steely resolve.

"Not that long." Her voice sounded defeated and meek.

"Where is he, Sheila?"

She gave a confused look and shook her head. Her voice recovered the steeliness it had lost, and she said, with each word a sentence in its own right, "I have no fucking idea."

Johnson gently placed a hand on the table. Neither one said anything for a while. He lifted a finger without even looking at the kid, who blazed back to the table with another bourbon on the rocks. Johnson downed the entire glass, slammed it hard on the table, and stood up. He peeled several bills from his wallet and laid them on the table next to his empty glass.

"You call me if you get anything else." Johnson turned and strode out of the bar.

Cadotte, her hands still shaking, went for the bottle. She managed to grasp it and tip it to her lips. It tasted bitter and ugly now. She returned it to the table and breathed deeply.

The kid came back. "Anything more I can get you," he asked.

She started to shake her head no, but changed her mind. "Yeah, get me a rum and coke in a tall glass, and don't be chintzy on the booze." She gave him a threatening look. The kid took note and hurried back to the bar.

CHAPTER 25

Hodges dragged. With every step, the rough terrain took a heavy toll on his body. If his back didn't hurt, then his legs, hips, or ankles did.

Cassie noticed. She felt tired as well, knowing that their lack of protein and calories was a major cause of their fatigue. She turned to offer encouragement to Hodges; instead, she found herself tumbling head over heels down the embankment they had been straddling for hours.

Hodges called out, but watched helplessly as she cascaded down the hillside, ending with her body wrapped around a jack pine.

"Cassie," Hodges called and started picking his way down the hill. He heard her groan and then saw her move a leg and an arm. "Don't move, I'll be there in a minute."

She ignored him, unwrapped her body from the tree, and sat up. She had been lucky. The pine had stopped her from plummeting over a hundred-foot drop off. She leaned around the tree, peeked over the edge and shuddered. The pine held fast to the rocky soil via a system of roots snaking out from its base.

Hodges edged closer, hanging onto thick limbs of brush to keep himself from tumbling down the hillside. He stopped and held fast to some brush when she called to him.

"Don't come down here. It's too steep."

He watched as she repositioned the backpack; it probably saved her from serious injury. She clawed her way to her feet and leaned into the hillside, groping for something to get hold of. She braced her feet against the pine she had slammed into and searched for the easiest pathway upwards. "Go back up," she yelled.

Hodges hesitated, but followed her command and made his way to the top. He wished he had a rope to toss down to her. "Careful," he yelled, and watched her pick her way up the hillside.

She appeared to be fine when she moved upward. It took her much longer to ascend, but she made it near the top without a slip. Hodges grasped her hand when she reached out, and he pulled her to the pinnacle of the hill. She planted herself on her backside.

"I have to eat something." She rested her arms on her knees as sweat poured from her forehead. A fly buzzed around her face and landed on her lips. She sputtered, shook her head, and slapped at it. "Christ, I can't believe I did that."

"You were tired and maybe a little distracted," Hodges said. He paused and added as an afterthought. "Don't be concerned with me. I don't need babysitting."

She said nothing.

He sniffed and handed her one of the two remaining energy bars that he had snatched from the backpack. She accepted the bar and stared at it, turning it over and over in her hand.

"If you need help tearing it open, hand it back and I'll do it for you," Hodges said in a playful voice.

Cassie gave a tired laugh. "No, I was just thinking. We're just about out of food and we've still got a long ways to go." She stared at him. "We're going to need more food." She didn't open the energy bar, but instead handed it back to him. He took it, but reconsidered and tossed it back to her.

"Eat it, you need the calories. We'll get more food."

She looked at him skeptically, but opened the wrapper anyway. She took a bite of the bar and chewed slowly, savoring each bite. *At least Mr. Karonen fed me well.* "How are we going to get enough food to get us to Canada?" She finally asked, more out of curiosity than anything.

"I'm thinking we can wait till dark at the next trailhead parking area, then walk and find a grocery store."

Cassie nearly spat out what she had been chewing and laughed.

"Listen, Gerry, you're not from around here, so you don't know much about the area. There are no grocery stores. There are some gas stations, like Holiday ones where we could find something to eat, but I really don't have a clue where they are in relation to where we are right now."

Hodges took a bite out of the remaining energy bar. "We could find one of the Holiday stations, buy some food, and be out of there in a flash," he said after swallowing a bite.

The plan appeared to be gaining traction with Cassie.

"We could do it, but only one of us, probably me, goes into the store to buy the food. You're too likely to be recognized. Your picture must be plastered all over the North Shore by now."

Hodges took another bite and mumbled his words.

"I'm sure your picture is out there too, but you're probably right about only one of us going into the gas station. Since I'm considered the dangerous one, it should be you."

"Alright, it's settled then. I'll go in and buy the food," Cassie said.

Hodges gathered the wrappers and stuffed them into the pack.

"Do you have any idea of where the next Holiday station is?"

Cassie pondered the question, one finger planted on her chin.

"We can't be far from Little Maris, and I know there's a station on the edge of town."

"You should be able to blend into the population with no problem," Hodges said.

She dropped the finger from her chin, turned to him, and shook her head. "Actually, it could be a problem. There's only about thirty people in the town."

"You call that a town?"

"It's a town for up here. Anyway, my point is that I'm not going to blend in with the locals. They know everybody. I'll take the pack and they'll ask about my hike, and hopefully, they won't connect me to what's happened around here."

Hodges didn't say anything for a long time, but stared into the woods.

Finally, Cassie asked, "You okay, Gerry?"

"I was just thinking." He picked up a pebble and threw it down the embankment. "Maybe you shouldn't come back for me. It would look better for you, if you turned yourself in, say you escaped from me and... let the chips fall where they may."

Cassie shook her head. "You know, I thought of you as a very smart man, Gerry, but the thought you just had, was about as dumb as I've ever heard. They'll find you right away, there's no question about it."

Hodges threw another pebble down the hill, shrugged his shoulders, and said, "Maybe it's for the best, Cassie. You'll be out of danger and there'll be no question in their minds that I forced you to come with me."

She frowned. "I can convince them of that after I get you to Canada. It's not a problem."

He gave her a pensive look. "Cassie, I don't want to be the cause of you getting hurt, or... going to jail for helping me. I've hurt too many people in this world, and I'm done with that."

"You haven't hurt me, and you won't. I know that." Silence. "Come on, we should get going."

Hodges slung the pack over his shoulders and followed Cassie down the ridge. Both watched their step more carefully.

Nightfall approached. They hacked their way through brush and back to the main trail, then down a short spur that led to the edge of Highway 61. Cassie had calculated correctly that they were near Little Marais. Hiding in the brush, and far enough back from the highway that they could not be seen, they finalized their plan.

Hodges made himself comfortable in a hidden area away from the spur and highway.

Cassie put the pack on and hiked Highway 61 for a couple hundred yards until she spotted the Holiday station, which doubled as a convenience store. Locals not only used it for gas, but as a small food market. Microwavable burgers, hot dogs, and sandwiches were available as well as some fruits and veggies. She browsed the aisles for food, candy bars, and trail mix.

The teenage clerk stood behind the counter and seemed surprised anyone but a local came in this late in the day. He said, "How's it going?"

She came up close to the cash register. "Not bad," she said, and continued inspecting the shelves of food. After going down another aisle, she said, "Hey, could I put my pack down by the counter and use one of the baskets for some stuff here?"

"Yeah, sure, I'll make sure it doesn't get stolen," he smirked. No one else was in the store.

She gave a good-natured laugh, said thank you, slipped the pack off, and leaned it against the counter. Cassie swept up a food basket and loaded supplies into it; a bunch of high-energy snack bars, four apples, a couple bags of baby carrots, candy bars—Snickers for herself. Having no idea what Hodges wanted, she guessed and threw in several Almond Joy bars for him. Concerned about weight, she loaded only two large water bottles from the refrigerated section, which they could use to filter water later, and one ice-cream sandwich for herself. *Might as well enjoy it while I can,* she said to herself.

She toted the full basket to the counter where he totaled it up.

"Comes to $22.78," the clerk said.

Cassie pulled out a twenty and a five that Hodges had given her. The clerk handed her the change. She loaded everything into the pack, and hoisted it onto her shoulders again. She had almost reached the doorway when the clerk called out.

"Hey, you going back on the trail, now?"

She froze, but managed to turn halfway around and say, "Yeah, I've got my tent set up back in the woods."

The teenager lost the enthusiastic tone and looked downhearted when he heard her answer. "Oh, I thought you might want to spend the night at our place. My mom has a room she rents out for the night, and I thought you might want to use it. It's got a shower and a soft bed," he added in a hopeful voice.

Cassie relaxed. She got the idea that his offer was about more than filling his mother's room for the night. She felt flattered, thinking he had found her attractive and wanted to be around her, which struck her as amazing, given the way she must look now.

"Thanks, but I haven't been out all that long and I've got a pretty comfortable sleeping pad. Thanks anyway."

The teenager nodded. "Maybe next time," he said and turned back to assume his place on a stool behind the counter.

Her gaze lingered on him. He looked forlorn.

"Yeah, maybe," Cassie said and walked out.

The light beaming down from the only street lamp in the parking lot made her squint. She adjusted the straps on the backpack, which was considerably heavier than before, slogged across the lot and onto the shoulder of Highway 61. Her pace slowed. She stayed on the far right side of the shoulder, and her mind wandered back to her conundrum.

A song popped into her head. *Should I stay or should I go?*

She sang the words over and over in her head, finally stopping and singing it out loud, but in a whispered voice. "Should I stay or should I go." *The song is catchy,* she thought, and the message was prescient.

She slipped the pack off and considered what Hodges had said before she left. Why wouldn't she leave him alone and tell the story he coached her on? Why, indeed? She put her hands together like she was praying, asking for guidance from an unseen god, but she wasn't. Her head dipped and she paced around the pack in a circle. *Why should I stay with him?* A good answer didn't come. She sat on the pack and considered her life.

"It's just me," she said, and then repeated, "just me." Cassie bolted erect. She said it one more time, "It's just me." She knew why she wouldn't leave him. He had invested himself in her, and she in him, like part... of a family. Now she needed to follow through. *Get him to Canada.*

Cassie coaxed the straps of the pack around her shoulders and trekked to the spur where she had left Hodges. A car's headlights shone from the south as she neared the trail. Her heartbeat quickened and her pace slowed, waiting for the auto to pass before stepping off the shoulder and onto the spur. The car seemed to slow as it neared. The headlamps blinded her when the auto turned round the bend and bathed her in a brilliant stream of light. The driver, evidently stunned to see something, slowed and then sped up again when he determined it wasn't a deer or wolf.

Cassie breathed in deeply. She hurried to the spur and scrambled up the trail until she was certain a car's headlamps would not illuminate her again. She stopped and waited, interested to see if the car would turn and slow in the same spot. Dual thoughts occurred to her. *I wonder if the driver knows about this connecting trail. Hodges should be waiting another fifty yards or so away.*

Five minutes passed before she felt comfortable enough to continue and connect with Hodges. The pebbles dotting the trail crunched under her hiking boots. It seemed so damn loud. She tried to walk softer, slowing her pace in the process. When she reached the spot where she had left Hodges, she stopped. Night was in full bloom with the sound of crickets, owls, and small creatures scurrying through the underbrush avoiding her approach.

"Gerry," she whispered.

No response.

She said his name again, only louder, "Gerry." It sounded strained and nervous. Again, there was no response. The pack seemed so heavy. She removed it and placed it near the rock she had last seen him, and walked off the trail a little ways. *Did he leave, figuring she was better off without him?*

"Gerry," she said in a voice too loud.

Hodges clicked off his phone and started toward her.

A hawk owl exploded from a pine bough above, transmitting a surge of fright through her body. She scrambled backwards, caught her heel on a jagged rock and ended on her derriere. Sitting there, palms resting on the dirt and pebbles that covered the trail, Cassie struggled to bring her breathing under control.

"Cassie?" Hodges asked.

"Yes, yes," she said, and scrambled to her feet.

Hodges emerged from an area further up the trail. He followed the spur down to where she stood, looking relieved.

He looked her up and down in the dim light to see if she was injured. She wasn't. "Did everything go all right?"

Cassie nodded. "Yeah, I was a little nervous, but it went fine." She remembered the bars she bought. "Oh, do you like Almond Joys?" She knocked the dirt off her clothes and did not see the smile that flashed across his face.

"I love them."

CHAPTER 26

Cadotte stared straight ahead while she waited for the kid to return with her drink. She checked her watch. It was 7:03 p.m. As if she were in a trance, she dug her phone from her purse. Her finger hovered over the touchscreen keyboard, not quite sure if she should call Hodges or not. She was just about to put it away when it rang. She let it ring several times.

"Hello," she answered.

"Sheila," Hodges said.

She looked around and paused. The kid was on his way back with her drink.

"Sheila," Hodges said louder.

The kid put her drink on the table, smiled, and returned to the bar.

"I thought we agreed we wouldn't talk again. I've done my part."

"I know, Sheila and I appreciate it. I... I just wanted to find out if Earl is all right. Did everything work out?"

Cadotte gave a furtive look around the bar before she responded.

"Yes, I think everything will work out for Earl, but... Lieutenant Johnson is skeptical of his story, and the details I told him, or didn't tell. He suspects I'm helping you." Her eyes searched the bar for Johnson or his underlings. For all she knew he could have left a listening device under the table. She did a quick check.

Hodges sounded regretful when he said, "I'm sorry I didn't tell you who I was sooner."

Cadotte dropped her gaze and she nodded as if Hodges was sitting in front of her. "It's okay. I might have turned you in if you had."

Hodges was silent.

She could still hear him breathing so she knew he hadn't clicked off.

"Are you... doing okay?" She asked.

Hodges hesitated. "Maybe," he finally said.

"Is Cassie Bandleson with you?" Cadotte asked.

There was more hesitation from Hodges. "For now, I think?"

An alarm bell went off in Cadotte's head. "What do you mean, you think?"

"I told her she should leave and tell the police she got away from me. They can't know she's been helping me."

"So... she left?"

"We needed food, so she went to a gas station to buy some." He paused. "I don't know if she'll be back."

Cadotte didn't say anything. She thought perhaps this whole thing would be over soon... if Cassie Bandleson left Hodges and contacted the police.

Part of her wished it were true.

"Whatever happens with me," Hodges said, "please make sure Earl comes out of this... okay. All right?"

Cadotte nodded again, as if he were in front of her. "You can count on it. The old coot is a pain in the ass, but he doesn't deserve jail time. I'll help him any way I can."

Hodges sounded relieved. He let out a breath, said thank you, and clicked off.

Cadotte picked up her rum and coke and nursed it for the next hour before she left for home.

She parked the Lexus in her attached garage, sat for a minute before getting out, and then rambled into the house like she had been up all night. She was tired, physically and emotionally. Cadotte took off her shoes and threw them to the side. She lost her balance and hopped on one foot before tossing her purse onto the sofa. She walked into her bedroom and collapsed onto her soft mattress.

Cadotte lay there, staring at the ceiling as her mind tussled with conflicting thoughts about Gerald Hodges and her decisions concerning him. Number one in her mind was the fact that he didn't seem like a killer. He seemed kind, gentle, intelligent, and concerned for his friends. *Was he really a killer?* He admitted as much when he told her who he really was, but...*can a person change so drastically? Maybe*, she told herself. She also told herself she should report her conversation with Hodges to Lieutenant Johnson.

In the morning... maybe.

Mancoat didn't feel as comfortable in his guest quarters as Johnson had told him he would be. It was a regular jail cell with an uncomfortable mattress, small toilet, and most importantly, nothing to do, except think and read.

Several magazines, People, Time, National Geographic, lay on one of two shelves attached to the wall near the lousy bed. He picked up the People magazine and started perusing it. *Oh, looks like George Clooney and his new wife were having problems.* He thought it wouldn't last. He never thought Clooney was the marrying type. He flipped the page. Something about Jennifer Aniston. *Now there's a looker.* He studied the pictures of her relaxing in her beach house. *What I'd give to be at the beach with her.*

He heard shoes clomping down the hallway toward his cell and he tossed the magazine back on the shelf. A few seconds later, Lieutenant Johnson appeared with the jailer. He stood in front of the cell for a moment, tie askew, and hands in pockets.

"Mancoat," Johnson barked.

Earl sat up and looked at him.

"Open it up," Johnson said to the jailer. "We're letting you out. We've checked out what you told us and everything seems hunky-dory. We picked up your friendly dealer and the teacher, Seinfelt."

Mancoat smiled and shook his head back and forth. "See, I told you Lieutenant."

Johnson frowned. "You just stay very available for the next few days. You still have a room at the Suites?"

"Yeah, I do." Mancoat walked through the jail door. Johnson turned his back and started walking away.

"Uh, Lieutenant?"

Johnson stopped, turned around, and laid an irritated look on Mancoat. "What?"

"Just curious. Did Seinfelt say anything when you picked him up?"

Johnson chuckled. "He just said that you and the other guy, I'm assuming he meant Hodges, were a couple of lying pricks."

"You just made my day, Lieutenant." Mancoat went to the locker area, picked up his things from the supervising officer, and left the station. He called a cab, which dropped him back at his hotel. An hour later, Cadotte called and asked if she could come over. Fifteen minutes later, she knocked on the door.

"You're damn lucky," she said when she burst through the doorway.

"Yeah, well, my mother always told me I was born under a lucky star. I guess I was."

"I got a call from Hodges," Cadotte blurted.

"What, when?"

"A couple of hours ago. Bandleson might have left him."

Mancoat's face dropped. He walked around the table in the dining area and sat down. He motioned for her to take a seat.

"If she left him, he'll never make it to Canada on his own," Cadotte said.

Mancoat raise his hands off the table like he wanted her to stop.

"Don't ever sell Gerry short. If she left him, he can still do it... unless..."

"Unless what?"

"Unless she gets ahold of the police and tells them where he is."

Cadotte's face darkened and her face lost expression. "He told her that might be the best thing for her to do."

Mancoat slapped a hand on the table, but his tone was weak and his voice was shaky.

"Gerry told me he'd be okay if he was caught. He said it might be for the best, and he could still do good things while in prison."

"We can help him," Cadotte said with an earnest look on her face.

Mancoat scoffed and shook his head. "I got strict orders by Johnson to stick around here and make myself available. I can't do anything. Besides, Gerry would kick my ass if I tried to help him now." He unconsciously kicked at the table.

Suddenly he stopped and looked at Cadotte. "Something I've been wondering, Sheila, is why you didn't run as far away as you could when you found out who he really was."

Cadotte squirmed in her chair. She looked uncomfortable.

"I can't really explain it, other than to say, there's something about him that doesn't match up with the narrative I've read. He's different from what you'd expect, and maybe I'm just buying into the old cliché. He's just so nice, I don't see how he could have killed anyone."

Their eyes met.

"Yeah, I know what you mean. I knew Gerry for several years when the whole thing in Rose Creek went on. The cops came to me and my friends and asked for anything on Gerry." He cleared his throat. "Well… we told them there wasn't a better man in town than Gerry. Then… we find out he did it, and it was like … Gerry? Unbelievable, is what it was? I do know this now, whatever went through his head when he killed those people, it's gone."

She kept her eyes locked on his. "How do you know?"

"Cause he told me."

"And you believe him."

"Yeah, I do."

Cadotte's eyes blazed intensely. "Let's get him to Canada."

CHAPTER 27

Hodges accepted the Almond Joy. He was methodical as he unwrapped it and took a bite. "Heaven, it's like heaven." He tipped his head back and chewed in slow motion.

After he took his last bite, he folded the wrapper into a square, creased and pressed it between his fingers, and then stashed it in the side pocket of the pack where they had placed all their other trash. "Did you see anyone else?"

"Just a teenage clerk, who hit on me, I think, and then a car slowed down when I came back up the road, but didn't stop."

Hodges sucked on the last bite of his bar, savoring every bit of chocolate and almond flavor. He looked up at the night sky. "You were gone longer than I expected. I thought... maybe you wouldn't come back." The stars dotted the sky, their light becoming brighter by the minute as darkness crept along.

"Gerry, I said I would get you to Canada. I meant it." She washed down the last bite of her snickers with bottled water and rinsed her mouth. It made a loud swishing noise. She expressed her embarrassment. "Sorry, I had to do that. I hate it when little bits of crap get stuck between my teeth. I haven't been able to floss since we've been in the woods."

Hodges took a swig from the other bottle and also rinsed.

"I feel the same as you, Cassie. My teeth hurt when I don't clean them."

She gave him a sideways glance in the starlight. His revelation struck her as a bit odd.

They took a couple more swigs from the water bottles, packed up, and hiked the spur to the main trail again. The night was crisp and the mosquitoes had disappeared except for the occasional lone assassin patrolling the woods.

"I know this part of the trail pretty well," Cassie began. "There's a couple designated campsites less than a quarter mile from here. We should stay at one of them and rest for the night."

"Hopefully, one will be open," Hodges said.

They hiked up and down the hills, almost missing the first site. No one occupied it. The campsite lay in a little clearing on the western side of the trail and there was enough room for a medium sized tent.

Cassie trudged into the clearing and slid the backpack off. Hodges followed her on spent legs and plopped himself down on one of the logs near the fire ring. He offered to help set up the tent as she dug it from the pack, but she declined, saying that he would get in the way. She put the tent up in five minutes. It was definitely a one-person affair, not even close to its description as a two-person shelter.

"I know it doesn't look very big, but both of us could squeeze in it," Cassie said.

Hodges gave her a skeptical look.

"No, really, we could," she said with a little more force in her voice.

Hodges walked over, zipped it open, and took a peek inside. He shook his head. "There is no way both of us fit in there. You take the tent, and I'll curl up beside the fire."

Cassie looked toward the fire ring. "What fire?"

"The one I'm going to make right now." He pulled a book of matches from his pocket.

"Okay. I'll get some twigs and wood." She walked around the edges of the campsite picking up dry twigs and dead pine needle branches. "The dead pine needles are the best," she said. "They light up like gasoline."

Hodges walked away from the campsite and back down the trail, calling back to her as he did so, "I saw a few larger branches on the ground a little ways back. They should last for a good share of the night after I get the thing lit."

He returned within five minutes hauling two dead branches about five feet long and four inches in diameter.

"How you gonna cut those up?" Cassie asked.

"I don't have to. I'll just keep feeding the unburned parts into the fire as the burned part falls off."

"Just checking," Cassie said.

While Hodges had been away, she made a perfect teepee of small twigs and sections of pine needles in between them. She had put an array of slightly larger branches nearby to feed the fire and burn longer as it progressed.

Hodges nodded his approval. Soon a small fire burned and crackled in front of them. Cassie handed him a light blanket she had stuffed into the pack when they fled Karonen's house and turned into the tent with the sleeping bag.

Hodges snuggled as close to the fire as he dared and wrapped the blanket around himself. He dug the phone from his pocket and turned it on. He waited for it to power up. Finally, one bar appeared.

He called Cadotte. It rang twice before she picked up.

"Hodges?" She said.

"Yes, it's me. Can you talk?"

"Yes, yes, I'm with Earl now. We're at the Suites, discussing you, and what we can do to help."

Hodges didn't let on how much that meant to him. "I don't think there's anything you can do."

"Where are you?"

"Somewhere on the hiking trail around Little Marais," he said.

"Well, you've only got about sixty miles to go before you hit the Canadian border."

Hodges sighed. "I thought we were a little closer than that."

"We might be able to pick you up and drop you off a little closer to the border," Cadotte offered.

"No, no, it's too dangerous. If you're caught helping me, it's the end for the two of you," Hodges said.

"What if..." Cadotte started to say, but Hodges cut her off.

"No, Sheila, please don't."

"Damn it, Hodges, hear me out before you shush me."

Hodges listened.

Cadotte took his silence as a victory. "What if I rented a car and met you two somewhere north of Little Marais at a trailhead, while Earl drove his car back into the Finland area to act as a decoy. The police will be likely to keep a tail on him and forget about me, especially if I'm not in my Lexus?"

There was more silence on the line until Hodges came on again.

"Sheila, I appreciate your thought, and your plan, but I would feel terrible if you were caught."

"Let me worry about that," Sheila said. "It'll work, I guarantee it. I could get you close to the border where you could hike across. You must have other contacts that could meet you on the Canadian side... right?"

Hodges started to soften. "I do," he admitted.

"Listen, Gerry. As you no doubt have figured out, cell phone service is a little inconsistent along the North Shore. There are pockets of good, bad, and no reception." She started breaking up, but Hodges could still make out what she said. "If you two can make it up to Tofte at the intersection of County Road 2, there's a trailhead just south of the town. Reception is good in that area. If you can get there by tomorrow night, I can call you and set a time for pickup."

Hodges began to feel a little hopeful. It actually sounded feasible. "All right, we'll try it," he said.

"Good, I'll clue Earl in, and we'll get things together here. It'll be tough, but I think you can hike that distance and be at the trailhead by nine o'clock tomorrow night. I've hiked that section with friends, and if you push it, you'll make it before nine. Okay?"

Cassie had emerged from the tent a minute earlier and could hear Cadotte explaining her plan. Hodges noticed her, and she told him, "We can do it."

"All right, Sheila, but be careful. Make sure you're not suspected," Hodges said.

"It'll work. Turn off your phone and conserve your battery. I'll call you tomorrow night."

"Okay."

Hodges turned the phone off and returned it to the side pocket of his trousers.

"I know we can do it. I just hope she can be there," Cassie said.

Hodges pushed one of the bigger logs farther into the fire, watched the burned end break off, and curled up beside the fire. He pulled the blanket tight around his chin. Exhausted, he fell asleep almost the moment his eyes closed.

Cassie went over their route in her head. She had been through most sections of the Superior Hiking Trail several times and wasn't worried about the timeline. Hodges though, was another matter. Although he had held up well so far, he was in his sixties, she thought, and she worried if she pushed him too hard, he might not make it. She listened to his easy breathing as he slept by the fire pit. *If I can get him to the rendezvous, my part is done.* The problem with her, though, was she wasn't sure she wanted to be done.

Cadotte had come up with the outline of a plan on the spur of a moment. Now she had to fill in the blanks and make sure Mancoat would be willing to do his part. She should not have worried.

"I'll do it," Mancoat said before she even spoke to him.

"Do what?" She asked.

"Whatever you got in mind. It sounded like I would be the diversion while you take care of the real rescue. Am I right?"

"Minus the details, yeah! You ready to help me work them out?" She asked.

Mancoat smiled. "There's not much of the night left, so we'd better do it right now. Shouldn't be all that hard for me to get the police to follow me and lead them on a wild goose chase. The question is where do I take 'em and how do you keep them from following you? I got the impression that Lieutenant Johnson doesn't trust you."

"Your impression's accurate, I'm afraid to say. I'm going to borrow a car from a friend when I get done with work tomorrow. I'll have to work it so if Johnson's got someone tailing me, he doesn't see me switch cars."

"Not to sound skeptical, but you sure you'll be able to borrow a car? Must be some friend, especially if you do it all cloak and dagger like for her not to get suspicious."

"It's not a her. It's a guy I know. He owes me, and I'll call him when I get home."

The plan they decided on was this: at around 6 p.m., Mancoat's job was to take his car and drive up Highway 61, turn off at Finland, and drive around the back country for a couple hours. Make a few stops, have coffee in Finland, and maybe a bite to eat. If he and Cadotte were correct, there would be a plainclothes officer or two, following him around at a safe distance, ready to pounce if he made any contact with Hodges.

Cadotte would get off work by five p.m., drive home and park her car in the garage. At 7, her friend would drop off his dark green SUV three blocks away, leave a key under the mat, and walk away. Cadotte would exit her back door a few minutes later, pass through the alley, cross two more streets, drive the vehicle away, and try to make sure no one was following her.

Neither could see a reason why it wouldn't work, which should have worried them.

Cadotte had a plan B just in case, but she didn't divulge that to Mancoat.

CHAPTER 28

Hodges got up before dawn and stirred the fire's ashes to make sure it was totally extinguished. As he did, Cassie crawled out of the tent and stuffed the sleeping bag and blanket back into the pack. She bundled the tent into its bag and crammed that in as well. They broke out a couple of energy bars and apples for breakfast, ate fast, and began their long trek to the rendezvous point.

Cassie noticed Hodges seemed refreshed and exhibited a bounce in his step this morning. She thought it was because he could now see a workable plan and a successful end in sight. She had the same thoughts. *This might just work.*

They hiked hard and fast. It could never be called a blistering pace, but for who they were, how long they had been at it, and Hodges' age, they did fine. Late in the morning, they stopped to rest and eat a snack along a ridge flanked by white pine on both sides.

The ridge had an abrupt three hundred foot drop off on the western side. The slope was gentle on the eastern edge. *Note to self,* Cassie thought, *I'd rather tumble down the eastern edge than the other side.*

By the time they started hiking again, the day was bright, sunny, and warm. They avoided other groups when they could see them ahead by hiding in the bush until they passed. Two times, however they were unlucky. The first encounter involved a group of teenage boys out for a day hike. Hodges and Cassie acted friendly and didn't visit long. The second encounter happened shortly after the first when they ran into a mother, father, and ten-year old daughter trying to hike fifteen miles in a day. *Good luck with that,* Cassie thought. None of the hikers appeared to suspect them as the fugitive and captive, or even know the authorities were seeking two individuals who matched their descriptions.

By early afternoon they entered Crosby Manitou State Park, a primitive area with only walk-in campsites. Again, the hiking was rough, but as they hiked, Hodges inhaled the sight of waterfalls, cliffs, and occasional deer.

Moose, black bears, and wolves also inhabited the park, but fortunately, in Cassie's mind, they saw none. She was feeling good about their pace and confident of keeping their appointment near Tofte.

They passed out of the park without seeing another person and paralleled Highway 61 for several miles. Cassie and Hodges observed darkening skies and felt a chill that began to creep into the air.

"God, I wish I had my rain gear," Cassie said as she gazed at the dark, rolling clouds coming their way.

Hodges felt a drop of rain. "It might be time to take shelter under a nice broad pine," he said.

Cassie felt a drop and said, "We have our pick of them, that's for sure."

A gust of wind hit with an abruptness that sent them scrambling. They found the perfect tree and huddled on the leeward side of its trunk. The massive branches, covered with pine needles, provided a decent roof.

Wind gusts devolved into constant straight-line winds, approaching the level of a tropical storm. Rain pelted the landscape like it was trying to destroy everything in its path. Hodges and Cassie huddled close, holding onto the trunk.

Twenty minutes after it began, the storm passed, the skies returned to a beautiful shade of blue, and the wind abated to almost nothing. Remarkably, the white pine had protected them from the rain, and they had stayed relatively dry. Hodges unwrapped himself from the tree as soon as the wind dropped and looked around.

Cassie did the same. The wind had blown the pack away from the tree and deposited it against another pine twenty feet away.

Cassie walked back and retrieved it. Though the pack had a water resistant material covering it, the driving rain had soaked through and drenched their energy bars. "I knew I should have bought the waterproof cover for this damn thing."

Cassie tossed a soaked bar to Hodges. It slipped through his hands and landed in the mud between his feet. He picked it up, and as he wiped the mud away, the wrapper disintegrated in his hands.

"Oh well, might as well eat this now." Hodges took a bite. "This is better wet than dry." He scarfed the gooey bar down in thirty-seconds.

Cassie shrugged and ate a bar too. When finished, she hefted the pack and they continued their hike. Whenever a search helicopter passed near, they hid in the bush until it was no longer visible.

Plainclothes Officer Chester knocked on the door. Lieutenant Johnson waved him inside as he continued talking on the phone. Chester stood off to the side and tried not to listen, but watched Johnson flail his free arm about and speak in a harsh tone.

"Damn politicians!" Johnson slammed the receiver into its cradle and slapped his hand hard on the desk.

"Trouble with the mayor?" Chester asked.

Johnson whirled around. "He'd be the least of my problems. It was the Chief. He wants Hodges, and he wants him yesterday."

Chester made his best attempt at a sympathetic expression.

"He says he can't understand how he slipped through our hands. Son-of-a-bitch!" He hit the desk again. "Damn politician is all he is. The guy didn't have to work his way up through the ranks, never really ran an investigation." He laid a withering gaze on Chester. "That bastard has had everything handed to him every step of his career, and now he thinks he's gonna be the Republican nominee for Governor. He says we need to get Hodges soon!" Johnson walked around the desk a couple of times before pausing and looking out the window. "We'll get Hodges all right, but it won't be because of the Chief, I'll tell you that."

Chester sat down when Johnson motioned for him to take a chair. He sat in silence. He could always tell when Johnson's brain was grinding, so he stayed silent and attentive until Johnson spoke again.

"You know Sheila Cadotte, right?"

Chester squirmed in his chair. He had dated Cadotte a few times before they had decided they were never going to be an item. "Yeah," he said, hesitating just a little.

"I got a feeling about her. I don't think she's telling us everything she knows about Hodges, Mancoat, and this whole thing with Karonen."

Chester looked up. "So... what are you saying?"

"I'm saying I want her watched, her and Mancoat. We need a guy on them all the time... not close, but around. Know what I mean?"

"Lieutenant, you asked if I knew her. You know that I dated her for all last summer. I really don't think she'd hold anything back." He looked up at Johnson. "She knows Hodges is a murderer and wouldn't protect him, if that's what you're saying."

Johnson studied Chester for a moment and then turned around, facing the window again. He turned to Chester and said, "Intellectually, I know that, but my gut says something else. It says she's hiding something and she can help us, whether she wants to or not. We need to keep an eye on her. She might just lead us to Hodges."

Chester started to protest, but Johnson held up his hand, stopping him cold. "Just get on it, twenty-four-seven." Johnson whirled around, signaling the end of the conversation.

Chester got up slowly, walked to the door, but turned to say he thought it was the wrong move.

Johnson had already circled his desk. He stood, holding a cup of coffee and staring out the window. Chester closed his mouth and walked out.

Mancoat bummed around most of the day. He walked down to

the Lakeside Cafe and drank two cups of strong coffee. From there, he walked around some of the shops, and then down to the Lake Superior Maritime Museum. The sea had always fascinated him and he spent two hours wandering around; looking at exhibits and reading about the shipwrecks that dotted the huge lake.

It was a lovely sunny day so Mancoat stepped out on the pier and watched the ships enter and exit the harbor. The lake breeze tossed his hair, but the sunshine warmed his face. *I could handle this for the rest of my life,* he mused. He didn't notice the plain-clothes officer shadowing every move he made, but he suspected someone would be near.

He checked his watch. It read two forty-five pm. *A lot of time to kill,* he thought, so he decided to go to the Great Lakes Aquarium. He walked back to the Suites parking lot, hopped in his car, and drove the short distance to the aquarium. It cost him more to get in than he thought it should, *but what the hell, you only live once.*

He loved it. He watched the shark tank feeding, and thought, *what the hell is a shark doing in the Great Lakes Aquarium.* He shrugged his shoulders and then took in the program about river otters. The presenter delivered an excellent narration, and the otters entertained the crowd with their water acrobatics. It took up most of the afternoon, and he was ready to go by five.

Mancoat thought he had seen the same person at the museum and the aquarium. It was either a coincidence, or he was being followed. He smiled. *This is going as planned.* Jumping in the car, he decided to have a little fun with his watcher who had seemed surprised when Mancoat abruptly left the aquarium and rushed to his vehicle.

Mancoat tore out of his parking space like a character from *Grand Theft Auto.* He watched in the rear view mirror as his tail scrambled to his car, hopped in, and tried to keep up with him. He didn't.

Mancoat sped down the street and took a quick left and then a right. He pulled into a parking space beside a small building and watched for the tail to buzz by. He didn't have to wait long.

Fifteen-seconds after swinging into his parking space, the officer assigned to keep track of him, sped by with his head twitching left, right, and ahead searching for Mancoat's car. He passed out of sight in another few seconds.

"Ah, that was kind of fun," Mancoat said aloud. He pulled away from the curb and drove back to the hotel where he planned to eat something and have a couple of beers before heading out to Finland.

He drove into the Suites lot and parked. As he walked across the street to the hotel, he spotted his tail driving toward him. He tipped his hat when the officer slowed to allow him to cross safely. *He won't have any trouble picking up my trail later,* he thought.

Cadotte finished work and drove home at five, stopping once to pick up a bottle of wine at her favorite liquor store, Morelli's. She figured it would look good to whoever tailed her... if anyone tailed her. She wanted to make them think she planned to settle in for the evening with dinner and a good bottle of wine. *Lull them to sleep,* she hoped.

Trying her best to be vigilant, she pulled into her driveway, and thought she caught sight of another vehicle parking a block away. It could have been a neighbor, she thought, but she couldn't be sure. *It might be a tail.*

Cadotte paused as the she waited for the garage door to open all the way, and then waited a little longer, keeping an eye on the suspect vehicle. She didn't see anyone get out. She waited a few moments longer, pretending to look for something in her purse. She could see a figure in the car. It stayed there, never emerging.

Satisfied it was probably a tail, she drove into the garage, shut the door and entered her home carrying a bottle of Petite Syrah.

Cadotte changed into more comfortable clothing and searched the refrigerator for leftovers. She found a slice of pizza with pepperoni, onions and green peppers, warmed it up, and luxuriated in every bite. She opened the bottle and poured herself a small glass. It was wonderful. She started to pour another one, but stopped, reminding herself that she had better be on her game tonight. She was still hungry so she ate three large olives stuffed with jalapenos and garlic. *Exquisite*, she told herself.

With more time to kill, she picked up the book she had been reading, *The Girl with the Dragon Tattoo,* and read until nearly seven.

The house was quiet, which made the abrupt ringing of her phone startling. She picked up on the second ring. It was her friend letting her know the package had been dropped off and the item she requested had been included.

She thanked him and hung up.

Okay, am I ready for this? She said it out loud, and then answered her own question by grabbing a hat and tucking her hair up under it. She made sure the front door was locked, left a few lights on, set the timer switch to turn the living room lights off and her bedroom light on at ten p.m.

Sheila put on her bulky long coat and walked out the back door. She could feel the dew on the grass as she strode across, stepped over the fence separating her yard from one of her neighbors, and continued on through their backyard. She pulled her hat low to hide her face, and unconsciously slumped as she made her way through the backyards. She passed into a front yard and traveled the sidewalk paralleling the street two blocks away from her house.

She crossed the street and went another block where the 2009 Chevy Equinox was parked where her friend said it would be. She checked the empty street again for any watchers before crossing to the vehicle, opening the front door, and grabbing the key under the floor mat. The car started on the first try, and she wound her way through the backstreets and onto Highway 61.

Her eyes kept checking the rear and side mirrors for any sign of being followed. She sighed when she pulled onto the expressway, and drove the speed limit. She did not want to be ticketed for anything tonight. The drive to Tofte would take a little over an hour. She figured she had more than enough time to get to the rendezvous point. She hoped Hodges and Bandleson could make it.

Mancoat left the hotel parking lot at precisely seven. He followed Highway 61 until he saw the sign for Finland. He turned off on Highway 1, keeping an eye on the rear view mirror for his tail. He wasn't disappointed. Right on cue, the same vehicle that had been following him before, turned onto Highway 1 a couple of hundred yards behind him.

Mancoat drove the speed limit. *No hurry,* he thought. In fact, the more time he took, the better. Keep these guys as far away as possible from Cadotte and her mission. He chuckled. In a few miles, a Finland sign greeted him. He drove into the little town and stopped for gas at the only station. *Do it yourself, of course,* he thought. There weren't any full service stations anywhere, anymore, and the price of gas was ridiculous.

The light was fading as he pumped gas and watched his tail drive by and pull in at the local pizza establishment. His shadow didn't get out of the car.

The driver had positioned himself so he could exit the parking lot as fast as need be.

Mancoat finished pumping gas and went inside to pay. A young lady, who had been texting, put her phone down as if she was embarrassed, and greeted him with a ton of fake warmth. He browsed around the convenience store part of the station, took his time paying, made some small talk with the girl, and walked out to his car.

Mancoat noted that the follower was still where he last saw him. He got in, started his car, and pulled out, driving by the shadow. On cue, the shadow pulled out a block behind him and stayed at a safe distance.

They gotta know I know they're following me, Mancoat thought. *Oh well. I won't disappoint them.* Highway 1 was a road with lots of bends, and it was always best not to drive it too fast. Mancoat ignored that truism and took his follower on the ride of a lifetime, ending in his car coming to a skidding, sliding stop in a widened part of the road where he got out and peed in the bushes.

The driver of the car behind him managed to stay in sight and slowed down when he saw Mancoat slide into the pull off. Earl stood exposed in all his glory, peeing as the dust from his slide settled around him.

The sky had darkened as Cadotte neared the intersection of County Road 2 on the south side of Tofte. *Perfect,* she thought. She turned off and headed for the trailhead where they were supposed to meet. She found it, parked, cuddled up in her seat, and started reading her book again.

It was eight-forty-five. Cadotte closed the book and punched in the numbers for Hodges' phone. It rang several times before commenting there was no voice mail. She waited a few more minutes and called again.

This time, Hodges answered. "Yes," he said, out of breath.

"Where are you?" Cadotte asked, the concern evident in her voice.

Cadotte heard some discussion between Bandleson and Hodges before Hodges came back on the line.

"Cassie says not far, but we'll be a little late."

"Is everything all right?" Cadotte asked.

"Yes, yes, we just got held up by a little rain storm. We had to take shelter for a while, otherwise we made good time."

"Okay. You should conserve your battery, so shut it off until you get here. We can recharge it for a while in the car if you have a charger with you."

"I do," Hodges said, and then he shut the phone down.

Cadotte reclined and curled up in the driver's seat. Darkness had spread over the trailhead parking area and she had difficulty seeing the words in her book. She leaned over and pulled a small flashlight from the glove compartment. "Much better," she said as she illuminated words on the page.

Hodges and Cassie hiked along a low ridge covered by speckled alder, blackberry, and currant shrubs. She recognized the area.

"We're really close," Cassie slapped a lazy mosquito on her

cheek. "Probably a couple of hundred yards, and the trailhead will be in sight."

Hodges' pace had slowed considerably since the early part of the day. "Good, I'm worn out now." It took a Herculean effort to lift a foot every step forward.

"Do you want to stop and rest a bit, Gerry?"

"No, I'm afraid if I stop I won't be able to get going again. It's not far, so let's just get there. I'll have time to rest in the car."

Cassie acknowledged him, but slowed her pace a little. She knew she could use a rest as well... and a hot shower... and deodorant... and the list went on.

Mancoat circled back from Highway 1, ending up near Lax Lake. He stopped at a little rest area, got out, and admired the calm water and the antics of two loons. The shadow drove by slowly, passed him, and continued on, presumably to the next drive off. Mancoat waited another ten minutes before getting back in the car and driving toward Silver Bay. The shadow pulled out when Mancoat drove by, staying a respectable distance behind.

Forty minutes later, Mancoat entered the parking lot opposite The Suites. He got out, walked across the street and reentered the hotel. He didn't see the shadow, but assumed he was near. He plucked his phone from his pocket and called Cadotte. She answered on the second ring.

Mancoat spoke first. "I'm back at the hotel. I led my shadow around Duluth, Silver Bay, and Finland. How about you?"

"I think my guy still thinks I'm at the house," Cadotte answered.

"You got her?" Johnson snapped. His impatience and desperate tone did not escape Detective Chester.

"I got her. She stopped at a trailhead up the road from Tofte. She's just sitting in her car. Looks like she's got a light on looking at something—maybe reading."

"Let me know pronto if you see Hodges. She's gotta be waiting for him. Probably been in contact and they're meeting there."

"You got it, Lucas." Chester put his phone down and continued watching Cadotte from his position in the woods. He had followed Cadotte, quite expertly, he thought, since she slipped out her back door and into another vehicle a few blocks away from her house. The other unmarked police car remained out front to make her feel safe while he watched her back door.

Now he had an excellent vantage point on the hill, just past the trailhead. His partner remained with the vehicle a hundred yards up the road, and could be at the trailhead within fifteen-seconds. Chester's only regret now was that the light had faded and he could not see as well as he wanted. He also kicked himself for thinking that Sheila would not help Hodges. He couldn't think of any other explanation for her sneaking out, driving for an hour, and pulling off on an isolated trailhead, other than she had been in contact with Hodges and would pick him up somewhere along the lower elevations of the Sawtooth Mountains ridgeline.

Chester also damned himself for not thinking of bringing a pair of night vision goggles, the newest acquisition of the Duluth police department, made available to units across the United States by the Department of Homeland Security. He could have used a pair tonight.

Moving slowly, Chester worked his way through the brush to get a closer view of Cadotte's car and anyone who might approach. He didn't count on his clothes being grabbed and torn by raspberry bushes, or slipping on rocks and greasy clay earth made worse by recent rain. A minute after starting down the slope, he slipped and fell, landing on his butt before sliding several feet down the hillside. With a butt full of greasy clay mud, Chester didn't notice the two figures emerge from the other side of the County Road 2 and cross over to the trailhead.

When he got up and tried to brush the mud away, he looked toward Cadotte's car, saw the dome light on, and the back door closing. He grabbed the phone in his pocket and managed to pull it out. It slipped through his muddy fingers and flipped onto the ground. He snatched at it in desperation as he watched the car pull out of the lot. He finally got hold of the phone and punched in the number for his partner.

"Get down here, quick," he yelled. "They're here, they're here." Chester watched in helpless desperation as the car turned back toward Highway 61. He slapped the mud off his pants, hands, and jacket as he ran down the hill to the parking lot. His partner skidded into the lot and Chester threw himself in. "Go," he yelled.

They tore out of the lot and raced back to the intersection of Highway 61 just in time to see taillights ahead turn and head north. Chester pounded the dash.

"There," he shouted. Chester called Johnson. "I think we got "em. They're heading north on Highway 61." Breathing hard, he added, "We're in pursuit."

In his excitement, Lucas Johnson slapped his desk and sent a paperweight flying when he heard the news. "I'll call Grand Marais and get a unit down there." It took him just a few seconds to get hold of the Grand Marais police department. He slammed the receiver in its cradle when he was told that the single squad car they had was involved in an accident ten miles up the Gunflint Trail.

Johnson called Chester back on his cell. "There's no units coming from Grand Marais. Don't lose Hodges. I'm getting two more units and we're heading your way now. I'm also calling the State Patrol, DNR, and Border Patrol to find out if they have anyone in the area. You hear me? Don't lose him!"

Chester hung up, squinting to make out the taillights clearly. There were two sets of lights ahead of them. One had to be Cadotte's car carrying Hodges.

"Get closer," he barked to his partner.

"We made it," Cassie said when she ducked into the backseat of Cadotte's car. Hodges slipped in after her.

Cadotte wasted no time chatting. She started the car and pulled out. She headed to Highway 61 north.

"Are you sure no one followed you?" Hodges asked.

"Hey, I've got a few tricks up my sleeve," Cadotte said as she kept her eyes on the road. "They had a car out front, but I went out the back and used a friend's car. Clever, huh?"

"Yes, but if I were them, I would have had someone watching the back too," Hodges said in his irritating, know-it-all voice. He turned around and watched behind as they turned onto Highway 61. He noticed a set of headlights south of County 2, but then spotted another vehicle turn onto the highway after the first set of headlights had passed.

"We may have company," he said.

Cadotte responded right away, "What?" She shot a glance in the rear view mirror. "Shit! Two cars!"

"The second one just turned onto Highway 61 from the road we were on. It could be they followed you from Duluth," Hodges said.

"Or, it could just be someone who lives past the trailhead driving up for dinner in Grand Marais," Cassie said.

"Well, it's not too late for dinner in Europe now, but maybe a little late for Minnesotans."

"I'd have to agree with Hodges on this one." Cadotte lifted a hand from the steering wheel and slapped it down. "Damn that Lucas Johnson. Why didn't he trust me?"

"Hey, we don't know for sure if that car's following us," Cassie said.

"Let's find out. Speed up," Hodges commanded.

Cadotte stepped hard on the accelerator and sped to up to seventy. The second set of headlights pulled out and passed the first, gaining on them in the process.

"Shit, shit, shit!"

"Maybe the guy just likes to drive fast," Cassie suggested.

Cadotte stepped it up to eighty.

Hodges watched the car behind intently before he said, "He's sticking with us, maybe gaining a little."

Cadotte cracked a smile the other two couldn't see. "Lucky for us I have Plan B." She sneaked another peak in the rear view mirror.

Hodges glanced at Cadotte. "This would be a good time to share."

"When I spoke with Karonen he said he dumped Hecimovich's body in Devil's Kettle."

Hodges looked perplexed. He clasped his hands together. Finally, he said, "What is Devil's Kettle and what does it have to do with Plan B?"

Cadotte kept checking the rear view mirror as she talked.

"It's a double waterfall. One side empties into the river and one side empties into a hole in the rock and goes... well, nobody knows where."

"Okay, I'll bite. How do the falls fit into Plan B?" Cassie asked.

"Simple, when the police are watching, we push Gerald over the edge and into the disappearing falls. They think he's dead and never go looking for him again."

Hodges waited a few moments before responding. "The only problem with your plan is that I will be dead, and I'm not okay with that."

Cassie tapped Cadotte on the shoulder. "Hey, they're gaining on us."

Cadotte depressed the accelerator a little more.

"Wait, let's try backing off a little and see how he reacts," Hodges said.

Cadotte backed off to sixty.

"He slowed down and matched our speed," Cassie reported.

Hodges thought out loud. "I don't think he'll try to stop us on this section. It wouldn't surprise me if they have another police unit waiting for us in Grand Marais, and then they'll trap us."

"My plan will only work at Devil's Kettle. We've got to make it there, and that's another twenty miles north of Grand Marais."

"You mean your plan to kill me?"

"Yes... I mean no. We won't really kill you. I've got a mannequin in the trunk dressed up in clothing kind of like yours. That's what's going into the Kettle."

"I feel so much better," Hodges deadpanned. "Honestly, Sheila, that's your plan?"

"Yes," Cadotte said, the irritation evident in her voice.

"You got a better plan?" Cassie asked.

Hodges didn't say anything for a few seconds.

"No," he finally admitted.

"Good, now that we've got that settled we can concentrate on avoiding being captured in Grand Marais," Cadotte said.

"We're toast if they block the road," Cassie said.

"If they block the road, we stop and I surrender. I won't risk you two being hurt. I'll show them the gun and explain that I made both of you help me escape."

"But Gerald," Cadotte began.

"No buts, Sheila, this can only end one of two ways, either I escape cleanly with no danger to you and Cassie, or I surrender peacefully."

Cassie and Sheila remained silent until Cadotte put out a strained, but positive statement, "We're gonna get lucky, get through Grand Marais, and make it to Devil's Kettle."

"We'll see." Hodges had already persuaded himself they would have to surrender in Grand Marais.

"One mile to the city limits," Cadotte said, adding, "get ready for anything." She slowed to forty-five and rounded the first bend.

A profound sadness enveloped Cassie. Had she done this for nothing? Sitting in the back seat, she shook her head and wiped a tear from her eye. *Why am I so wrapped up in this?*

Hodges turned to the women. "It's okay. I'll be fine."

Neither woman said a word.

They rounded the second bend near the Grand Marais municipal campground. Still no roadblock or any sign of police vehicles. Cassie turned to the rear to see if the car behind was getting any closer. It wasn't. They were almost through town.

Hodges spirits rose along with the women's. The town was quiet as they passed through. When they left the city behind, Sheila let out a whoop.

"Chester!" blared Johnson's voice over the phone.

"Yes sir!"

"Where are you?"

"Just left Grand Marais. They're continuing north."

"We're fifteen minutes behind you. Keep them in sight, but do not engage. Wait for us. We've got three squad cars behind you."

"Our guy is still behind us," Cassie said.

"In fifteen minutes, it won't matter. We'll disappear from view and get on the hiking trail to Devil's Kettle. It's a mile long so we'll have to move fast up the trail and set up at the falls. Gerald, you'll get out of the car immediately and hide near the parking lot."

"I don't understand how they're not going to see me get out of the car and hide," Hodges said.

"I'll take care of that."

Fifteen minutes later, Cadotte turned her lights off and began coasting.

"Jesus," Hodges yelled.

"Wait for it, wait for it. There," Cadotte said. She coasted into the turnoff for the falls and into the parking area before tapping the brakes once and coming to a halt. "Don't get out yet. Wait for them to go by."

Several seconds passed before Chester's vehicle went by.

"Now!" They flew out of the car and Cadotte retrieved the mannequin. They said quick goodbye's to Hodges before he ran, stumbled, fell, got up, sneaked and hid between two large boulders a hundred feet away. The women ran up the trailhead with the mannequin and a twenty-foot section of rope, but Cadotte waited a few more seconds to give Chester's car a glimpse of a figure running up the trail.

"We just lost their tail lights!"

"What the hell?" Chester said. "Slow down." Their eyes searched the highway ahead, but saw nothing.

"Pull over, turn around. They switched off their lights and turned off somewhere."

They made a quick U-turn, and this time, noticed the sign for Devil's Kettle.

***

"There, pull in there." The headlamps of Chester's vehicle illuminated a figure running into the bush.

He called Johnson and told him what had happened.

"Keep the vehicle in the parking area. Block the in-drive. We'll be there in two minutes."

In less than two minutes, the three police cars pulled into the in-drive. Chester's partner moved his car further into the lot to give them room.

As Johnson stepped from his vehicle, his cell rang. He didn't break stride, flipping his phone open and answering the dispatcher.

"What?" Johnson yelled. He listened for half a minute. He flipped the phone shut, and shouted, "Find him."

Chester, who had emerged from the unmarked police car, hurried to meet Johnson.

Every light on the three police cars was flashing, brightening the parking area.

"Sir, as we pulled in, we saw one of them run up the trail over there," Chester said and pointed to a trailhead sign directing visitors to the Devil's Kettle.

"All right, secure the parking lot and do a sweep of the immediate area. I'm leading the rest of the team in."

CHAPTER 29

odges watched the scene unfold and slunk deeper into the bush. He thought about Cadotte's plan to toss the mannequin into the swirling waters of the Devil's Kettle, and hoped she could pull it off convincingly. Timing would be everything, as she would have to have the mannequin in position to look like he was holding her and Cassie hostage.

The trick would be for her and Cassie to appear to struggle with him and push the mannequin over the edge of the precipice into the water below. The darkness of the night would obscure the view of the officers. Before the police got to them, they would also have to find a rock, tie it onto the mannequin's ankle, and make sure it was large enough to make sure the mannequin went under water so it would go on its journey to who knows where.

The plan sounded entirely lame to Hodges as he thought about it, but... stranger things had happened in his lifetime. If it worked, he would be dead to the authorities, and Cassie and Sheila would be in the clear. He sighed and shook his head. Right now, he could only stay hidden and hope things worked out the way they had planned.

Cassie took the lead as she and Cadotte ran down the trail. Bushes along the trail tore at the mannequin, almost ripping it out of Sheila's hands several times. Grunts and epithets emerged from their mouths as they raced up the narrow pathway. Cadotte had a headlamp, which she had given to Cassie. She followed as closely as she could to take advantage of the dim light. *Damn low batteries! Should have checked that.*

They didn't say much, trying to conserve their energy as they dashed toward the falls. Cadotte hoped that Hodges had not been discovered, or worse yet, given himself up. What a waste of effort all this would be if that turned out to be the case. *Follow the plan!* That was all she could do for now.

Behind them, Lucas Johnson and three officers were pounding down the trail, gaining ground with every step. They carried floodlights, which shone a hundred feet in front of them. Johnson almost salivated as he and his officers rushed toward the falls. He wasn't as familiar with the area as he would have liked to have been, but was certain the trail ended at the falls about a mile from the trailhead. Hodges was trapped.

The trail bobbed and weaved close to the river, always pitching uphill toward the falls. Neither Cassie nor Sheila experienced fatigue. Cadotte half carried and half dragged the unwieldy mannequin. Only Cassie's dim headlamp illuminated the narrow pathway.

Adrenalin and desperation drove them forward. *We have to have everything in place and be completely ready*. At last, Cadotte heard the distinct sound of water hurtling over the Devil's Kettle.

Cassie heard it too.

"We're almost there!" Excitement reverberated in her voice.

Cadotte glanced behind them. She saw the flicker of a floodlight illuminating a portion of the woods two hundred yards back.

"Move, we gotta move!" They quickened their pace, sweat streamed from their faces. Two minutes later, the roar of the falls blasted their ears and they felt a mist on their faces as water rose from the churning falls.

Cassie veered left.

"What are you doing?" Cadotte followed her.

"We've got to get in the right spot to make this work," Cassie screamed above the tumult of the falls. Without warning, Cassie stuttered to a halt, and stood on the precipice above the screaming river as it tumbled over the fork in the falls; the falls that flowed into a cauldron with no discoverable outlet.

Cassie had stopped so abruptly that Cadotte almost plowed

into her. She threw the mannequin down and immediately began searching for a rock large enough to tie the mannequin onto.

The light behind them was getting brighter.

"This one, here, this'll work." Cadotte dug at a partially buried boulder a foot in diameter.

They dug furiously, trying to loosen it from the ground. They rocked it, clawed it with their fingernails, kicked at it. Finally it broke loose from its bed. Cassie seized the rope and looped it around the rock three times, quickly tying it off. Cadotte tied the other end to an ankle of the mannequin and maneuvered the rock to the edge of the cliff, balancing it precariously so that the slightest push would send it, and the mannequin, over the edge and into the gurgling water below.

"They're almost close enough to put their lights on us. Hold the dummy up."

Cadotte held an arm of the mannequin around her neck. Cassie stood on the other side, ready to nudge the rock and mannequin over the edge.

"When they shine the lights on us, we scream like hell."

Suddenly, Cadotte realized Hodges' hat was not on the dummy's head, understanding the illusion would not be as effective if the mannequin's head and face were not obscured. She looked around in desperation. The floodlights were getting nearer and they could almost see the squad of trackers bearing down on their position.

"There!" Cassie plucked the hat off the ground in front of them and slapped it on the dummy's head, pulling the brim down to partially cover the face. She quickly moved back into place.

"We're here, we're here!" they screamed in unison, making their voices sound as frightened and desperate as they could. The floodlight flashed, fully illuminating the trio.

"Now!" Cadotte said in a quiet, but firm voice. She flung the arm away from her neck as Cassie simultaneously kicked the rock over the edge of the precipice, pulling the mannequin over with it. They hoped it appeared as if they had thrown off their attacker, and sent him over the edge of the cliff.

They did it to perfection. The illusion was of two women fighting off a man ready to sacrifice everything, and failing.

Cadotte and Cassie dropped to their knees, crying and hugging each other in apparent relief.

Lucas Johnson and Walter Chester cautiously made their way to the women, shone their lights over the edge and into the roiling waters below. Johnson breathed hard as he repeatedly swept the floodlight over the edges of the watery grave. There was no sign of the mannequin... or Hodges.

He turned to Sheila and Cassie. "It's okay." His voice was soft, even gentle. He and Chester helped the women to their feet.

Cadotte slowly turned and looked over the edge. Her body shook. "He made me pick him up at the Tofte trailhead, said he would hurt Cassie if I didn't help him." She turned to Johnson. "I couldn't say anything, Lucas. I was afraid he would hurt her." Cassie hugged her and the two cried.

It was one of the best acting jobs either of them had ever performed.

Johnson turned toward Chester. He spoke above the din of the Devil's Kettle.

"Walter, would you mind escorting them back to the trailhead?" He nodded toward the women. Johnson had never called him by his first name... ever. Chester wondered if it was Johnson's way of apologizing to him for doubting him.

Chester and another officer walked the ladies back to the trailhead.

Johnson lingered near the edge of the falls shining his light over and over the legendary bottomless pothole called the Devil's Kettle. He couldn't believe it was over... just like that.

He scanned the perimeter of the cauldron hoping he would see Hodges clinging to the edge. He didn't want it to end this way, and yet it had.

One of the remaining officers approached Johnson. "You okay, Lieutenant?"

Johnson bit his lip and sighed. His body slumped and he suddenly realized he was exhausted. He had been running on pure adrenalin for the past thirty-six hours. "Yeah, I guess so..." His voice was weak and shaky. He hesitated before moving, flashed his light once more over the water below, and seemed to regain a small measure of strength. His voice was strong when he said, "Let's get back to the cars. I want a team up here in the morning looking for any signs of life."

The officer nodded. "We'll have a team here bright and early." He doubted there was anything to look for or find. They shone their spotlights on the trail and walked back to their squad cars.

CHAPTER 30

Cadotte invited Cassie to stay the night with her. Chester dropped them off in front of her house and left, eager to file a report and get home and catch the end of the Wild game.

"I can barely believe we pulled it off," Cassie said as they both collapsed onto the sofa in the living room.

"It was close, no doubt about that. When we lost the hat I was so scared we wouldn't find it, and Lucas would have known for sure it wasn't Hodges," Cadotte confessed.

A thump against the wall behind Cassie startled them. They both turned and stared into the twisted face of Peter Karonen. He held a butcher knife in one hand and a boning knife in the other.

Cadotte's throat tightened.

Cassie tried to seize the moment. "Peter!" she swallowed hard. Before she could say anything more Karonen interrupted.

"Surprised?" he said in a quiet voice, walking nearer the sofa. He stood ten feet away from Cadotte who shrank away, closer to Cassie.

He pointed the knives at them, holding them belt high. "You shouldn't move. It upsets me."

She stopped.

"Mr. Karonen, what are you doing here?" Cadotte asked. "And how did you get away from the hospital—and find my house?" She was positive her voice cracked and wavered, giving away the panic she felt.

He chuckled. "Police, and more importantly, nurses take breaks. I was able to slip out between shifts, and you know, telephone books still come in handy. They are an underutilized resource in this day and age." He cocked his head and then took two steps closer. The women trembled, but tried their best not to show it. He stopped, lowered the boning knife in his left hand and raised the butcher knife in his right. He rubbed his cheek with the back of his hand, massaging it slowly.

"There, I feel better now. I've had this terrible itch all over my face since... since I was in the hospital and realized Methodist had died." His voice was sad. It seemed detached.

"That's a good step, Peter!" Cassie said right away. "Accepting what is real is progress."

Karonen scratched his cheek again. "I'm connected to reality now, Cassie. I know my daughter is gone because of a man you knew... and because of what you did to her."

"But, Peter, that was an accident. I didn't cause the power to go off and the machine to stop working... I didn't."

"Cassie, stop," Karonen said. "I accepted the reality of her death, and the cause. You'll have to pay the price because you contributed to her death. That's also part of my reality."

"Mr. Karonen," Cadotte blurted. "Methodist was dying. When the power went out, Cassie had nothing to do with it, you've got to know that."

His face became stone. "She was there," he rasped between gritted teeth. He stood, glaring at Cassie and taking in shallow, quick breaths. Then he calmed and his breaths became even. "No more talk. Get your keys. We're going for a long ride." He motioned with the knives. When they didn't move, he took a menacing step toward them and slashed the air with the boning knife. His eyes blazed.

The women, holding onto each other, stood and walked slowly in front of the sofa. Cadotte reached down and plucked the keys from the bowl sitting on the coffee table. Karonen backed away a couple feet so they could pass by. Not knowing if Karonen would lunge, they leaned away from him as they passed by. He followed, holding the knives at waist level again.

Cadotte unintentionally stepped on the gas hard, and the

Lexus started with a roar. She shook so badly she could hardly hold onto the steering wheel. Karonen sat in the back seat. He pricked Cadotte in the back of her neck with the tip of the boning knife. She screamed and blood trickled from the tiny wound.

"Stop, leave her alone," Cassie yelled. She swung her arm backward nearly slashing her wrist on the boning knife.

Karonen spoke in a calm voice. "That was a warning, Ms. Cadotte. Cassie knows about my warnings." His next words were quiet, almost inaudible. "Don't you, Cassie?" Cassie placed her hand on Cadotte's knee, and held it there for a moment.

"Don't do anything unless he tells you to," she said. "He means what he says.

Peter, please let Sheila go. It's me you want. All she's done is try to help everyone." Her pleading voice seemed to affect Karonen.

"When we get to the Devil's Kettle, I'll let her go, but not until then."

They shot worried glances at each other.

"Go. Go now," Karonen commanded. Sheila backed the car from the garage and out into the street. Cassie staunched the trickle of blood on Cadotte's neck with a tissue, and the journey, perhaps their last, began.

CHAPTER 31

Hodges remained hunkered behind the boulder until the last police car left. Yellow crime tape had been stretched across the entrance to the parking area. The authorities had taken longer than he figured to mark the crime scene by the falls, return, mill around the trailhead, and then leave. He assumed they would be back at first light.

He had also watched Cadotte and Cassie return with an officer, get in his car, and leave. It appeared everything had gone as planned. His skepticism, he thought, had been well placed, but he couldn't quarrel with the outcome. To the authorities, he was dead and his body would never be recovered. *I am born again.*

All he had to do was make it into Canada without being caught. Once there, Lucille was only a phone call away.

He turned the cell phone on. *Plenty of battery left, but no signal.* He would wait until the border to call her. His last contact with her had been on the trail with Cassie. It had been a brief conversation, but enough information was exchanged for a plan to be formulated.

If he was lucky, a car would be waiting for him across the border, and he could drive to Winnipeg, catch a flight to Vancouver, and be free to start a new life without fear of capture. He could scarcely believe everything had worked out as well as it had, and he shook his head as to why he deserved such a wonderful outcome.

Hodges put a hand in one of his coat pockets and felt the smooth skin of a very hard apple. Smiling gratefully for having grabbed it from Cassie's backpack before jumping out of the car, he removed it and took a huge, satisfying bite. Quiet laughter escaped him as he wiped away the juice with his free hand. It tasted delicious.

Hodges finished the apple and tossed the core into the trees. He rose from his resting place with thoughts of paralleling the highway. Headlights appeared to the south, stopping him in his tracks. He watched as the vehicle slowed. If they're thinking of turning into the parking lot, they'd better think again, he thought.

But the vehicle did turn into the lot, blasted through the yellow tape, and then stopped fifty feet away. He thought it looked like Cadotte's Lexus. *By God, it is her Lexus!* He waited behind the rock. *Maybe they've come back to help me get across the border. I can't believe they took the chance.*

A door cracked open. Cadotte emerged from the driver's side and just stood there, waiting. Cassie emerged from the passenger side at the same time a third person emerged from the back.

Hodges pulled back a little from the rock. The person in the back seat was a man. He watched as the man jabbed Cadotte in the back with something. Sheila let out a pained cry.

What the hell? This is not good.

Cadotte yelled out, "Run, Cassie, run!"

The man behind Cadotte stepped around his open door and grabbed Cadotte's wrist.

"If you leave, your friend will die now. Stay and I'll let her go when the business between us is done." Karonen poked Cadotte in the back again, eliciting another cry from her.

"I'm not going anywhere," Cassie said. She walked around the front of the vehicle and stood beside Cadotte, taking one of her hands.

Cadotte shook her head. "You should have run."

Karonen nudged both of the women toward the trail leading to the falls, and they shuffled along in silence.

Hodges watched, eerily fascinated. Karonen had somehow escaped from the authorities and had found Sheila and Cassie. He knew the man was conniving and clever, this was almost too much for him to believe.

Hodges emerged from behind the boulder and followed the trio at a safe distance. No matter what Karonen planned, it couldn't be good for either woman. Whatever it was, it most certainly involved the Devil's Kettle. *Why come back here, if not to send one or both of the women into the cauldron below the falls.*

Just enough moonlight filtered through the evening clouds to outline the trail for Hodges. It also helped that he could see the flash of light Cadotte used to show the way for her traveling mates.

Hodges' mind raced, trying to resolve how to surprise Karonen without the women coming to any harm. He had no weapons. He wondered if he should sneak as close as he could, rush him, knock him to the ground and disarm him. Or lay a blow to the back of his head from a log, if he could find one, and never expose his face to the man.

He decided to wait until Karonen's plan became obvious before he intervened.

Risks accompanied every option, but he knew he did not want to permanently harm Karonen, or reveal the fact that he was still alive. He had fifteen to twenty minutes to make up his mind, so he resolved to follow and watch for the right opportunity.

Cadotte cursed herself for always keeping her knives expertly sharpened. Every time she breathed in, the knife penetrated her clothing, not enough to pierce her skin, but enough to let her know he meant to jab the knife through her if she tried anything. She knew her kidney would likely be the recipient of the blade, a blow she could probably survive if that were the only wound, but there was no guarantee of that.

It felt as if they walked for an hour before they began to hear the rush of the water tumbling over the dual falls. Cadotte was not a churchgoer, but she believed in God. She said a silent prayer.

Cassie knew she could escape if she just took off running, but she was unwilling to sacrifice Sheila's life. Karonen would surely make good on his word to kill her. She wracked her brain trying to figure out a plan to get both her and Cadotte out of this alive, but nothing came to her. The night air generated an uncharacteristic humidity and sweat trickled down her face and stung her eyes. Her hands trembled, and her legs felt like lead. Thoughts of sacrificing herself actually played across her mind, if only she could be sure he would let Sheila go. She would do anything—throw herself into the Devil's Kettle, let him stab her, if only he would let Sheila go. Maybe her life could finally mean something.

That's crazy, she told herself. *There's gotta be a way out of this!* *There had to be.*

They were close. Cassie felt the mist before the other two. She trembled as she approached the edge of the falls.

Cadotte followed, lips tight, eyes pleading, and the knife firmly pressed against her back.

Karonen breathed hard. Whether that was because he had decided he needed to work himself up to a killing task or he was actually out of breath seemed irrelevant at this point. He planned to kill Cassie. Both women knew it.

Cassie stood near the edge of the precipice, seemingly resigned to her fate. Karonen gently pushed Cadotte away from him and the ledge. He was ten feet away from Cassie. She readied herself. He would make a move soon.

"My word is good. Ms. Cadotte, you may leave." He motioned for her to go and pointed the knife toward Cassie.

Cadotte took two hesitant steps away from Karonen and looked for a rock, a stick, anything she could use to stop him. The ledge seemed devoid of any loose debris.

Desperation consumed her. "You can't do this!" she screamed.

A body flashed across the rocks and slammed into Karonen, sending him and the other person over the edge and into the Kettle. A bewildered Cassie watched the two figures descend twenty feet to the swirling waters below, not understanding what had really happened. A shocked Cadotte hurried to the edge and stood beside Cassie. The roar of the falls was deafening, and they strained to make out the figures in the water.

When Hodges had seen what he deemed to be Karonen's final solution, he reacted. He ran and hurtled his body into him. He felt the mist on his face as they both tumbled over the cliff and into the water. He heard a sickening clunk and felt himself sink into the swirling surge of water emptying into the cauldron. After the initial descent into the water, he kicked with all his strength. Straining against the undertow of the water, his head broke the surface where he struck out in desperation and grabbed onto a log jammed between rocks on the surface of the pothole. He hung on, gulping water, and nearly out of breath. The undertow pulled and sucked at his legs. He managed to turn his head and look around. There was no sign of Karonen. He assumed he had descended into the abyss.

A moment later, he became dimly aware of screams erupting from above and forced his gaze upward. The pounding rush of the falls generated a mist, compounding the difficulty of seeing anything in the dark. He managed to meekly wave an arm.

"Hodges!" The women yelled in unison. Squinting through the dark and the mist, Cadotte could see a figure clinging to a log below them.

"It's him. We'll help," she screamed, trying to assure Hodges.

Cassie turned toward Cadotte. "How, how do we help? We can't get down there."

"I have more rope in the back of the car. Stay here. I'll get it." Cadotte took the light from Cassie and raced down the trail not daring to guess how long Hodges could hold onto the log, and fearing the pull of the water emptying into the cauldron would drag him under. She hoped she could return in time to save him.

Twenty-five minutes passed before Cadotte charged back onto the precipice with the rope.

"Here, I found this." Cassie pointed to a tree impossibly rooted in the crack of a boulder near the edge of the cliff.

Cadotte tied the rope around it. She tested her weight against it, and it held. She hoped it would hold Hodges, who outweighed her by sixty pounds.

She tossed the other end into the cauldron. It reached Hodges with feet to spare.

He struggled against the sucking action of the water as it sought to pull him into the depths. Furiously kicking his feet and grasping the log with one hand, he finally managed to tie the rope around his waist, and use it and the rope to pull himself onto a slim edge at the bottom of the pothole.

The women watched in frustration as Hodges tried to climb up the smooth sides of the Kettle, but kept slipping back to the ledge.

Cadotte and Cassie grasped their end of the rope and pulled.

Hodges, with the women lugging hard, managed to work his way up. Soon, Cassie took hold of his hand as it appeared above the rim. Finally, Hodges flopped onto the top end of the precipice, like a played out fish in the bottom of a boat.

He lay there, exhausted and panting.

"That was a bit much for an old geezer like me."

Cassie knelt beside him. "You're not a geezer. You saved us."

"Again," Cadotte added.

Hodges smiled wryly as he sat up. "Just trying to even out the ledger. That... and the world would be a poorer place without you two."

Cassie's heart melted. The simple words he said struck her as the kindest ever directed to her. She cried. She knew there was more to it than that. He had feelings for them, as they did for him, and even though it shouldn't have been left unsaid, no one verbalized the obvious. They were grateful for having had Gerald Hodges in their lives and wanted him to live.

The feelings were mutual.

EPILOGUE

Hodges guided the Hyundai Elantra into the parking lot of the international airport in Winnipeg. He had picked the car up just across the Canadian border. After rescuing him at the Devil's Kettle, Cassie and Cadotte had driven him near enough to the Canadian side to enable him to sneak across the border. He found the vehicle exactly where Lucille had said it would be. One of her friends arranged to deliver the car, along with a change of clothing, food, water, a bottle of the best Cabernet Sauvignon he could find in Thunder Bay, a flight schedule, a new passport, and a ticket to Vancouver. He read the name on his new passport, Oliver Payne.

He would have to get used to it.

Hodges breathed in the crisp air while walking to the terminal. He thought of the heartfelt embraces he had received from Cassie and Sheila near the border and relived the joy it had brought him.

He paused before stepping into the terminal, turned, and looked at the world around him. This was the best he had ever felt in his life, and he was ready to *do good,* as he put it to Cassie and Cadotte when he said goodbye to them in Minnesota. There was a smile on his face, and a spring in his step as he bounded up the stairs, bag in hand.

He was free and he would make good on his vow.

ABOUT THE AUTHOR

This was J.J. Ollman's fifth novel, and the second one to feature Gerald Hodges. Hodges' character has evolved from an odd, obsessive man with a killer past in *The Book Club Murders* to a strong and somewhat sympathetic, grandfatherly figure in *The Devil's Kettle*. Will there be future novels involving the man who is now Oliver Payne? Maybe.

Ollman is considering writing a non-fiction book in the future about growing up in a family of atheists. In the meantime, he will paddle his kayak down the Red Cedar River, camp in the Boundary Waters Canoe Area, golf, write stories, read, enjoy a nightly glass of wine, and most of all, enjoy life with his wife, Cindy.

CPSIA information can be obtained
at www.ICGtesting.com
Printed in the USA
JSHW020356060723
44279JS00005B/23

9 781478 786207